THE DAY ENDS LIKE ANY DAY

Timothy Ogene

Holland House

www.hhousebooks.com

Paperback ISBN: 978-1-910688-29-8
Kindle: 978-1-910688-30-4

Cover image: Antony Gormley, SUBLIMATE XIII, 2007, Photograph by Stephen White, London, © the artist

Cover design by Ken Dawson Creative Covers
Typeset by handebooks.co.uk

Published in the UK

Holland House Books
Holland House
47 Greenham Road
Newbury, Berkshire RG14 7HY
United Kingdom

www.hhousebooks.com

For JPH and SES

I remember my childhood names for grasses and secret flowers. I remember where a toad may live and what time the birds awaken in the summer – and what trees and seasons smelled like – how people looked and walked and smelled even.

John Steinbeck, *East of Eden*

PART ONE

I

If you were a lazy stroller like me, doing the ramble from block to block, you would spot Pa Suku sitting on a stool in front of his door, reflectively raptured into the squeal of his transistor radio. He lived two blocks away from us. And whenever I paid him a visit, which was as frequent as the daily return of dawn, I would stand by his window admiring the copper wire that was the antennae of his radio, as it rose from where the radio's original antennae used to be, ending its sinuous rise as a small coil around a nail hammered into the window frame. I would watch him fiddle the dial through the frequencies until it settled where the BBC was gong clear. I remember wondering why the BBC commentators rattled like they had hot potatoes under their tongues, always in a hurry to leap from sentence to sentence.

Rwanda was in the news that year. Stories were read as they came from sources on the ground, from Tom Carver, Mark Doyle, and other names I do not remember. Pa Suku followed these reports and would try to explain what was going on: the savagery, the horror, the implication on world perception of Africa. I was more interested in the rattle of what I called radio voices. Rwanda was nothing to me, a mere name from the distant world of radio voices. I was young. Years later, I would be fed details of that genocide, after it had fizzled into conference talks and jargons in cities where death could be detachedly discussed with cups of fair-trade coffee. After the news I would say goodbye to Pa Suku and walk home, silent and trying to imagine a world outside the blocks, what the news reporters looked like with hot potatoes under their tongues.

*

I have perfected a new way to visualize O., my place of birth. The trick is to hold still, close my eyes, and pretend I was hovering above ground, a vulture scouting for decaying flesh. And each time I try this trick, the result is always the same. I see O. as a bottle-shaped space, blurry, with roof-dots sprinkled inside, lying east of Port Harcourt, south of the new highway that runs from Aba to Port Harcourt, and west of the murky Imo River. I do not know how I came to associate O. with an empty bottle, but that is exactly what I see in my mind's eye. And if pressed for details, as I expect would happen someday, I would say a quick word on daybreak and nightfall, since both were clearly marked by events that etched themselves on the walls of my mind. Nightfall was an outstretched hand blanketing us from the rest of the world, shielding us from what we were: curious figures roaming in search of nothing, herded into rooms that may well be cubicles for bodies waiting for the knacker's stretcher. But we fought those cruel nights, the absence of electricity that amplified our feeling of isolation. Sitting in groups outside before midnight, if your parents were liberal enough to let you roam loose and free, you resisted darkness with a kerosene lamp by your side, and traded stories with your friends before heading home to sleep. That lamp, its flames fluttering as we walked through the night, was a cut in the belly of darkness, and each small glow, darkness expelled, was a triumph against all forces, real or imagined, that kept electricity from us.

There were nights I played the flâneur, stopping to peep into the narrow doors of poorly lit and scantily furnished rooms. I once saw two shadows swaying and trashing against a wall, glued together, dissolving into the wall, reducing and increasing in height. I lingered for a minute or two to see what would become of this show, to sort what it was all about, a staged fight or a mere night-dance. There were nights the stars sagged so low we could nearly reach them with the tips of our fingers, and nights they recoiled from us, banished from the sky by monstrous spells of gas flaring from oil plants across the new highway. There were also nights the moon tore grim clouds apart, prolonging playtime for us kids. In those moonlit nights, our faces beaming as we galloped without care, our kerosene lamps, those weapons of mass resistance, were declared useless, forgotten.

*

We called them the blocks, our corner of that bottle-shaped space, twenty-six rectangular buildings of various lengths shaped like chocolate bars, each room a slim slice off that bar: block a, block b, block c,… block z. The letters were written in black, and were slanted and skewed, with paint dripping below each stroke, congealed by time. From the old road and the entrance to the blocks, you could see the alphabets on each wall, running from z to a. Each small letter was a curiosity in itself: k was an emaciated r, b was a 6 with a straight back, g was a 9 begging to stand straight, and z—with lines of caked paint underneath—was a swastika. Some alphabets were gone, consumed by the passing years, others were gradually fading into the walls, becoming shadows. But they belonged to us, the blocks and all they represented, and if we were groceries we would have labels that read: Boy, Aged 12, Made in the Blocks; Girl, 10, A Product of the Blocks. I sometimes imagine our parents, knocked over by whatever they drank in those days, gyrating at the edge of block x, or between c and d, gyrating until we were safely inserted and thereafter birthed in a room in block a or q or z, and then I picture a midwife holding us up to face life for the first time, holding us up by the left leg, tossing us without care until blood streamed to our brains to announce a new, odd world, and when we opened our eyes the vague faces of our parents offered us our first smile. Then the strange odours would welcome us from clogged gutters and dumps, smacking our fragile nostrils awake. In the years to come, we would walk those blocks sniffing our umbilical cords in the nearby bushes, where they were hastily discarded for dogs or rats to consume. And when we finally left to face the world, to universities and big cities, we would fight to forget those peculiar odours, but they would linger, reminding us that the past was as present as our flesh.

*

At the blocks...

The roofs leaked like loose baskets. When the walls or the floors cracked, they were patched with a mix of cement and sand. The cardboard ceiling bulged with dirt and dust, including rat excrements collected over time. Septic tanks overflowed into clogged drainages, and when it rained the drainages surged, overflowed their banks, and flooded our doorsteps. Resourceful tenants dug pit latrines with square slabs that had cylindrical holes at the top, where the toilet-goer squatted and went to work. Zinc shacks were erected around the holes, held steady by bamboo poles. Ten to twelve feet deep, they were shallow enough to release their contents as gas, close enough for us to inhale that gas against our will. Then the slabs aged, gave, and became death traps. A boy once disappeared but was later found in an old latrine, dead. He was fished out and bathed and buried in an unmarked grave. He was an only child and was my age. God wanted him to die that way, they said.

At the blocks…

We were our own comic relief, soothing each other's pains with numbed grins from the corners of drawn lips. Childbirth, which occurred so frequently I assumed it happened every day, was never about the child or its mother, but an occasion to break from the gradual, collective rot inside. At the naming ceremony, with its customary open invitation, the crying child would be passed from hand to hand, from stranger to family friend, from aunt to cousin, from the tailor's wife to the barber's daughter, rocked and tossed in the air, pinched on both cheeks, tickled, whistled to, clapped to, sang to, the overwhelmed child, struggling to breathe in a room with sweaty bodies, would bleat in exhaustion, the more critical ones would aim vomit at the faces of their handlers who, disgusted but constrained by watching eyes, would offer thanks to God for showering his blessings via baby puke.

*

From block z to a…

Ours was a convergence of tongues. A crucible.

11

Somewhere between a salmagundi and a hodgepodge. Neighbours were not distant, ethnic brands, neither were they exotic curiosities on public display. There were no minorities, no majorities. Our ethnicities disappeared into that single crater called poverty, which subsequently defined how we saw and received each other. Your next door neighbour drank from the same well down the road, or trekked the half mile to the nearest tap for the not-so-clean water. He or she, like you, did not enjoy the luxury of an air conditioner when the sun beamed its worst. There were no exclusive restaurants at the blocks, no boutique tea shops and high-end fashion stores to mark class. We were, you might say, a people united by the shallowness of their pockets, their distance from all resemblances of the good life. United also were we by a mutilated, foreign tongue, which we spoke with the improvisational rush of jazz, notes skipped here and there, with convenient clichés inserted as each occasion demanded. Our English, owned and considered the lingo of our birth, with its ruthless rule and nuances peculiar to the blocks. There were times that lingo gave way in the face of deeper sentiments and native tongues emerged to show that one's ancestral roots ran deep and still alive.

*

We lived in block v room 7. Across from our living room was the backyard-cum-litter space of block w room 7 and all it offered: unwashed pots, puddles collected over time and the enduring stench of stale urine levitating like mad ghosts. When we had guests, mostly from the other blocks, they tiptoed across the puddles, as though their neck of the woods was much better. We occupied two rooms like most families around the blocks. The door between the back room and the living room was shut at 8 PM, separating us from our parents. I believe it was their way of taking a break from us, a way to detach themselves from the burden that we truly were. The back room was theirs. The living room was ours. There were nights we heard laughter from the other side, and nights when the silence was frightening, causing me to pray and hope my parents were still alive. There was a rectangular table in the centre of the living room, its shape a mockery of the shape of the blocks: long and uninteresting. Its varnish had vanished over time, leaving a grotesque surface we covered with a floral tablecloth. Three upholstered chairs—black—surrounded the table like knights on guard. Those knights held a collection of bed bugs, which we fought with kerosene and petrol sprays to no avail. Bed bugs and mosquitoes will take over the world someday, my father used to say. I believed him then and still believe him now.

A bed the size and softness of a billiard board occupied the space between the table and the only window. A dust-covered mosquito net, with two cone-shaped holes on either side, hung over the window. The mosquito nets were more or less a novelty, at least they appeared so in those days, which was the only reason my parents installed them. The conical holes, from where we reached to pull and bolt the window, let the mosquitoes in before nightfall. The nets were useless.

During the day, the living room was a place for guests and all. At night it was a furnitureless sleeping space. The upholstered knights were piled up in a corner and the table placed on top. Then we took the floor, Kor and Leab flanking me on either side snoring away. Pan, the oldest, had the bed to himself. Ricia was outside this mix; she slept in the back room with our parents. I would often ask her how it felt to sleep where the bed was soft and no one snored, and would remind her that I once occupied that position but was booted out by her unwanted presence (the way I ousted Kor who had ousted Leab who had ousted Pan). She would shrug, fall silent and smile like grown-ups patronizing talkative kids. I was bothered by this attitude, which I thought was an affront on the rest of us who had been banished to the living room. It especially bothered me that Ricia pretended not to have an idea or an opinion about anything. But as time would later reveal, she was of a different kind, one of those who say little but mean every word. The older we got, the more I saw how her mind, tucked away behind that silence, ran two times the speed of light. If only she had not been prematurely uprooted by the leprous hands of an unknown illness.

*

The long walk to State School One, seven kilometres west of the blocks—under the burden of our bags, the mild morning sun behind us, crawling overhead to overtake and position itself in our faces—was a lesson in endurance. One way I pretended to enjoy the journey was to point and talk about the objects and people we saw along the way, an activity that bored Ricia but she indulged me: the number of electric poles on either side of the road, erect like frozen policemen caught collecting bribes; the bean-cake woman and the man who sat behind her pounding black-eyed peas into thick paste; the preacher we saw every morning, a megaphone strapped to his left shoulder, his astonishingly big bible clutched under his arm, his steps dramatically urgent, on his way to fish men for Christ; the motorbike that delivered meat to street-side restaurants, a bloody carcass tied to the passenger seat, denuded of its skin for flies to taste, its head (goat or cow) baring charred and clenched teeth, nodding as the bike sped along, leaving a blood-trail. And then, not too far from our school, the lumberyard or what we called "timber shed," about ten acres of logs in different stages of death, with machines clacking away in open sheds and shirtless men hefting logs and planks unto waiting trucks. At the Jumbo Gardens, or what was left of Mr Jumbo Doku's garden of herbs and tropical flowers, I would stop to watch bees fluttering atop overgrown flowers, and observe how they hop from one petal to another, careful not to perforate fragile anthers with their bee-strong thrusts. Of all the flowers at the Jumbo Gardens, the blood lilies—round conflagrations contained in oval pots—were more inviting. I secretly wished I could pick them by the peduncle and sniff away like a bee. I would often stand for a few seconds staring at the brown, earthen pots scattered about, some empty and broken, others containing unpruned but lush gloriosas and scented herbs with petals aglow as flames, some drooping over the pots, or defying their poor states by holding up their necks.

It was rumoured that Mr Jumbo had lived alone for many years and had taken care of his flowers like they were his kids. But after a fatal accident left him half paralyzed, the flowers were abandoned to die or grow wild. There were days I spotted him crouched between pots, an unlit pipe dancing on a side of his lip, his ash-grey wigens hat tilted back, a pair of secateurs in his only working hand. And all he did was look at his flowers, his wild and dying children, unable to prune or move the pots. But there was always a wavering grin on his face, which I never understood. Whenever he was there, Ricia would run ahead, "He looks dead, he is a dead man," she would say. But the day old Jumbo died, a Thursday morning, Ricia stood and watched his body, stiff on a wooden stretcher, carried off to a waiting van. When the van reversed and headed east, she turned to see where it was going. And then, as if possessed by a demon, she jumped the gutter between the street and Jumbo's garden, went straight to the pot of blood lilies, plucked two fiery heads, handed me one and inserted the other in her kinky hair. Then she broke into a trotting dance, offering me broad smiles as we wove our way through a group of mourners, mostly aged men, their faces drawn by what must have been a realization that they too were as close to the grave as their departed friend. I, on the other hand, felt my skin freezing in fear. Why must he choose to die on a day like this, I thought, and to do so when he knew we will be on our way to school. How inconsiderate. I knew a week's worth of bad dreams awaited me in the nights ahead. Ricia continued to bounced along but stopped when we heard the hollow sound of the school bell in the distance, about two poles away from Jumbo's garden. We were late for school. I could feel her fear.

Each school day, the punctuality prefect picked someone to ring the bell, a terrible job it was, one I would not do for a bucket-load of cash. The bell itself was hideous: the wheel of a truck sliced in half and strung up an almond tree, where it dangled like a lynched criminal, its jagged edges an image of bloodlust. To beat the bell with a short rod, the bell-ringer climbed a wobbly stool that was as old as the school. Many crashed from that stool, occasionally breaking a bone or two. I did wonder if the crash was by chance or if the bell had some invisible powers with which it exerted vengeance. The bell itself was significant in two ways. Officially, it signalled the start of school day, when early comers stomped off like robots to the great hall to sing from the hymnbook, pray, recite the national anthem, and listen to announcements. For latecomers, its sound at nine meant that punishment by the cane or whip was nigh. And on this particular day, the punctuality prefect, a bespectacled, lanky lad with almost flat forehead, had positioned himself at the gate, waiting for latecomers. There were a good number of us already kneeling before him. Ricia had her blood lily in her hands, the soft stalk between her thumb and index fingers, rolling it gently as the lily's ball of fire dimmed in the morning sun. The prefect would occasionally pause to cast a careless glance. The gate was where he fed the despot I saw in him. He looked at us and, perhaps seeing us as hell-bound devils, crossed himself, his rosary drooping on his right wrist. His whipping cane on his left. He held it up, wagged it, sniffed it, smiled, and began to pace up and down. While we waited, he asked us to sing the punctuality song. We sang hesitantly like heretics forced to recite scriptures before facing the stake: *Punctuality and regularity is our motto,/ punctuality and regularity is our motto./ Oh pun-tu-ah-li-ty and re-gul-ah-ri-ty is our m-o-o-o-to-o-o…*

"Again, again," he yelled.

We sang for the bastard. He started from the far left. His first victim was a brittle teenager whose shirt was already wet with tears. I spat in front of me. When it was my turn to face his cane, I looked into his eyes, not to beg for pardon but to see if he was human. There was nothing to see but a pair of sharp eyes guarded by thick glasses. Behind those glasses I saw a boy weighed down by years of enduring a similar fate. By whipping us, I believed he was slowly relieving himself of his own pain. While his whip worked, the voices of early comers came to us from the great hall, rising from the vaults of the chapel, bearing "All Things Bright and Beautiful." *All things bright and beautiful, / All creatures great and small, /... The Lord God made them all*, they sang, as if to remind the prefect that we were all equal, big or small. I hummed along, my eyes wet and shut. There were no specifics to my tears. I suppose it was the sting of his whip or the fact that I was a child. We got fifteen strokes each. Our crime? We were late to school. I opened my eyes, wiped the tears and turned to Ricia. She was also wiping a tear, and brushing dirt from her knees. The blood lily was lying next to her, as helpless as we were. She looked at me with unreadable questions in her eyes. Did she expect me to do something? The more I looked at her, the more powerless I felt. She had sustained a cut and was licking her own blood.

That same day, at recess, I saw the prefect running towards the football field with three other boys. There were no traces of the serious-faced, cane-wielding boy in the person I saw at noon. He rather looked vivacious and genuinely normal, as though that morning was from another time in history. Looking back, I would say he reminds me of that bizarre old man in a story by Joyce, who went from discussing girls and the weather to sharing how boys "ought to be whipped and well whipped."

*

There were mornings when, having exhausted my routine stops and commentaries on the way to school, I would raise questions about the back room where Ricia slept. She would fall silent, smiling, making me feel like a failed comedian on a stage of straw. In one instance, I retaliated by making fun of her wrinkled skirt, its undone hems, how it never fluttered, how it hung still like raffia palm baskets turned upside-down. "See," I began, "it does not move at all. It is stiff. It is a bag. No, it is a basket." She paused, stepped back, pointed at the two conspicuous holes in my shorts, and asked, "Are those eyeglasses or the headlights of a car? Oh, I see, they are rabbit holes. Careful before rabbits jump out of your shorts."

"All the boys in my class have holes in their shorts," I cried in defence—more of a self-consolatory argument than a defence.

She had hit a nerve. I was not the only child with torn shorts, but the other boys did not care when jokes were spun around their tattered uniforms. I used to be that way, indifferent to what was said about my school uniform or my person, until Pa Suku said it was not okay to walk around in rags. He killed my ignorance, shredded my innocence, and since then, when the subject of torn shorts and shirts was raised, I would draw away from the conversation or angrily note that there was nothing funny about the rags we wore to school. The other boys would hush as though seriously considering my remark, look me in the face with open mouths and then, done with their silent mockery, fall over, cackling. The seeds Pa Suku had sown became a torment, a burden that never went away. He made me see the holes for what they were: the face of indigence.

At the end of school day, pupils from my school would walk on the left side of the old road, aware that the rich kids would flow out of their private school, which was not far from ours, and would walk on the other side. Their parents and teachers had warned them to stay away from us. And they did stay away from us. We were not told what to do; our parents and teachers did not care who we mixed with. But we knew exactly where we belonged and stuck to our side of the road, sweating and stomping home. They, on their side of the divide, walked gently, lightly exhausted and quiet. They were children of the new middle-class—auto spare-part dealers, oil company workers, importers of used and new electronic gadgets, senior civil servants—whose parents had broken the spell of poverty, swearing to pave a smooth path for their own kids. So they enrolled their children in private schools, flew them abroad for holidays and summer camps, and most importantly taught them how to despise the rest of us. They lived in flats with multiple rooms and gated walls that rose to the roofs. They had houseboys and gatemen who sat outside waiting for cars to crawl in and out. As a child I wondered why their houses were called flats. Not that the roofs were flat, anyway. But as Pa Suku would say, theirs was a different world where one could spontaneously, perhaps after several glasses of wine, invent and appropriate words at will.

There were days I walked home alone from school, noting signposts and lintel signs on shop-fronts. At the intersection of the old road and Timber Shed Street, I would linger before the fantastic sign announcing *Umezuoke and Sons International*. Under the italicized and unspaced lettering was the sketch of a cell phone, followed by three different phone numbers. Written below the numbers was the name of the general merchant himself: Chief Umezuoke Onuoha, KSM. On the walls, on both sides of the double door, were illustrations of what the Chief's international business offered: to the right, a ship perches warily, its mast disproportionately larger than the ship itself; next to the vessel, several bags of produce are stacked, high enough that they are the same size as the ship, perhaps waiting to be hauled abroad; to the left were paintings of spark plugs, car filters, motorcycle tires, and a portrait of the Chief beaming behind a pair of glasses so tiny they competed with his irises. Across from *Umezuoke and Sons International* was the coffin place with its fabulously radiant signpost. Umezuoke had employed two colours for his signpost: white for the background and black for the letters. The coffin dealer's sign had blue, green and a third that change from orange to red. I once stopped to closely examine one of the coffins under construction. It was reasonably wide and long, with humps like the ridges on the back of a camel. On the edges were gold glitters and little protuberances that looked like fat horns.

"Is there someone in that box?" I asked the coffin maker. He was surprised that I was there but offered me a smile. "Is there a rich person in that box?"

"Yes, there's a man there," he answered, his teeth as brown as the coffin.

I was not convinced, so I asked to see.

"No, no. The man is asleep," he said.

"But I want to see."

"There is nothing much to see," he said. "The man is not only asleep but has a permanent frown on his face. You want to know why?"

"Yes."

"Because he wants to be left alone."

"Why?"

"Because he is on a journey, one that requires solitude and silence. But the world keeps tugging him here and there, including his wife and relatives."

"Why?"

"Who knows? He never said a word before locking himself in that box."

"Do you have the key?"

"No."

"Where is it, in his house?"

"It's in there with him, I think. Or in the bushes somewhere."

Seeing the effect this had on me—that I was completely buying his story—he asked if I wanted to see the inside of an empty coffin, and made sure to add that he regularly napped in "the one over there." I declined but accepted the Tom-Tom sweet he offered and ran along. When I turned, I saw him grinning, both hands on his hips, a yellow 2B pencil sticking out of his overgrown hair. I had a bad dream that night. The coffin-maker, cloaked in a white robe, astride a black coffin, came flying towards me. That ugly grin was still on his face. When he landed, he opened the coffin. It was painted white on the inside and contained the decaying body of an unidentifiable animal, with maggots swarming. He dipped his hands in the porridge of maggots; they crawled and slid between his fingers.

There was a story about the coffin-maker that I thought was instructive and sordid. It was said that on a Sunday in December, before Christmas, he went to church for Thanksgiving. With a fat envelope, two goats and several tubers of yam as offerings, the church did not wait to ask who he was or what his testimony was about. They took his offerings and added him to the list. When it was his turn, he thanked the lord for favouring his business, bringing him customers from far and near, including customers who, under the good lord's direction, showed up three to four times a year to purchase products for loved ones embarking on a long journey. The church erupted in praises to the lord, claps and nods and measured shrieks. Moved by the coffin maker's words of gratitude, the preacher called him forward, asked him to kneel before the altar, placed a hand on his shoulder, and invited the church to pray for more blessings on the grateful businessman. The enthusiastic preacher, as bearers of this account contended, should have left it at that. But he was so moved that he asked the man, "What is this business of yours?" Perhaps waiting for this moment, the coffin-maker rose from his knees—they said he almost danced at this opportunity—brushed dirt off his knees and started with what he called his favourite bible verse, "In everything give thanks, for this is the will of God in Christ Jesus concerning you." Then he announced his trade, at which the church, caught off-guard, released a heavy gasp that—as the story went—was heard several kilometres away, startling passers-by and everyone within range.

Having thus accomplished his goal, the coffin-maker—rolling his shoulders—gleefully walked through the church to the back row, where his two assistants were waiting with the goats, picked up his bible, and disappeared. According to another version of the story, he had slowly broken wind on his way out, and so loud and violent was his flatulence that it struck down a curious child trailing him from behind.

There was yet another bizarre story about the coffin-maker. It was said that on several occasions where customers asked for discounts, he would tell them not to worry, that he would do something if they showed up again, at which the mortified customer flee from the scene before death got wind of those words. I did not believe these accounts but they confirmed my suspicion that the coffin-maker's sense of humour bordered on the sinister.

*

It was on one of my lone walks from school that I first met Pa Suku. He was walking at the same pace as me but on the other side of the road, both hands folded behind him, absorbed, picking his steps gingerly, as though the flat earth was plagued with invisible ditches. A bit hunched, with broad shoulders that curved forward, it seemed as though an irregular weight, strapped to his shoulders, was pulling him back. I do not recall the colour of his trousers but remember how tight they were, with a folded magazine rising from his back pocket. He was a conspicuous figure at the blocks where I lived. Everyone knew him, the man who spoke to no one, except when spoken to, who, in his white singlet, would sit outside his door, fiddling his radio or pensively reading a book, smoking a cigarette and occasionally looking up to examine the heavens.

He crossed to my side of the road and started a conversation. I am sure he knew I was from the blocks and may have spotted me loafing alone around, as I do when I am not in school or trapped at home by my boring family, humming odd tunes as I walked, stopping to draw abstract figures with my big toe.

"Hello, my friend," he greeted. "Do you mind if I walk with you?"

I shook my head. We walked five poles in silence. I studied his feet. His flat shoes had a visible hole on the side of the left leg. He retrieved his hands from his back, shoved them in his pockets and began to whistle. The sun, on its way west, positioned itself behind us, and I could feel its departing scorch on my neck. The clouds rumbled, suddenly, enveloping the sun in one quick swoop, validating the saying that in the Delta the weather changes without notice, like the moods of a pregnant woman.

When we got to Uwana's Calabar Kitchen, he paused and asked if I was hungry. I was not sure if I was hungry but nodded all the same. I had been walking for nearly ninety minutes, half of which was past the intersection where I was supposed to turn left and enter the blocks, which of course meant that lunchtime had passed. We turned right towards Uwana's Kitchen, a street-side shed with benches arranged in no order. Three cauldrons were boiling over an open fire: one was heavy with tomato stew, with chicken feet peeking out like old rakes; the second cauldron had a metal lid, making it whistle and spit bubbles that reminded me of a kid who had convulsed and spat bubbles in school; the third cauldron was full to the brim with white rice, from which Umana, her bosom heaving over the steaming cauldron, sweat-beads threading down her breast path, scooped onto a stainless plate. Then she moved to the tomato stew, scooped three times, fetched two chicken feet and placed them atop the plate. The customer whose order was being filled had four empty bottles of Gulder beer before him, on a green plastic table that was missing a leg. When the plate of rice and chicken landed on the three-legged table, the poor thing almost collapsed. The customer uttered something incoherent and wedged the table with a knee. The bottles fell over but did not break.

We sat on a short bench. Behind us the cauldrons hissed. I could feel the steam, a little too warm for comfort, and I could hear the slow cry of burning wood. The sun beamed once more as the clouds gradually dispersed, perhaps off to the adjoining towns—Etchie on the north side, Imo River town on the east, Umuebulu across the new highway.

When Madame Uwana finally came to our table (a tray atop three cement blocks), I saw her eyes were bloodshot but mild. Her forehead shone with sweat, and there was something unrecognizably different about her skin: its ambiguous fairness, the unevenness of the blackness around her knuckles and elbows. I concluded she may have compromised her skin by standing too close to fire or may have, as was the case with a man I used to know, adulterated her blackness with some abrasive nonsense.

"The usual?" she asked Pa Suku, who had not said a word to me since we took our seats.

"Yes, please," he answered, "and ask the young man what he wants."

"Rice?" she asked.

"No," I said.

"What, then?" she asked.

"Water."

She turned to Pa Suku, who simply shrugged and said, "Get him water, thank you."

To my surprise, the "usual" for Pa Suku was not a plate of rice and chicken but a bowl of vegetables, half a cucumber planted in the middle. As Uwana returned with this bizarre lunch, the other customers could not hide their contempt. The man next to us, vigorously crunching chicken bones, squinted at Pa Suku's bowl and my lone cup of water. He shook his head and called for a beer.

"I do not come here for food," Pa Suku finally said, not exactly talking to me but merely speaking to the space we shared, within earshot of everyone in the small shed.

In time I would become accustomed to his manner of speaking, but at first it struck me as too odd and detached.

"You see that house over there?" he said

I turned to see what was left of a razed bungalow. A part of the roof was gone, with sheets of zinc flapping or curled backwards. Half of the building seemed to be gradually collapsing, with a mound of rubble by the side, and two wide doors, shut tight as though they led to secret chambers. One was painted black. The other was white. Perhaps for balance, maybe not, for the white one had a black poster with the drawing of a hollow-nosed skull.

"You know what that building is?"

I looked at the white door with the skull. I do not recall what or how I responded to his question, but I remember he too did not know what it was. Uwana returned to our table. She fished out a pack of cigarettes from the pocket of her chequered combat shorts, offered Pa Suku a stick and a matchbox. One of the customers called for a cup of water. She was working alone that afternoon. The cauldrons demanded her attention. The feasting men demanded her attention. She betrayed no signs of exhaustion.

"That building reminds me of a house I used to know in Port Harcourt," Pa Suku was saying, "a house that collapsed during the Civil War, in the same month that Port Harcourt fell. I was too young to know what exactly happened, but I'm sure it wasn't bombed, neither was it shot at. It just collapsed. It was not the collapse itself that compels me to come here and stare at this crumbling building. You want to know why I come here?"

I nodded.

"That house, as insane as this may sound, tells me that the past, unresolved, is still with us, lurking, that war, those frightened soldiers, the massacre at Elelenwo, that putrescence is still here, and will one day come to a head, at which, like the house I used to know, the present would implode without notice."

And so began my relationship with Pa Suku. He would later introduce me to his transistor radio, and would also introduce me to the books he read. "This one," he started, the day he introduced Walser's *Jackob von Guten*, "was originally written in German. I will share a line from —" he flipped the pages "— from… Okay, here goes: *There is no worse behaviour than that which comes from disgust and ignorance.*" He closed the book and returned to his transistor radio.

2

Lose Your Mother.

Is that a command? I read it again. And step back to study the book itself. On the cover is an archway, an imposing passageway made of brick, leading nowhere, ghostly. The author's name sounds African. I assume she is African.

"Lose Your Mother!" the bookseller yells from the other side of the book-pile, where Faulkner and Fitzgerald snuggle with Achebe and Ellison on a mat.

This is where I buy my books.

"It's a great book," he adds.

I grunt a reply, drawn into the world the title conjured up. *Lose Your Mother.* A lacerating command. I will read it later, I say to myself. The edges are worn. The spines are broken, a sign of its transatlantic journey from New York to Nigeria. The pages are pulling away from the stitching, weakened by the journey and the rough handling at ports on both sides of the Atlantic.

*

Mother.

I must have been two or three when she started telling me stories. The first that stuck to my memory was that of the tortoise and the birds, in a kingdom that disappeared long ago, where critters could speak, and there were no distinction between them and us. An invitation had been made to birds of all kinds to a lavish dinner in the skies. The tortoise, the most cunning of all creatures, the glutton of all gluttons, got wind of this exclusive dinner, and swore he would either attend or die trying. So he went from one bird-hut to another, borrowing feathers, concocting stories to back his bizarre feather-gathering quest. He would leave each bird-hut with an instruction not to share his visit with anyone, since his mission was sacred. Two bird-streets later, he had enough feathers to travel to the sky. And he did, to the shock of the bird community. Since the host was not an earthling, he had no clue which bird was real or fake. And the real birds were too polite to start a fight with the sly tortoise who, to their distress, was already taking charge. "See," he began, "I know these people and their strange ways. I also know you're upset that I'm here, but it's too late to kick me out. You simply can't. So you may well make use of my wisdom. First things first, we must pick new names. Yes, it's the culture here. They invent new names for themselves each day, and that's how they live. Don't ask me why. You over there, pick a new name. And you over there." They all did. And then it was his turn to pick a name. He rolled his neck, moved his shell from side to side, and announced that his name, which they must not protest, was 'All of You'. "I know, you think it's a strange name, but believe me, it's a name I identify with, it's indeed a name that's been in my family for centuries. There's always someone with that name. The last bearer, my uncle, passed a month ago. I pick the name to honour him and maintain a family tradition as well. So, there, the story behind my new name. Second and most important point to note, you must wait to hear your name before you eat anything here. Trust me, it's the culture. You'll see what I mean. They'll call your name as they walk through that door with whatever they're serving."

He was still talking when the server appeared with a keg of palm wine. "For all of you," the server said and walked away. The dwarf bittern, known for her insatiable thirst for wine, leapt from its seat to pour herself a glass, but was hushed back by the tortoise, who had already moved the keg to his side of the table. "You must be deaf, my friend, or you were not listening to what I said about the ways of these people. This keg here is for All of You."

"But how did they know to mention your name," cried the dwarf bittern, "we did not give them our names?"

"They know your name. Things work differently here. These people know what you're thinking. God lives here. These are God's tenants, and they are supernatural beings. Excuse me. I need a glass…"

The server returned with a steaming pot of nut soup. "For all of you." And the tortoise pounced on it, cleared the whole thing. "Patience, my friends. They'll mention your names."

This went on and on, course after course, until the birds could take it no longer. It was the weaverbird who launched the first offensive. He walked straight to the tortoise, whose sides were covered in feathers of all sorts, browsed through and plucked back its feather. The others followed and soon the tortoise had no feather to fly back to earth. At the end of day, full and heavy with food, he was left to find his way home, stranded in the sky. Luckily, the cattle egret forgot her purse and flew back to pick it up.

"My good friend," the tortoise began, tilting his head to the side, "please, I beg you in the name of my ancestors, do me one favour…"

"What?" the cattle egret snapped, all the time casting the tortoise a curious stare, wondering what it was that drove his appetite and fuelled his treachery. "What do you want from me? If it's a feather, forget it. And it won't do you any good, since you need more to fly out of here. If it's a ride back to earth, that's also not possible. You are five times my size, not to mention the weight of your stomach after all that food. You look like a cow this minute."

"Please, only one favour. When you are down there, please kindly inform my neighbour, the hare—"

"There are two of them, which one?"

"The one with a short left ear, who narrowly escaped death last week. Tell him to rent ten mattresses, wide and bouncy ones, and put them outside, near the market square."

"You plan to jump?"

"I'll face my fate, my friend."

"I'll tell him."

The cattle egret left. He did not go straight to the hare's, but stopped at a small party organized by cows outside the city, where he drank, ate, and danced from one cow to another. "They love me here," he kept saying to himself, as the cows let him jump on their backs, fanning him with their tails. "They love me here." When he eventually made it to the hare's, tipsy, he delivered a different message: "Your neighbour asked for a stage to be erected at the market square. He's going to perform, an exotic dance I think. Prepare the stage with whatever you have, straw or wood or iron. And be sure to show up." On the way home, he stopped at every door to announce that the tortoise was planning a grand performance at the square, inviting them all to attend. The day came. The stage was set—not made of straw, but with scrap metal and wood. The tortoise looking down from the sky, saw a platform, but could not tell if it was made of mattress or not. He jumped. The crowd, anticipating whatever magic he was planning to perform, watched. The crash was hard. The crowd waited. Perhaps he would emerge, alive and triumphant. But that was not the case. He did live. His shell, however, was shattered. It was the snail, the benevolent snail, that took him in and used her slime to patch him up. "That," Mama concluded, "was how the tortoise got his shell." In another version of the same story, the birds hauled the tortoise down, split him in half, one half left on land, the other thrown in the ocean, which explains why we have the tortoise on land, and its relative—the turtle—in the ocean. I believed her. I believed everything she said, even when she retold or re-interpreted biblical accounts to make a point. In one instance, after a sermon on the exploits of the apostle Paul, she came home and shared her version, and left us her little doubts by way of interpretation. It was the story of Paul in Ephesus, where he had gone to spread the word among Jews and gentiles; and there, he was given the powers to heal, so much so that those who touched his handkerchief or apron were instantly healed of whatever ailed them— even evil spirits were expelled. "God is great," Mama added, "but this thing about handkerchiefs," she sighed and shook her head. She reread the entire nineteenth chapter of the book of Acts, thanks to her moderate reading skills, which she always praised for placing her on the same level as the Bereans who, as Paul recounts, "were more noble than those in Thessalonica, in that they received the word with all readiness of mind, and searched the scriptures daily, whether those things were so." "I wonder why Pastor D. didn't talk about the Seven Sons of Sceva," Mama continued, "that would've been more entertaining. It's in the same chapter, but he left it out."

Several days later, she returned to those Seven Sons of Sceva, and wondered why the Lord sat back and watched them humiliated for invoking his name, not as if they did so after drinking themselves senseless or emerging from a whorehouse, but had simply done so to dispel an evil spirit in the name of Christ. They had commanded the evil spirit to leave the possessed body, in the name of Jesus Christ whom Paul preached. The possessed man had replied, "Jesus I know, and Paul I know; but who are you?" And went ahead to beat the living daylights out of them. "I don't understand it," Mama said, "at least the lord would have honoured his name." I also did not understand why the Lord abandoned them. My confusion was total when, many months later, our pastor mentioned a portion of the new testament where Paul declared that it did not matter if Christ was preached out of envy or love, "whether in pretence, or in truth," and that the most important thing was for the name and message of Christ to spread. If that was the case, why then did he abandon the Sons of Sceva? Did it matter if they had mentioned Christ as part of their incantation? Was it not to the Lord's benefit that they had invoked his name as the ultimate dispeller of evil spirits? The whole thing was a puzzle to me, the same way I could not fathom why God would decide to destroy the world with water after investing so much time to create the intricate creatures he left to roam freely.

It was Mama who planted Noah's account in my head, but for a different reason; the equality of all creatures, irrespective of how humans choose to group them. "On the fifth day," Mama said, inching towards her in Noah's account, "God created the beasts of the land. All of them. He created them as equals. Size did not matter. Ants were as good as bats, lizards as good as gators. And many years later," she paused for effect, drawing back as though to emphasize the colossal passing of biblical time, "many years later, when he wanted to destroy the world, he instructed Noah to save a pair of each, male and female: goat, dog, cat... Now tell me," she paused again, nodding instructively, "tell me, if the creator considered them equal enough survive the flood, why do we create classes between animals?" Ricia and I exchanged glances but kept quiet. I was older at this point, and had long discarded the innocence with which I embraced her early stories. She had replaced most of her tortoise stories with biblical stories and events from real life: her day at the market, a neighbour's daughter that went and got herself pregnant, a boy that was caught smoking cigarettes and was flogged and expelled from school. The use of real life experiences, I suppose, was to drive the lesson home, to make the moral of the story more palpable. In retrospect, I would say some of her stories were rather traumatizing, since we were too young to figure out the context within which they occurred.

"So tell me," she continued, still talking about God and Noah, "where do we get this idea of separation between these animals?" Ricia and I made no reply. I was more interested in God's decision to destroy a space he created and called beautiful. I did not voice this interest. I listened. Our job was to listen. Mama was preaching to herself and had only summoned us to simulate a sermonic atmosphere: a preacher and her flock. "It's right here in Genesis, see?" She tapped the bible on her lap. As if assured by the sheer feel of the book, she laughed and reached out to pinch my nose. He fingers smelled of the raw onions she had chopped for the chicken stew she was preparing for dinner. She had asked if I wanted to chew a tiny piece, repeating her usual homily on the gastro-cleansing powers of onions. I declined and opted for what I loved doing with chopped onions: bow over the bowl and open my eyes as wide as they could go, holding still for a second or two before dashing off with teary eyes, pretending I was crying. Ricia thought it was a dangerous act and warned that I would go blind one day, and then find it impossible to convince anyone I was truly blind and in pain.

"Noah was a great man," Mama continued, her breath reeking of onions.

We listened attentively. I imagined Noah the way Mama described him, the way she had been conditioned to describe him: foreign, distant, strong, infallible. It rained that night. It was more of a deluge as I imagined it that night, with lightning visible through window cracks and thunderclaps ripping the darkness without. I struggled to sleep. The room was soot-dark. I feared the roof would give and the bulging ceiling would give too. I pictured a roofless, flooded room illuminated by lightning, with millipedes crawling about. I was eventually wrestled down by sleep and dreamt an incomplete dream. Noah was there in my dream. I knew it was Noah. He introduced himself to me the way personages announce themselves in dreams—a synchronized knowing. He was garbed in blue. Short hair. No beard. No walking stick. What an impostor, I thought. I struggled to reconcile the man before me with the image Mama had planted in my head. You are not Noah, I cried, disappointed. Noah is not black. You are not Noah, I wept. Your nose is flat and ugly. You are not Noah. Where is your beard? Mama said you were in white when the floods came.

Blue is ugly. You are not Noah. Where is your walking stick? Where are your sons and their wives? You should be taller than this. You are not Noah. Why are you black? You are not Noah. Then the floods came, rising from pores underneath our feet. "Move on," Noah instructed, his voice as thunderous as the growling clouds. I was paired with a cat, Ricia with a bat. I turned and saw men and women paired with creatures of all kinds, marching up to a waiting train, singing, dancing, happy to be rescued. I went along, completely confused.

I shared my dream with Ricia on the way to school. This was before Old Jumbo died. She asked if I genuinely thought Noah was white. How could she ask such a question? "You think he was black?" I asked.

"There is no Noah. He does not exist," she announced.

I could not believe what I was hearing. How could that be?

"How do you know?" I asked.

"Do you think the tortoise once borrowed wings from birds and flew to a meeting in heaven? Do you believe the woodpecker once bragged about burying its mother in the trunk of an Iroko tree?

"I don't. Those are ordinary stories," I said.

"Noah's story is also an ordinary story," she said, her head tilted like an old school teacher correcting a child's homework.

"How do you know?" I asked.

"How could he have gathered a pair of every living creature and organized them into a single ark? It's all made up." This time she looked straight ahead, her voice flat and full of certainty.

I fell silent.

My backpack felt heavier.

I passed Jumbo's Garden without waiting to admire the flowers. Ricia stopped, perhaps hoping I would pause as I always did.

I did not.

I locked both hands in my pocket, pondering whose account to believe: my mother's, the uninvited dream that forced itself upon my mind, or Ricia's argument. Someone should at least agree with me that Noah, real or not, was not black. Later that day I went to Pa Suku for answers. "You have to believe in creation to believe the story of Noah," Pa Suku said when I raised the topic. Then he went ahead and said something about evolution. Names were dropped. Charles Darwin, etc., blah, blah, blah, and digressed to share multiple versions of the same flood narrative, starting with some obscure Native American account and going on to the Epic of Gilgamesh. Too much for me to handle. I listened but was rather more confused than I was when I came to him.

*

Mama named her goats. There was Uta, a brown she-goat with one broken horn. And there was Ogoamaka, Mama's favourite. Mama had a theory: the God of the cuddled cat is the God of the goat. If cats and dogs were named, goats and cattle deserve names and special treatments too. There were dogs around the blocks that roamed and sniffed trash, and at night slept under discarded tables. If those dogs, Mama argued, as smelly as they were, could have names, or once bore names to which they answered, what about goats? But there was more to Mama's position.

Her take on goat naming was an allegorical attack on the new middle class whose material worth, contrasted with our lack, glittered like polished pebbles. As it turned out, Ogoamaka was also the name of her boss's daughter, the brat who ordered Mama around because her dad paid Mama a pittance to clean bathrooms and rugs. Mama would return from those duties exhausted, her eyes red and teary from several hours of inhaling bleach. As soon as she walked through the door, tossing her handbag, we would rally around her, waiting for the leftovers she brought from the flats. Once she handed them over, she would go outside, yell Ogoamaka's name and toss her crumbs to chew. We would pounce on whatever it was she brought home. In that moment, face-to-face with those rare crumbs we so cherished, everything else ceased to exist. We would giggle as we tore them apart. Mama would be looking at us. There were days she smiled as we munched on those crumbs, and days I saw pain in her eyes. That expression of pain, as I see it now, was the unutterable sadness of knowing that a better life existed outside the blocks. It was a life she could not attain, that she had accepted as unreachable, a life she sniffed but could not ingest. As an employee of the new middle class, she shuttled between two worlds, inhabiting one and not the other, hence in despair. I think her pain—I may be wrong here—was because she could not understand the workings of that other world, what it truly entailed, how it was constructed, how it came to be alienated from the world she embodied. How, for instance, could an individual own two cars, a big house with servants, a wardrobe that might as well be the retail outlet of a luxury brand? How is that possible? As an adult, knowing the things I know about class in Nigeria,

I imagine Mama asking those questions and running into a blockade in her mind. Are we destined to stay poor, to serve the new middle class? Will my children also serve their children? Those, I believe, are some of the questions that must have crossed Mama's mind.

Ogoamaka was unusually smart for a goat. Whenever her named was mentioned, she drew closer, especially when yam peels or breadcrumbs were in sight. I thought goats were dumb, doomed, and destined for hell as we were told in church: "… and He will separate them one from another, as a shepherd divides his sheep from the goats. And He will set the sheep on His right hand, but the goats on the left." It has increasingly occurred to me that Mama was, perhaps, also mocking the foundations of her faith when she started naming her goats. By naming and humanizing them, one could argue that somehow she excluded them from the biblical goat-to-hell narrative, conferring them absolute grace and eternal equality.Ogoamaka was more than a goat to my family. She was a named presence that trotted on all fours. She had a life and so did we. The thought of selling or slaughtering her for Christmas never came up. She died a peaceful death and was buried next to a group of plantain trees. That was a long time ago. But by reason of her active presence within our household, memories of her glorious and adventurous life still lingers. Just a few months before she died, for instance, I recall seeing her walking towards Ma Ike's open kitchen, where yam and plantain peels were scattered to dry on a mat. The incident that followed, as bitter-sweet as it was, became a fixture in my memory, not only reminding me of Ogoamaka but also marking a pivotal moment in my uncertain relationship with Ma Ike, who lived alone in the single room next to us.

Ma Ike did not enjoy the luxury of two rooms with a dividing door in the middle. The landlord had walled off her middle door, the other half occupied by a different tenant, one Mr Obono from Ugep in Cross River State. Her side of the divide faced the small stretch of shrubs and bushes, the only oasis of fresh air we shared. Between that stretch and her door, was a door-less kitchen she built by herself, a simple shed with a low wall made of planks and a zinc roof. Ma Ike and I did not get along. I was not sure if she hated me or if I simply misunderstood her. Her unreadable eyes made it difficult to see or know what was on her mind. Whatever it was, I had my misgivings; and that evening, those misgivings kept me from stopping Ogoamaka's avaricious walk into her kitchen. The fresh yam and plantain peels were there. In a few days they would turn earth-brown and Ma Ike would pound them into consumable powder for lunch and dinner. Everything was useful in Ma Ike's world: the yam and its peels, the plantain and its peels. It was rumoured that she used cassava leaves as a vegetable, a delicacy that was not popular in the Delta. Her frugal ways with yams and plantains, as admirable as I thought they were, did not put her in my good books, as I wondered why she stared when I flipped old newspapers on our front porch. I suppose her stare was the consequence of proximity. Those strange stares were often followed by barely audible but stabbing comments, which made them even more ominous. "Small boy... he will not play with his mates... now he talks to himself like the old fool he chats with." Hearing those words, I would swell in an anger that deflated as soon as it started. I am still baffled by how sad I was when she moved, and how much I wished I had the guts to stop the new neighbour from tearing down her kitchen afterwards.

There were days she sat on her front porch combing her hair, peering into a handheld, sickle-shaped mirror. And from our porch I would steal glances at her, making sure she did not catch the direction of my eyes. She would hum and sway, a smile on her face, adjusting the mirror's distance from her face. And then she would touch the sleeves of her blouse, steady her weight on the dwarf stool, and what must have been a flirtatious glance would be tossed my way. Was she putting on a show for the two of us? Was there something she wanted me to know that I did not? Was there a hidden lesson? I wish I knew what she saw when she looked into that mirror, and what her thoughts were about me. I once assumed she expected me to throw in a compliment, to say I liked her thick eyebrows, which I did like. But I was twelve and clueless. And then there was the bra and sheer underwear incident, which I do not remember well but will reconstruct here in fragments. It was a Saturday afternoon. I was home alone, out on the porch, reading an old newspaper I had borrowed from Pa Suku. She knew I was there. I made myself believe she knew. What else could make her do what she did, emerging from her room, clad in nothing but a purple bra and a transparent underskirt, pretending I was not there? The sun fell on her chest and lingered long enough. Then she turned and disappeared into her room as if nothing had happened. Not even a small wink to signal or signify her intentions, if there were any intentions. I replayed that scene every night, impressing it upon my mind until it became a recurrent dream. In one dream she turned to face me, her bra fell off. I expected both breasts to emerge, but instead I beheld two pistols positioned to shoot my eyes off, her head replaced by the coffin maker's. I woke up to a slimy patch between my legs.

She was right. I did talk to myself. But there was a method to my madness. What she did not know was that those conversations were repetitions of sentences and phrases from the BBC programmes I listened to, my small attempt to sound like the reporters, which proved extremely difficult, for all I had were fragments, often misheard, since the "radio voices" neither slowed down nor repeated for my benefit. I remember going to Pa Suku and asking him to help me sound like a radio voice.

"They are not called radio voices," he said, "they are called reporters."

"I want to be a reporter," I said.

"Well, you can be whatever you want to be," he said, waxing dreamy as usual. "When I was a kid, I wanted to be a civil engineer. It was after the war and the nation was rebuilding itself. New roads and houses were springing up everywhere. In Diobu, it was rumoured that civil engineers made a lot of money." He smiled as memories trickled through his mind. "I will tell you something a famous writer once said," he branched out. "This American writer, John Updike, said he once wanted to be an animator for Disney." He paused. I waited. The evening clouds thickened and gathered. I anticipated a downpour. A small burst of wind passed with the grace of many shadows, ruffling nothing but a few cellophane bags. It was a grey evening, slowly stripped of light by the slow approach of dusk.

"John Updike. Yes, I know you are lost there."

He had seen it on my face. The names he dropped—Brecht, Dostoevsky, Sartre—were often so farfetched that they made me stare blankly, unable to conjure mental images to match the names.

"You will meet Updike someday," he continued, "You will meet him on the pages of his books. I met him in '76, at the University College in Port Harcourt. I was on a visit there and had gone to the library to browse their collection of American novels. They had quite a few those days, including everything Updike had written up to that time. Well… where was I? Right, you will meet Camus and Calvino, Faulkner and Flaubert. They will be out there on the shelves of bookstores, in libraries, and street corners. They will be waiting for you and the generation after you. It doesn't matter whether you are a slum bumpkin," he laughed, "they will be waiting for you, my boy.

As I was saying, things change. Today you want to be a journalist, the next day you are a pilot. Ever thought of flying planes? I'll tell you something. When my crush on engineering waned, the thought of flying airplanes took over. In those days we made paper planes, tied them to small sticks and ran the streets of Diobu pretending we were pioneer aviators. Do you know how to make one? I can show you how."

He pulled a page off the newspaper he was reading. The first three folds were familiar. The clouds, about to yield their contents, growled. Wind in mild gusts came and passed. His hands trembled, with veins erect. He squinted to see where the folds went and bit his lips as he fastened and tucked a flap. The last two folds were unfamiliar, though not hugely different from what I would do. At the final fold, his product was the same as the paper planes we made. He offered me the plane. It surprisingly felt heavy, as though he had stuffed it with pebbles. I thanked him but secretly wished we ran the blocks together with our new plane, playing pioneer pilots. Would that not be a sight? Pa Suku and I, paper planes in hand, running between blocks to the bewilderment of residents. Ma would have been mortified, and I swear she would have dashed after me, screaming my name until I screeched to a halt, waiting for a smack to land on the back of my head.

"Does it look familiar?" he asked.

"It does," I said.

"There's nothing new under the sun," he said. "Here's an example. In this country, there've always been coups and counter-coups. And you know what? There'll be another one. What year is it? '94, right. There'll be another coup. The signs are everywhere." He studied his feet and mine, perhaps pondering what he had just said. His mouth parted, as though about to speak. He excused himself and walked into his room. I heard his feet shuffling on the carpetless floor, and the rustle of plastic bags followed. When he returned, I sensed he was slightly irritated. Was it exhaustion? The jitters were more pronounced.

"What is a coup?" I asked.

He was not listening. He was off again without answering my question. I could hear him moving stuff. I pictured him rummaging... He returned with a half-finished cigarette and a full smile. Clutching the cigarette between his fingers, he swayed, puffed, and chortled for no reason. His sway brought me his body scent: the smell of untreated timber left to soak and rot, the same smell that enveloped you when you passed the lumber yard. I may have imagined this smell, or may have amplified it. His gaze was up in the sky. The clouds had regrouped and were descending and dispersing. He rocked his knees. I saw strands of greying hair on his bare legs, his toenails were over-grown, digging into the ground like claws.

"I will break it down for you," he began, returning to my question. "When a government is corrupt, as they always are here, soldiers show up from nowhere and kick them out. That's a coup, in a nutshell. But it never always works out smoothly. The new guys end up becoming worse than those they've removed. It's human nature as we know it now, until there're enough reasons to think otherwise.

So, where were we?" he asked. His cigarette was now a small stub and he dropped it and crushed it with his big toe. "Ah, okay. After all the dancing around with decisions, I became a freelance writer and thinker."

A grin took over his face at this point. A freelance writer. A thinker. Both sounded right and on point, since he always had a thinking pose and scribbled all the time. I left it at that, aware that he would return with further explanations. He never left a thought, a random word, to stray too far. "An unfinished thought," he used to say, "is as dangerous as a child left to grow wild, without a sense of right and wrong."

*

Two baby goats from the corner of our block emerged and joined Ogoamaka as she made her way to Ma Ike's kitchen. It appeared they had been waiting for her to pave the way. Ogoamaka stood for a minute or two at the entrance to the kitchen, as though in reverence for the peels that would soon be chewed into cud-ready pulp. I wondered if she was giving thanks. After this solemn pause, she strolled in and started with a moderate mouthful, her jaws grinding, zigzagging, her ears twitching and shifting like revolving satellites, her eyes scanning for threats. She saw me and halted in mid-chew. The others were going at the peels with abandon. Assured that I was not a threat, Ogoamaka returned to the buffet. She changed her position, turning her rump to Ma Ike's door, a wrong move, a fatal miscalculation on her part. Ma Ike had heard their controlled bleats and had concealed herself behind the curtain. I could hear the faint shuffle of Ma Ike's feet as she angled in readiness to strike. The young goats, overjoyed, were beginning to bleat above the cautionary volume, skipping in small circles, giving each other little shoves. Ogoamaka did not care, the coast was clear enough and all was going well. Before they could say Jack Robinson, disaster was upon them. Ma Ike ran out of her room wielding a long spatula. Ogoamaka fled first. The others followed. The spatula was swung at one of the baby goats. It missed. My Ike lost her balance. The fall was hard. An audible chuckle escaped my mouth. She ignored me and sprang up like a cat. Her hair, tousled, had collected sand and dust. She tossed the spatula aside. It landed next to a line of scattered peels, where the baby goats had had their last chew. Then she turned to me and started addressing the goats, as though I had become a representative of goats.

Breaking from her tirade, she asked why I was laughing. Unaware that my chuckle had progressed into a laugh, I was taken aback by her question. I buried my head in the sports section of the old newspaper. "I'm not surprised," she said, "you are like that mad man. You better stop visiting him or you'll be worse." She retrieved her spatula and retreated to her room. Her remark hung there, a dense presence that successfully defeated my laughter. I felt anger building up. I closed the newspaper and shut my eyes, quivering as though I would disintegrate in no time. I was confused at the effect her remark had on me. She had only issued an advice, more of a warning, but I took offense; for her words, as simple as they sounded, were an onslaught on the man I respected and considered wise. My outrage was however tampered by a streak of fear and a jolt of self-examination. I wondered what it was about Pa Suku that disgusted her. I knew he could barely afford his cigarettes. And when he did, he smoked them slowly, smothering them in-between puffs to ensure they lasted longer than usual. I knew the single room he occupied had nothing but a table, a slim mattress on the floor, books in boxes and on the floor, sheets of paper. His stove was never lit. What did he eat? I did imagine him munching old newspapers and thick books, regurgitating them whenever hunger struck again. If I continued to visit him, read his old newspapers, follow the news on his five-band radio, would I wind up in the same position? I shuddered. Me, an old man, hunched over piles and piles of scribbles, hair spiralling out of my ears and nostrils, engrossed in a fat hardback at noon, reading as though life is nothing but a set of texts. But now, having moved into the larger world where I hear stories of men with Pa Suku's kind of learning and exposure, who seize every chance to wag their intellectual tails and carve society up with their tongues, I am of the opinion that Pa Suku was a rare case: a saint. He must have so hated the world outside, its range of pretension, that he abandoned it for the dirt and stench of the blocks.

I shared the day's drama with Ricia and told her what Ma Ike had said to me. I warned her not to tell Mama, knowing how opposed Mama was to my friendship with Pa Suku. Ricia swore to keep it to herself, but that was not the case. The next morning, while preparing for school, I heard Mama's voice outside. It did not sound like she was singing to her goats or chanting praises to her God. Ricia and I ran outside. A group of women from the adjoining blocks had gathered, their hands folded across their breasts, with mock-serious faces feigning concern when, in reality, they wished for a fistfight, which then would suffice as their dose of entertainment for the day. Ma Atta was in that group, almost kissing another woman's left ear as she "authoritatively" explained what was going on. Her listener, eyes open wide in excitement, was nodding in agreement, as though Ma Atta was privy to the whole matter. I shot both women a contemptuous eye, but they were too absorbed in Mama's outburst to notice my disdain. Mama was calling down fire and thunder on evil neighbours next door. Whatever evil they wished her son would return to them tenfold. "Evil neighbours that use their lips to destroy destinies, evil neighbours... ." Ma Ike's door was tightly shut. Not a whisper, not a sigh. I had expected her to bounce out of her room, tighten her wrapper around her waist, position herself at her door and mount a counter attack. She did none of that. Not even a murderous cackle to infuriate Mama. She surprised me. She disappointed Ma Atta and her band of "concerned" neighbours.

But how did Mama find out what Ma Ike had said to me? Ricia was not supposed to share. I trusted her. I felt the sting of betrayal and was scarred by that brief feeling. I was the sensitive one. She, on the other hand, was impervious and bold. But in this instance, having read the sign of pain on my face, she caved and avoided my eyes. Mama came for me, her chest heaving as though it would burst. I felt Ma Atta's eyes on me, explaining me to her listeners. Mama pulled my left ear and dragged me inside. Ricia followed, sniffling. "You, this tiny rat," Mama started. Rat. I can still hear her rolling the r in rat. RRRRRAT. Her face was covered in sweat, smearing the invisible layer of powder she had dusted on her face. I expected her to react the way she did, but I did not expect the name-calling. She never called us names. "I don't know what you want to become," she continued, examining me from head to toe. "Stay away from that… from that hopeless Pa Suku. He does nothing but read those books that are heavier than his skinny body. He is nothing but bad luck. Whatever that stupid Ma Ike said was because of him. He's already bringing you bad luck! I don't know where he comes from and cannot say where he is going. Let him carry his own load. Stay away from him." Her eyes were damp, but she managed to keep the tears from falling. She left the room in two quick strides. I knew she was off to work, where she would spend the whole day cleaning kitchens and bathrooms for the new middle-class. I stood where she left me, confused, frightened, torn.

The walk to school was different that morning. Ricia was quiet as usual. But this time her silence seemed rooted in what had happened. In my confusion, I temporarily paid no heed to both sides of the road, though I noticed how empty the road was that morning. In normal days, I would have paid close attention to this strange silence, perhaps stopped to ask Ricia—who was better at drawing inferences—to attempt an explanation, but I was not in the mood, neither was Ricia. Mama's face that morning had done something to me. Her words and the look on her face shook me up. It was a look that encompassed more than the issue at hand. It bore anguish repressed, fear unuttered. I would see that look two more times. The second time was a few years later, when she saw a copy of *Playboy* under the basket where I kept my clothes. She did not know what the magazine was (neither did I) but she knew it was no good for a boy my age. I had turned fourteen then and was beginning to let my eyes trail and fall on images that tickled me. So when I saw this magazine at the vendor's stand nearby, prominently displayed a sight away from a primary school, it caught my attention. A day later I left school before Ricia, bought it and hurried home. The vendor had grinned and winked as I handed him my little savings. It was an old issue from '71, with Darine Stern on the cover. I was not home the day Mama saw Darine Stern under my basket, I was away with Pa Suku. It was the same day Pa Suku said something about Quentin Crisp, speaking as though they both knew one another, had shared drinks somewhere, "QC's bright toenails," "QC's witt." When I returned from Pa Suku and his QC tales, I met Mama's stare.

"Where did you get this?" she asked.

An invisible glue sealed my lips.

"Are you deaf? I'm asking where you got this?" she asked, shaking the magazine.

Ricia was standing behind her. I sank my face to the earth and each grain of sand seemed magnified, each with its set of eyes and glistering teeth, jeering as I fought off the shame that enveloped me. I hated them. I hated myself. I hated everyone. I despised Darine Stern. I studied my toenails. Ma Ike, who was positioned at her door, shuffled herself into her room. I swear I heard her laugh. Ricia stepped forward, came close to me and walked off. And when I raised my face, I saw Mama's lips quivering. She held out the magazine to me, begging me to say something, to offer an explanation.

"You are not like your brothers," she said, nodding. It was a random statement but it was at the core of her fear and anguish. I was a different child, frail and fragile, and she was afraid I was going to turn out as "miserable" as Pa Suku. "You are not like your brothers."

And she was right. I was indeed not like my brothers, and I am still not like they are. Kor left school to apprentice at a cobbler's shed and now runs his own small shed in O. Leab got a place as a machine hand at the lumber yard and now operates his own machine. Pan had worked with Uju the vulcanizer and took over Uju's workshop when the latter died in a car crash. I, on the other hand, am certainly on my way to becoming Pa Suku. Mama saw it then and was afraid. I, too, was afraid but since come to terms with the fact that I would rather die poor than become someone else.

The third time I saw that look on her face was when I said I was going to study English literature and History at university. At first she was glad I had been offered a place and had managed to secure funding for myself, which of course meant she and Papa would not have to agonize over how to pay for my education. Then she asked what a degree in English and History would do for me—the entire family, that is. I hesitated. She waited. I said I did not know what I would do with a degree in English and History, and hazarded a few possibilities: write for a newspaper somewhere, maybe in Lagos; edit books for a publisher somewhere, I don't know where; write my own books, maybe not. She squinted at me. Have I thought of becoming an accountant? Her boss's friend was a chartered accountant and worked for an oil company. Accountants make money. Have I considered "bank work?" I said I was not interested in banking and finance. She squinted again. Then I saw that look in her face.

Ricia and I were late to school that day. Instead of blaming our mood, which kept us from quickening our pace, I put the blame on the white man we saw at the entrance to Pipeline Street. It was Ricia who saw him first. She froze and lingered. I saw him and my eyes almost fell off their sockets. He was standing next to a white Hilux pickup with a yellow oyster shell drawn on its side, a familiar logo to anyone raised near oil installations owned by multinationals. His white helmet also had a yellow oyster shell logo. There were two black men, one in a red overall with the same oyster shell on the back of his boiler suit. They both were shovelling a small strip on the side of the street, pointing and shovelling as though an Ogbanje's *Iyi-uwa* was buried there. The white man was taking notes and smoking a cigarette. He was the first white person I saw up close. I wanted him to talk. Here was my chance to hear the exotic version of English that came clear though Pa Suku's radio. For a moment I forgot the earlier incident with Mama. The road was beginning to come alive. A Coca-Cola delivery truck pulled up a block ahead, and I could see the delivery boys readying themselves to do the rather intriguing toss-catch-and-stack routine. Two exciting things at once: a white man and a Coca-Cola truck! I waited. Then he spoke, more of a mumbled instruction to the two diggers who, by the way, reminded me of the men who dug the grave for the kid who died in a pit latrine: same humiliating bow to break the earth with a shovel; same flood of sweat streaming down their faces, dripping like fresh blood from the side of those dogs slit open by the butcher and dog pepper-soup man in block d. He spoke, this exotic stranger, and I thought I had misheard. I lingered some more. He passed another instruction. It barely sounded like the type of English I expected. The two labourers had to move closer to understand him. I flinched. Where is this one from? I thought. Are not all white people supposed to talk English? The ones in Pa Suku's radio talked English. Who is this impostor? I moved along feeling disappointed, so disappointed that I passed the coca cola truck without paying attention to those muscular delivery boys.

3

I continued to wonder why Mama and Ma Ike disliked Pa Suku. How could they not see how brilliant he was? How could they not see how much of the world he knew, how he captured that world in words so sweet one could listen to them all day?

I did not know, as I now know, that their repulsion was the result of their inability to understand; Pa Suku was a conundrum, a round peg in the square hole that was the blocks. They may have also wondered why his obvious brilliance hadn't won the material lushness that existed outside the blocks. If he knew what the rich folks knew, all that fancy English and manners, why was he not over there where houses were fenced and gated?

I decided it might be better to hear his side of the story. So I went ahead and crafted a chain of questions for him: Are you as poor as they say you are? Are you as useless as they say? Where are you from? I simply wanted him to clear my doubts.

The day of questioning came. I hastily ploughed through my lunch and walked to his block, juggling the questions in my head. About a block to his door, Dan appeared. Dan was the tailor's son and was known to simply appear everywhere, and I believed he vanished and surfaced wherever he pleased. He was about fourteen, one of those kids who turned up at every event around the blocks. You could spot him at night on his way to the local football bars behind Pa Suku's block, where grown-ups, adorned in their team jerseys, brawled over beer and laid claim to the

FCs of England. His parents did not care where he went or when he left their sight.

Dan was also known for his multicolour, multi-fabric shorts and shirts. This particular evening he was wearing a pair of blue, pink and green shorts. One of his designs, I presumed. He knew how to work his father's Singer treadle, and would frequently scavenge scraps of fabric, mount the machine and treadle away. One of his best designs was a pair of *ankara* shorts, which he wore on special occasions. I thought Dan was a genius. Now I think he was a Michael Kors who never became what he was destined to be. This was not the popular take on Dan. He once showed up at a naming ceremony in his *ankara* shorts and a lipsticked lip. The moment he stepped in, everyone stood still. He smiled, innocent and unaware of what he was to the world, ignorant of the uncertainties that enveloped his person. He was quickly bounced. It was Achu who lifted and dumped him outside. Like Pa Suku, Dan was a curious case. No one knew what he was or why he acted the way he did. On normal occasions, Dan would stop to chat. But in this instance he ignored me. He appeared weak and emaciated. His shoulders were hanging rather low. His eyes closely watched his feet, as though to stop them from trailing off. He could have easily passed for an exile striding softly on foreign soil, careful not to trample or be trampled upon.

*

Pa Suku was sitting in front of his curtainless door when I got there. Up close, the stool on which he sat looked grotesquely old and fragile. He rocked with its wobble, smoking his St. Moritz, possibly a leftover from the previous day. His eyes were tightly shut, a foggy grimace on his face, as though he was listening to a distant song. Left leg crossed over the right, he air-tapped to the music in his head. There were times I wanted that music to explode into our shared space, blasting forth in measured beats. It never did. It was solely his, a personal buzz in his head, perhaps keeping him alive or reminding him of times past.

There were times he hummed and whistled between talks, which was the closest he got to sharing the music in his head. Those infrequent hums and whistles stuck to my memory and became the scale on which I weighed songs .The day I heard a piano version of "A Tea for Two," many miles away from the blocks, I stood and wondered where I had heard it before: in the musical punctuations of Pa Suku's conversation.

His room lay empty behind him, a rectangular void peopled by nothing but his grim-looking table, a mattress, books and papers. On the wall, right opposite the door, the dimming evening sun illuminated a framed photograph of a man in a grey hat, standing in the shadow of brick houses dimly lit by odd street lamps. If I squinted, I could make out a few details from that photo: cars parked on both side of the street; men and women in heavy coats, some in motion, others posing with newspapers beside storefronts, with neat garbage bins in close proximity. There was a vague resemblance between the man in grey hat and the bearded man I had come to question, but the paved street in the photo was nothing like the uneven grounds and puddles he now shared with the rest of us.

His walls were painted deep blue, an unusual colour around the blocks. Ours was whitewashed. If you touched our walls, the paint left marks on your fingers, which was why the walls were called "touch and follow" after the love charm that supposedly fetched men as many woman as they could touch.

"Good afternoon, Pa Suku."

"Hey, son." He opened his eyes.

Having acknowledged my presence, still air-tapping his left foot, he closed his eyes and rocked and swayed on his leather-top stool. Then he picked up from an old chat, knocking me off my pre-planned start.

"I said something about me the last time but did not elaborate."

I felt my questions dissolving like Styrofoam in petrol. My mind went blank He had this effect on me.

"I did not tell you what I did as a freelance writer and full-time thinker. I thought it would be important to explain that. But to do that and to do it well, we must begin from the beginning."

My questions were now far from me. I tried to reel them back but they were gone beyond my reach. I do not remember feeling disappointed or frustrated at this turn of events, not that it mattered anyway. What mattered was the space I shared with him, the world he created with his words, a world he helped me in to, a world we both escaped into. With him I was an individual, a person with a voice and a working mind. He listened when I talked, and conversed with me in words not coated with cant. The other grown-ups were busy being grown-ups: shooing us away as though we were fruit flies on ripe plantains; smacking us in the head at the slightest provocation; shoving us aside when they bantered and we vied for a piece of the joke.

Pa Suku never dismissed me. I did, in many occasions, wonder why the other kids avoided him, why they never came close when he sat outside with his radio. Were they warned to stay away from him? What did their parents think and say about him at dinnertime? Ricia's friend once asked me where he came from. I told her I did not care to know, and asked why she wanted to know.

"Because people come from somewhere," she said, "they don't drop from the sky."

I never thought of it that way. People come from where you meet them: at a restaurant, at a bar, in an alley, anywhere; and now, as an adult, I would include the bookstore, strip clubs, abandoned railway stations, anywhere. Ricia's friend thought I was beginning to lose my mind, and was acting like my "old friend."

"People come from somewhere," she insisted. "My father is from Ahuoda. My mother is from Bonny. Our next-door neighbour is from Buguma. My English teacher is from Isiala Ngwa." She went on in this manner, mentioning names and placing those names in specific towns, cities, and villages.

I walked away from that conversation but never forgot it.

"As I told you earlier," Pa Suku was saying, "I thought I would be an engineer. But by the time I was in senior secondary two, that fantasy was swept away by literature."

Now he was the one sweeping me away. My long list of questions, which I thought would put an end to the seeds of doubt about him, had been blown from my mind.

"My literature teacher, one Mr Tunji from Okigwe, was a brilliant young man with a degree from Durham. Durham is somewhere in England. This Mr Tunji was a large man with a comic face and an unusually curved moustache, which added to our fascination with the subject he taught. In the months after our first class with him, he

59

read us Dickens, Joyce and Woolf, and taught us how to read poems with emphasis on how and where the stress was on a line."

Dickens, Joyce, Woolf. Who are these people, I thought. He took a deep breath. His greying eyebrows moved up like he was questioning his own recollection.

"Those where the good old days," he said. "By the time I left for university I was sure I wanted to study literature. Two semesters into the program I switched to philosophy."

He had lost me somewhere, though I followed his moving lips. Regaining my grip on his tale, I asked:

"What is philosophy?"

"Philosophy? Let me see. Philosophy is as complex as complexity itself."

He uncrossed his legs again and opened both eyes, lowered his head and stared into my eyes. What I saw were not mere eyes but pearly tunnels emptying into another world.

"I will not commit the crime of using the complex to explain the complex," he said.

"What is sophistication?" I asked. It was a random question, but I had heard him use that word a few times and had stashed it away, waiting for the right time to ask.

"Let's see. Sophistication." He asked me to repeat it. I did. "Sometimes words are better understood by exploring what they are not. You see that woman over there?"

It was Ma Deborah, a well-known troublemaker. She was about fifty feet away from us, sitting on the ground, with two teenage girls braiding her hair. Her most recent fight was with a girl of about nineteen who she suspected was receiving gifts from her husband. I remember hearing a loud roar at the entrance to the blocks and running out to see what it was. Squeezing my way through the crowd that had gathered, I emerged on the other side to see Ma Deborah atop the girl, pummelling her. The girl was trying to fight back but Ma Deborah was three times her size.

"She is not sophisticated." Pa Suku said firmly

Having pictured Ma Deborah on the day of that fight— the sheer immensity of her violence—I got the idea. She is not sophisticated. That was enough explanation for me. I extrapolated the idea to include Mr Empire who got his name from the small cigarette shop he ran. Mr Empire was notorious for punishing his sons with ground pepper sprinkled around their genitals. The boys would go mad, howling as they ran around the blocks. At times he chased them with a whip, lashing as they sprang from block to block. Mr Empire was not sophisticated.

"What about philosophy?" I asked.

"Yes, philosophy. The word itself comes from two non-English words. But I'll not bother you with those, for that would be tantamount to using the complex to explain the complex.

"What is tantamount?" I asked.

"I knew you were going to ask that question."

"You knew?"

"Yes. Some words, like *tantamount*, are music unto themselves. Saying them is engaging in that musicality. Words like 'tantalizing' and 'titillating' are like jazz. They rise and fall and swing in wide circles. I used to write poems, you know." He branched out again. "For inspiration I would hunt words with music in them. They occasionally came looking for me and I would let them sink into my heart, and later empty them into a poem. I hope you become a writer someday, my boy. That way you will see what I see, and these words will mean more to you. I think you should start writing. You're not too young to start. Just write, anything, any word. Anyway, 'tantamount' is another word for 'equivalent.' But you must know that no two words are the same, like no two humans are the same. But all words, as mere words, are equal, the way all humans, as humans, are equal."

He committed the crime he was avoiding; 'equivalent' and the metaphorical ramble that followed were of the same weight as 'tantamount.' I pocketed my ignorance. He returned to philosophy.

"Philosophy is the love of wisdom. With the tools of philosophy, you are able to think critically, offer a balanced interpretation of what you see, make sense of the spaces and experiences around you."

I wondered if philosophy was the same as full-time thinking, since both, freelance writing and full-time thinking, were his primary occupations. If both were the same, it must be a hard job, I thought. If you cannot explain your own profession in one word, then it must be a difficult job. There were several ideas and stories he shared that, although he broke them down for me, were still complicated and obscure. He once shared something about Kafka and I thought he was discussing the kaftans worn in parts of Nigeria. All he said afterwards dissolved into the image of free flowing kaftans swept about in the wind. It was a story he told three times over. But each time he repeated it, I pictured Karl Rossman in a toe-touching kaftan, or encased in an oversize garment, struggling to break free, to see the world.

"America is not only a country, but an idea," he had said after his first summary of "The Stoker," but I was lost to a different trail of thought that, unbeknown to him, was stirred by a word I had misheard—Kafka as Kaftan.

From explaining philosophy, he returned to his days at university.

"My professors were good," he started, "and they loved what they did. Those were the days when universities were well funded, and scholars were happy and loved their jobs." He shut his eyes.

Pa Suku was not the only one who smiled or shut his eyes when he discussed the past. Papa did the same. Whenever Papa dropped his famous line, "We used to groove the bars around D-Line with a few Naira notes," he would add a lavish smile at the end.

"Back then," Papa would say, "our currency was as strong as Mama Charlie's papers." Then he would laugh, almost knocking his beer bottle over.

"What are Mama Charlie's papers?" we would ask, pretending he had not told us before.

"That was what we called the British pounds," he would say, returning to his beer for a gulp or two. "Mama Charlie is the Queen. She used to be our Queen too. But we got tired of a Queen we never saw."

We would ask if the Queen was invisible, or a hermit like the witch doctor of Abonema, the medicine man who lived alone in the swamps. He would fake a frown, clench his fist and say "she was visible, but now she is not." Then we would launch the next question:

"Was that when our money fell and hers rose to become stronger?"

He would shake his head and grunt as though in pain, "Bloody politicians. We should round them up and have them whipped."

I did wonder if alcohol and cigarettes fuelled nostalgia. Papa did not drink much. But whenever he did, the perfect pasts stretched out before him like mats, and he would long for those early days when he and his mates were full of pride in their fatherland.

"Where are the groundnut pyramids that towered to the heavens? What happened to cocoa and rubber? What about cotton? Do these idiots think with their heads or with their testicles?" He would end with the crude oil and politics analysis: how politicians went crazy over oil and the rest was history. "Tough disease, tough, tough disease," he would say, "this country is dying of tough disease." It was only recently that I realize what he meant: Dutch Disease! It would be interesting to know if he deliberately, for sheer effect or whatsoever, replaced "Dutch" with "tough." I never asked and do not intend to.

Unlike Pa Suku, Papa's moments of recollections were short, taking the same time as it took to finish his drink. After the last sip he would fall silent, deep in thought. Then he would trudge to the back room and we would try not to talk too loud. He never drank more than a bottle, perhaps to ensure he did not spend more than an hour with us. His words were few and he dropped them casually in-between swigs. It was hard to think of him without seeing the shape his lips made when sucking a beer bottle. I still see him that way. I have tried to dismiss that image but it will not go away. He was a strange man. I never understood him beyond the faces he made when wielding a whip, beyond the vast absence he left everywhere, every day, as he left for "work" before we woke up at dawn. I did not know what and where that "work" was. I only remember the despair on his face when he came home from "work" and the swift change in mood when beer was introduced to the equation, the brief levity, the stories. I secretly wished he would drink more than a bottle, maybe three or four, so that we could talk more. I wanted to know his past, what he did when he was my age, if he hid magazines with racy covers under his pillow, if he dreamt of faraway places like I did, countries where people spoke English like they were drinking tea in haste. I wanted to know about his parents, my grandparents who I never met, who he never said a word about, whose ancestral home I never visited. I badly wished his beer would never run dry.

Pa Suku did not drink at all. He smoked. And whenever his cigarette was lit, the past came in gusts and sheets. There were moments the violent rush of recollection threatened to drown him, and his whole body would shiver in the cold arms of memory.

Unlike Papa, Pa Suku did not whine about the past. He engaged it philosophically, which made it more fun to be his audience. If Papa descended haphazardly upon the past, ploughing through without a compass, serving up chopped pieces of history, Pa Suku did the opposite, gently and carefully treading and picking routes, with a chart, his eyes on plotted lines of memory, how those lines connect, where they connect, and how to harvest the past for the benefit of his audience.

"In my final year at university," Pa Suku was saying, "I met one Dr Isodje. He was a lecturer in my department. Fresh from Yale with a doctorate in philosophy, his head steamed with ideas, some of which were new and too radical at that time. I was swept away by his brilliance. He was an intense fellow and a lucid scholar. He was young too."

Yale. I pinned it to a corner of my mind and waited for a perfect time to ask where and what it was. He broke into a wide grin, the grin of an old man recalling and re-streaming the bliss of a love lost to time. He tapped his almost-finished cigarette with his index finger. The ash fell into a small heap next to his feet.

"I loved him, this Dr Isodje."

Love. It sounded light and delicate on his lips, which he pursed and licked afterwards, perhaps savouring the word itself for what it was and meant to him.

"It was a good experience," he added and heaved.

The cigarette, now a baby stub, was pinched between his thumb and index finger, nearly concealed but visible enough to show the border that separates the gold band from what was left of the actual cigarette.

"Before I met Isodje," he continued, "he had just written a fine book on the systems of African thoughts. Do not worry about that one, my boy."

For a second his hair, separated in knotted strands, distracted me.

"Are you here, son?"

"I am," I answered.

I liked it when he called me son. I did wish he were my father or a near relative.

He tapped the cigarette again. There was nothing left but the butt concealed between jittering fingers. There was a stick of cigarette left in the pack. He tossed the butt and pulled out the remaining stick. His lighter was not there.

"Please see if I left it on the table inside, next to my radio."

It was where he said it would be.

He continued:

"Sometimes I think I'm doing you a disservice by sharing all these stories. Life is in stages and in phases. A leap into another phase by way of stories may have adverse effects, maybe not. At this age, your mind is still fresh, fragile and unburdened by the weight of knowledge. I envy you, but will encourage you to enjoy that innocence while it lasts, for as long as the heart pulsates and the senses receive signals, innocence will die a natural death. Innocence is transient, a fleeting phase that disappears with time. It comes at birth and goes as we grow. Time depletes innocence, consuming it from bottom up.

"Innocence is inversely proportional to time. The older we get the less innocent we are. One day you will be like me. Time ate my innocence, leaving me with a pile of learning. The things I know are now my burden. They also make me human. You will understand this later and will realize that the more you know the more you want to know. The thirst for knowledge is insatiable. In the end we are victims of what we know, victims of the sweet-sour fruit of experience, in the same way that we are potential preys in the hands of that which we are yet to discover. I choose to know and be burdened. Ignorance is a horrible alternative."

He continued to talk, effortlessly, in measured beats and breaths, as though he was speaking a song. Once in this mode his voice became brisk and fluid, alternating between both states, assured like a bugle in the hands of a royal messenger. He would go on in small chunks of words, throbbing like drums, swelling and waning. I fell a thousand times for that cadence. The cigarette was gone. His fingers were still hanging, jittering as usual, positioned like the stubs were there. Then he slowly moved his fingers as though he was tapping out ash, the way a pianist would finger keys in sleep.

"So, where was I?" he asked. "Where did I start? Did I tell you about my freelance writing and thinking? How about another day?"

"Another day," I repeated, stood up, dusted the bottom of my shorts, and walked home.

4

On the way home from Pa Suku's place, I saw a semi-circle of people—men, women, children—at Jide's door. Not an unusual sight. But this time the semi-circle seemed in a state of shock. There was a woman in black holding a child to her hip, clutching the child as though it would bolt on release. The child tossed vacant stares over its mother's shoulder, its unblinking eyes wide as if dilated by a drug. Next to the woman was a teenage girl running her fingers through her half-loose braids, her mouth agape. A boy my age was holding a plastic bag, perhaps on the way back from the grocery stand. He too was immobilized by Jide's coloured television.

Jide's television was a magnet. There was hardly anyone at the blocks—excluding Pa Suku—who did not find time to go see the latest movies at Jide's place. Jide enjoyed the attention, and strutted with the air of an aristocrat. Each time he raised his curtain and smiled at the semi-circle outside his door, his ego expanded. He was the proverbial rich man in a famished village who, emboldened by owning the only bushel of grain, wielded a godlike influence over everyone.

I was there when the VCR player was hooked to Jide's black and white television, and was old enough to remember Solomon, the electrician, doing the installation. I recall how Solomon, unboxing the VCR player and untwining the chords, mumbled something about electronics that "change every day." Jide celebrated his new appliances with crates of beer positioned outside his door.

The drinks were free for all. I recall someone yelling at us children to stay away from the drinks: "Get away from here, you little mushrooms!" In the end some mushrooms smuggled bottles and disappeared between blocks, only to return with a different glint in their eyes and a disorderly gait that gave them away. Papa said Jide worked as a cook for one of the oil companies, where he earned more money than he could spend in a lifetime. A near-empty beer bottle propped on his knees, held steady by the neck, Papa said: "Those oil companies, hmmm, they spit money like no-man's business. They talk and out comes money, they break wind and out comes money, they sneeze and the floor is covered in naira notes."

Jide was an enigma and a local champion. Boys wanted to be like him. They practiced his steps, the way he dragged his feet with no sense of urgency. He was the man they saw themselves becoming. When he walked into a room he would rattle his key holder to announce his presence. It was rumoured that those keys, which we may as well call Jide's tambourine, were for his fleet of cars and a house somewhere, none of which anyone claimed to have seen. These rumours added to an already towering presence at the blocks. It was collectively agreed that his decision to live among the poor was the hallmark of humility. His potbelly was considered an evidence of wealth, and so was the toothpick that dangled at the edge of lips to announce he had just had an expensive lunch somewhere. Pa Suku called him "an empty barrel rolling down a gravelled path, all noise and no substance." Once, looking at Jide from a distance, Pa Suku remarked: "When you are his age, remember to be everything but what he represents: a brain underutilized, a body put to the wrong use."

What Jide presented as his life was public knowledge. And this was because he constantly spieled on the whens, the wheres, and the whats of his job. We all knew his work schedule: two weeks offshore, two weeks off work; two weeks away on the Bonny Islands, or on the Escravos River, and back to rest for two weeks. It was from him that we knew about swamps that yielded more money than the government. "My people," Jide would rattle, throwing and catching his key holder, "oil is God's own spittle and we have been blessed with a fast flowing river of that spittle." It was also from him that we learnt of swamps that attracted more visitors— "overseas visitors"—than any tourist attraction in Nigeria.

"They say it's not safe here," he boomed, "lie, lie, lie they tell. Go to the swamps," he pointed the beak of a key in a random direction, "they are there drilling oil and taking breaks with our girls."

His stories of faraway orgies on sea vessels with expatriates and their "high class women," were swallowed hook, line, and sinker. He, like everyone else around the blocks, made no effort to filter the explicit contents of the stories shared; kids and adults were treated to the same wild material.

Whenever Jide returned from his rivers and swamps, he would raise his curtain to the public. His was the only room with a rug carpet, a functioning ceiling fan, and a standing lamp—never lit—left between two intricately designed cane chairs. We were not allowed inside his room but were free to form that semi-circle at the door, where we fought for a perfect view. There were days the weather got in the way, and the rains would threaten to disperse everyone. Some would scamper off; others would bravely dare the rain to do its worst. It always did. Drenched, they would continue to follow Arnold Schwarzenegger or Sylvester Stallone pounding the enemy with bullets.

During those two weeks of leisure, Jide would frequently stagger home with different women. These were strange women with red fangs and stilettos. And they walked delicately like goliath herons in the delta swamps, with handbags that glittered against the hueless blocks, their chests thrust forward as they tiptoed, leaving the earth punctured and frightened. Witches! I thought they were witches. What else could be? I was afraid for Jide. He was, in my opinion, courting death.

"They are not witches," Ibe once said to me.

"No?" I asked, genuinely surprised.

"Witches only walk at night," he said, grinning conspiratorially.

"That's exactly why I said they are witches. They show up at night."

"You are a small boy." he said with a condescending wink.

"I am not a small boy," I announced, "I know they're all witches."

"You will know what they are when the time comes." He closed the conversation and ran off in the opposite direction.

5

My childhood nights were long and vast, with dreams that, in retrospect, I believe were induced by a lack of space. Four boys in a room was not a joke. Those nights were endured with sighs that smacked of hope, hope itself was reinforced by the cry of roosters at dawn, a reminder that daylight was set to triumph over night. There were mornings I woke up before the rest and walked to my secret place, a small lake outside the blocks.

As a child I saw my journey to the lake—and the lake itself—as a private affair, my little secret. Stepping out at dawn I would inhale the crisp air, involuntarily sniffing the assortment of odours from pit latrines. I would stand for a second or two, for no particular reason, and then turn left and walk between blocks on my way to the lake, observing the row of doors on both sides, some tightly shut, some ajar. I often wondered what happened behind those doors, all of which, except for one or two, looked the same: plywood with numbers at the top left corner. I once saw a woman, an unknown, puffy face with ruffled hair, coming out of Jaja's room. I knew Jaja's wife was not in town. And the woman I saw looked like Jide's witches.

After the last row of doors, at the tail of the blocks, a bush path ran north, leading straight to the lake. The path wound through cassava plots, emptied and cut through a patch of tall elephant grass. Burdened by the weight of morning dew, the grass would fall across the path, making it impossible to walk without getting wet. Their leaves, sharp at the edges, would lacerate the skin around my shin.

I saw them as conspirators who, cursed with immobility and vulnerable to the vagaries of weather, took it upon themselves to stop me from exercising my liberties as a mobile being.

At the lake I would sit on a deserted anthill, hugging my knees, the morning breeze tumbling over me as the sun etched my shadow to the side. It was agreed that a young woman with the features of a certain Bollywood actress lived in the lake: her hair black and long; a thick, red dot on her forehead; her feet without the webbings of a mermaid. I had heard the other boys talking about her, how she trapped men with her beauty. Those who played hard to get she enticed with treasures and carted off to her residence under the lake, where they were forced to work for her, hewing wood, polishing rare stones, working until their strengths faded, until their minds disappeared—at which point she spat them out sapped of their sanity and unable to recount their underwater experience. Sharing a version of this story with me one afternoon, Ibe asked:

"Do you know the mad man that runs naked from block to block?"

"There are mad men all over the place, Ibe. Which one?" I wanted to know this man who had seen the lake woman. The fact that he was already mad made Ibe's narrative more irritating but no less intriguing.

"I bet you know him," he cried. "Tall, with sharp, frightening eyes? Always chasing little girls, trying to touch their breasts?"

"The one who was recently chained to the mango tree behind block b?"

"Yes! My father said he was in the lake for three years." Ibe's eyes almost fell out of their sockets as he stretched his face to emphasize this point.

James Fire, as the story goes, used to fish in the lake. Then he went missing one night. His fishing line, still intact, with a dead tilapia rotting from head down, was discovered in the bushes around the lake, lying next to a pair of khaki trousers and a shirt, with no traces of the man. Three years later, after he had been declared dead, he was sighted one morning loitering in the bushes around the lake, near the same spot his fishing line was found. (There was a wrap of marijuana behind his left ear, a minor detail that was not accounted for in the whole tale.)

There also was the story of Kalu, who was strolling by the lake and saw a wad of cash. On picking up the bundle, he was turned into a tuber of yam. As the tale goes, the search party found the yam and was suspicious of a random tuber of yam by the lake. Perhaps irked by the disconcerting disappearance of a full-fledged grown man, someone struck the lone yam with a stick, and at the exact same time, a moan was heard behind the search party. When they turned, Kalu was crawling out of the lake, naked.

But it was James Fire's account that frightened and piqued my curiosity. Since the day Ibe shared Fire's story, I doubled the number of times I went to the lake in a month. I wanted to see her, to hide in the bushes and watch her bathe in the shallow corners of the lake, her hair soaked and dripping. I made sure to pick sunflowers on the way there, just in case.

She never showed up but my longing did not wane. I convinced myself that she existed, even when the fantastic tales surrounding her existence said otherwise: that she was—as I now believe—manufactured by men to explain whatever shade of madness or calamity that befell them.

In one instance, my daydream at the lake ate into my return time. The blast of what must have been a gun startled me back to reality. I picked up my flip-flops and dashed back to the blocks. I hated running home from the lake. I preferred walking back the same way I came, enjoying how the field of elephant grass, in the face of sunlight, sprang up and pushed aside the heavy weight of dew; how birds took off, spreading their wings in the first flight of day. Those return walks were also good times to chew over pressing thoughts.

The day after spotting Dan trudging between the blocks in despair, my thoughts as I walked home from the lake were solely about him. So strong were my preoccupations about him that I broke into a quick trot and thought of visiting Pa Suku to find out what was wrong with Dan. I knew there was something going on with him. I recall an incident where a group of boys pinned him down and wiped his make-up with their group piss. I remember how he lay still, smeared in a piss-made puddle, allowing them do what they wanted. From a distance I watched his assailants whooping in triumph, their penises—turgid black fingerlings—ejecting liquid in squirts. Then they sprang off towards the old road. I had wanted to bounce out and fight them off, or scream until they came for me while Dan escaped. But I held still, frightened by their audacity, by the assumed authority over the life of another. They could have killed him right there, and I would have lived with the sight of his body convulsing to the last breath. In their eyes he was an object, a piece of dried corncob on a kerbside. Covered in dust and dripping piss, he managed to give me a smile. If there was any feeling of shame and humiliation, he did not show it. There were no tears either. He stood up, wiped his shorts and walked straight to where I stood.

Reeking of fresh urine, he asked if I wanted to dance. "I'll sing and we'll dance, yes?" There was a spark in his eyes, like he had just walked out of a wild party. His question, a far cry from what had just happened to him, staggered my imagination. Unable to respond, I walked away from him. When I turned to have another look, he had both hands in his pocket, circling where the boys had rained piss on him. What I felt afterwards was a combination of shame and regret, both of which continue to haunt my memories of him. I could have dispelled both feelings by doing something when, a month or two later, I saw him being attacked by the same set of boys. This time he was walking home from school and they were trailing him, taking turns to smack him on the head. I saw this and kept quiet, bottling my anger hurrying home without a single word.

6

Pa Suku and I sat outside his door, silently wondering what had happened to Dan. A motorbike screeched along, leaving trails of thick smoke, an echoing wail. My left toe began to itch from a mosquito bite. I looked at where the itch had started before spreading upward and downward, resulting in a bump that mapped the dimension of the spread. I ignored it and lifted my eyes to a park of egrets scattered across the evening sky. Pa Suku went inside his room and I was left to reflect on our conversation about Dan. "They will not understand him," Pa Suku had said earlier, "poor kid."

"Understand what?" I asked.

He cocked his head and sighed without responding to my question.

Understand what? Dan was just a boy who struck me as odd, a puzzling character, like he did to everyone else. I was not yet aware of his sexuality, which, I'm now supposing, was obvious to the other boys, hence the attacks. Were they really aware? Did they see his difference as an affront on their fledgling masculinity? I did wonder what his parents thought of his personality. They did not seem to care, or were exceptionally good at not showing how they felt about their son. What did they make of their son's ordeal in the hands of neighbourhood kids? This, too, I was not able to find out.

Pa Suku emerged from his room with a book.

"*Giovanni's Room* by James Baldwin," he announced,

sounding like a teacher introducing a new topic. "I read this book a long time ago." He crossed his legs and tapped his bare feet.

"May I see?" I asked.

"Feel free," he said and offered me the book.

I took the paperback. Sniffed it. It smelled old and mouldy, like the inside of the box containing my parent's black and white photos: the smell of abandonment after rigorous use, the smell of loneliness. The pages were almost brown, the colours of cinnamon and mustard brewed, left to assume an autonomous hue. I ran my hands on the cover.

"It was a gift from Dr Isodje," Pa Suku said.

I sniffed it again and inhaled deep enough to have my nostrils assaulted by invisible grains of dust. I sneezed.

"What is it about?"

My eyes were still on the cover. I rubbed my nose and turned to the first page. I read out loud, hesitating between words and sentences: *I stand at the window of this great house in the south of France as night falls, the night which is leading me to the most terrible morning of my life.*

"What is it about?" I asked again, and finished the rest of the paragraph.

He did not answer straight away. When I looked up from the page his face was a volcano of smiles, beaming and flaring in pride. There was something more in his eyes, something fatherly.

"You will go far," he said through his fiery smile. "Well, I will start with the author. Baldwin was an African-American writer. African because his ancestors were from here, American because he was born there, in America."

"Black-American?"

"Yes, African-American. And he looked just like you and I. Hold on. I have a book with an illustration of his face on the cover." He went back inside.

I continued to turn the book from side to side. I wrote the title in sand, followed by the author's name. I wiped the name and replaced it with mine. I wiped the title with my left foot and replaced it with *Dan's Room* and swore that someday, when I was old and wise enough like Pa Suku, I would write a book with that title and send Dan a copy.

He returned with another book.

"Here," he said. "That's James Baldwin on the cover."

I handed him *Giovanni's Room* and took the other book—it was Stanley Macebuh's critical study on Baldwin, which meant nothing to me then. The man on the cover looked like my father: the lips, pursed and drawn; the forehead, furrowed, with a receding hairline; the eyes, staring ahead.

"He looks like my father," I said.

"I bet he does. Now, back to your question. *Giovanni's Room* is about a young American in Paris torn between two loves… "

I continued to study Baldwin's face. Then I returned the Macebuh and retrieved the Baldwin. This little exchange fascinated me. I wondered if this was how one grew into a well-spoken, wise person. I flipped through the pages and stopped where two italicized words in the second chapter caught my attention. *Le milieu.*

"What is this?" I asked, tapping both words with my index finger.

"*Le milieu!*" he exclaimed. "It's the French for 'surroundings,' depending on how you use it. There are lots of French words in that book. The story itself unfolds in

Paris."

"They speak French in Paris, right?"

"Yes, French in France."

"They also speak French in Rwanda, right?"

"Rwanda, yes, yes. I'm glad you remember. Nigeria itself is surrounded by French-speaking countries: Niger, Chad, Benin Republic, and the Cameroon. Rwanda is on the far side of the map, far from here. There are probably more French speakers on the continent. Let's find out."

He went inside for the third time.

I wrote in sand: *le milieu, le milieu, le milieu, le milieu.* I wiped the last, then the third and the second, leaving the first. How is this French spoken? I asked myself. How does one dream and think in French? What is *Ogoamaka* in French? I searched for more French words in *Giovanni's Room.* The next after *le milieu* was longer: *Je veux m'evader.* I wiped *le milieu* from my sand-board and replaced it with *Je veux m'evader.*

Pa Suku returned with a map the size of a notebook pinched between his fingers. He literally had the world between his fingers, which reminded me of a song we sang in Sunday school: "He's got the whole world in his hands, he's got the whole wild world in his hands, he's got the whole wild world in his hands…" Dizzy lines zigzagged everywhere on the map, running from one corner to the other, crossing shades of blue and yellow, with patches of green and brown in-between.

The map we had in school was ceremoniously posted next to the blackboard, and we were not allowed to touch it. "Under no condition are you to place your fingers on that map," the teacher had said, her twig of a whip smacking the tip of North Africa as if to claim it for school and principal. We were only free to watch and observe the world from the fringes, from our ignorant corners, pointing at the lines like the poor, peripheral bastards that we were. But Pa Suku gave me the map, and with that gift came the freedom to touch and cross all those dizzying lines. He offered me the world and everything in it.

"We are here," he was saying, "tucked in the middle of those French speakers."

He was delicately holding a matchstick. And with the matchstick he tapped and circled the blue and yellow colours.

"And over there is France, the home of the French language. Paris is somewhere here."

I touched the map. He let go. I held it. I held the world in my hands. I tried to magnify what I saw, fill it with places, with the murmur of waterfalls, the roar of lions, with the tremble of the earth when lorries ran, with the BBC voices that counted deaths in Rwanda, with my mother's happy face when she pounded okra in her narrow mortar. My eyes travelled from France to Nigeria, from Nigeria to lonely yellow patches here and there. And then there was India. China. Russia.

"How come we don't speak French?" I asked.

"Good question." He took the map. "See, that is England over there, the home of the English language and the BBC. We got our English from there."

I knew we got our English from somewhere. Everyone knew that. I looked from England to Nigeria, from Nigeria to France, from France to Togo.

"How did it happen?" I asked. "How did they give us their language?"

"Long story," he said. "It all happened a long time ago.

You see these blue areas? That is the Atlantic Ocean. It used to be as busy as the sky with all the planes. It was busy with ships sailing from here," he placed the matchstick on a random dot in England and drew a line that cut through the enormous blue space, "to here…"

For a second I thought I saw the matchstick trotting arrogantly into the blue expanse, brandishing flags, ready to force-feed its language to whatever or whomever it ran into. He left the map in my hands and fished out his cigarette pack. He lit a stick, stuck out his lower lip and liberated the first smoke to the heavens.

I continued to run my fingers on the borderlines and rivers and mountains and forests on the map. I tried to look for Rwanda, a name that never ceased to gush from the mouth of the news reporters, but my search was cut short by a riot of voices coming from where the motorbike had headed. We both turned and were frozen by a sight that was not unfamiliar but in this instance made strange by the peculiarity of the characters involved. I could see Dora, a girl of about fourteen, among them, crying. Her eyes were puffy from shedding tears and her hair, half braided, spiralled up like antlers. Next to her was her mother, a taciturn woman who was hardly seen lounging with other women, but was now walking with her wrapper sagging around her waist, her head tie perching on the tip of her dishevelled hair, the sleeves of her green ankara blouse falling between her shoulder and her elbow. Mother and daughter were flanked by neighbours. To the right was Tina the fishmonger, marching next to Lola the seamstress. To the left was Chisara, whose clean-shaven head was a routine subject of local gossip. Ma Dora's voice was loud but incoherent, like a shriek within the ululation of many mourners. A few words dropped between but whole sentences were flattened into simple notes. Pointing ahead, she spoke to no one in particular. It seemed it was Dora, her daughter, who was being led somewhere.

Dora wiped her eyes with the overflow of her red gown, which, torn along the waistline, swayed as she trudged along, sashes blown askance, her bare feet covered in dust. From stray words heard as the group passed, I began to speculate what the march was about.

As they marched on, crossing the blocks, curious children joined them. I watched as they increased in number. With each addition, Chisara did the storytelling, offering the newcomers a background to the unfolding tale. Chisara was a force to reckon with. The sprinkle of hair on her chest, almost at the funnel of her cleavage, the spattering of moustache between her neck and chin, and her stampede-ready calves all gave her a menacing look that earned her an equally menacing name: Madam Gunpowder. She lived up to that name and did explode from time to time. I recall she once punched a man to pulp for stealing a widow's box of savings. In this instance, as the march progressed, one would assume the battle was hers.

The march continued. I disengaged and looked down. *Je veux m'evader* was still there, in the sand. What does it mean? It stared back at me in my own writing, jagged and porous like sand itself. Pa Suku looked on to where the march headed. I wiped *Je veux m'evader* with my left feet, replacing it with the now familiar *Le Milieu*.

I returned to the moving figures. They had crossed blocks m and n, and were turning right at block o. At this point I left Pa Suku and dashed off to catch the action. It was no longer the fierce march of a few women, but had evolved into a mass movement of curious men, women, boys and girls. I saw Ibe, the carpenter's son, waiting alone at the entrance to block m, sitting on a moss-covered brick that was half buried in sand, fanning himself with his shirt, his chest dripping sweat. Unlike the excited marching crowd, Ibe was calm, cutting the pose of one who was waiting for someone.

"They will come back here," he declared with a certainty that was almost authoritative, as though he was the writer of the play. "They will come back here," he kept saying as I slowed down next to him, having suspected that his quiet manner was a hint of privileged knowledge.

He pointed to an arbitrary spot on block m and returned to fanning himself, his back slightly hunched like his father's, whose hunch came from many years of wielding smoothing planes and hefting furniture.

I backed up.

"What's going on, Ibe?" I asked and positioned myself next to him.

"It's Jide," he said.

I noticed the sprouting hair around his navel, with fledgling strands descending downwards, disappearing where the bunched band of his shorts concealed their destination.

"Jide put the thing inside Dora," he added without looking at me.

The mass movement emerged from block o, as Ibe had predicted, and they were now walking towards us, with Chisara leading. They emptied into block m and paused at Jide's door. Chisara planted her feet on the ground—tied her waist wrapper—loosened it—re-tied it until it was fastened to her taste. Then she stepped on Jide's porch and banged the door as hard as she could.

No response.

"He's inside," Ibe whispered in my ear, his breath reeking of something I could not place. "He is in there," he emphasized for my benefit.

Chisara continued to bang the door. The crowd murmured and buzzed the way they did when, at that same door, they gathered to watch Schwarzenegger rip his enemies apart like cellophane bags. Lola joined Chisara. They both pummelled the door until it creaked open. Jide looked genuinely shocked by the audience. While he stood there gaping Chisara lunged at him, aiming for his thick neck, but she missed. He slipped back into his room and closed the door. Undeterred, Chisara again hammered at the door. He opened the window, peered into the crowd and asked to know what was going on. The crowd fell silent.

"Can someone explain what is going on here?" he asked.

"See that girl over there?" Chisara asked, "she *is* what is going on, you useless man."

Having been dragged along and drilled for more information about her encounter with Jide, Dora was rather exhausted. She studied her feet and fiddled her sashes. Her mother was equally exhausted. Chisara did the talking. Ibe gave me the lowdown. Dora was pregnant. Jide was responsible. It happened the day she returned from school early having been whipped and sent home for not paying her school fees. Bored, she walked the blocks as most kids did. Jide's window was open and the television was on. He invited her inside and offered her a can of coke. It was not clear if she was drugged, not as if anyone cared enough to investigate further.

Chisara lunged again, slamming the window on Jide's face. He ducked. Two men rushed forward and grabbed Chisara on both sides. She yanked free and positioned herself for another attack. Jide declared his innocence: "I don't know what you're talking about." Dora lifted her head and shot him a piercing look. He averted her eyes. She continued to stare at him, trembling. I thought she would collapse or throw up or dash off and disappear. Her mother came forward, spat at Jide's feet, turned around and tugged Dora along. They left the scene. The crowd began to disperse. I looked around and wished Dan was present.

7

The path to the lake was not as dewy as usual. I surmised someone had walked the path before me that morning. I hummed and drew long breaths as I ventured off to spot the lake princess. The morning air was surprisingly fresh and free of its usual stench. As I walked across the field of grass, I wondered what Jide was up to that morning. I had seen him tiptoeing to the main road with a suitcase. At the lake, where the path ended and the clearing began, I saw a figure. From the shape of its hair I knew it was a girl. Her bare back stared at me. I recognized the hair, locked and alert like antlers, and the dress, unzipped to the waist. The sashes, splayed in defeat, cuddled the earth. I picked a safe spot several feet away from her but close enough to see her in profile. I wondered why she was there and what she was doing. Ripples ran over the lake, with ducks sailing leisurely between water lilies, paddling in a straight line. She stood up. And her dress, already halfway down, fell. I felt my heart beating quickly.

She walked down to the lake, squatted and stirred the water. I moved closer. She turned. I wanted to say something but felt a lump in my throat. Her eyes were red, like ripe peppers. She offered me a smile; I tried to smile but could not. I wanted to ask what Jide did to her. There were many questions on my mind but none found expression in that moment. Our silence filled the morning with words that would later become my side of Dora's account, an account I never shared and never forgot. She picked up a rock and grabbed a fistful of sand, stood, turned and walked straight to me, naked. Confused and alarmed, my legs froze where they were. What was I to do with the approaching pointers, dark at their tips, and the v between her legs? And why was shy coming to me? There, in front of me, she neither spoke nor touched my hands. Her eyes, sharp as knives, lacerated my forehead.

Then, as if on a second thought, she took my left hand, emptied the sand into my palm, and gave me the rock. She smiled. I squeezed out a weak smile. Hers disappeared. She turned and returned to the lake. She walked on. The lake rose to her knees, to her thigh, and her waist. She stopped and said in a soft voice, "Run home, please." I ran. And to this day, each time I replay that scene, I feel myself in motion, running away from what I could have stopped.

*

The crowd was back at Jide's door at noon. They had taken up positions in small, expectant, groups. Ibe was at the same spot, shirtless. Jide's door was ajar. Chisara was at his doorpost, her head tilted to the side as though contemplating her next line of action. No Jide at the door. No Jide at the window. Why the gathering? The crowd was not of the same spirit as yesterday. An unusual calm loitered. It seemed they had been instructed, for once, to offer silence to the earth on which they stood. I sat next to Ibe and studied their faces.

"Jide is gone," Ibe announced.

I had seen him leaving at dawn, and felt a knot tightening in my stomach. Ibe was beginning to say something else. I grunted as though I was listening.

Chisara pushed the door. It yielded. I did not bother to

look inside. Chisara entered the enemy's room and shut the door behind her. What followed is best described as the sound of fury. It started with a ripping noise, the curtains, perhaps. Then came the shattering wail of glass, or was it chinaware? The crowd did not move. The explosions ended with a big bang. The television? It was the bang that moved the crowd. There were gasps: mouths opening as if to collect rain; eyes zooming in on the door, as if to penetrate and take stock of the wreckage. Chisara emerged, sweating, her chest rising and falling. Her eyes were damp. For the first time I saw Chisara sobbing in public. She lifted her eyes to the sun and bit her lips. When her eyes fell, they fell on the cold crowd. I saw questions in her eyes, words she could not utter words that were meant to express how much she loathed them for enjoying the show, a show that began in the room she had wrecked and ended with an absconded man. What I saw in her eyes did not mean much to me then, but was vivid enough to leave impressions on my mind. Years later, I saw it for what it was: the strong stare of the first feminist I knew.

She walked through the crowd and disappeared between blocks. The curtain was drawn. The crowd lingered, perhaps dismayed by her brief but knowing stare. I began to think of Dora. She had asked me to run, to leave her alone. Why would she ask to be left alone? Not as if I had asked to stay with her. I began to speculate what her reasons were but could not draw any conclusions.

"Where is Dora?" I asked Ibe.

"I don't know. They say her Ma is looking for her."

For once Ibe did not know someone's whereabouts.

The crowd was beginning to buzz again. Word had gone out that Dora was missing. Did she leave with Jide?

Someone had seen her crossing the road at dawn; another "eyewitness" sighted her thirty kilometres away, somewhere between St. Peters and Okeke's barbershop; a lugubrious fellow with sunken eyes announced that he had seen her near the police station. Her stone was still in my pocket. I touched it. And could still see her red, ripe eyes. I tightened my grip on the stone and left the crowd to its confusion.

*

I returned to the lake before nightfall. And waited. The walk was slow as I turned sideways at each step to see if she was hiding between clusters of grass, or crawled into a ball on a side path, dead or alive. Why did I think she might be dead? That idea was surprisingly strong, and I recall the sudden heaviness that I felt in that moment. It was the same feeling that overcame me when, one school day during the morning assembly, it was announced that a pupil was missing, and that we all should "report" whatever we knew that might be helpful to the search party dispatched to look for him. They found him a day later, alive and well in his grandmother's house, about twenty miles away from his parents'. His disappearance, however, left me drained for days. In Dora's case, that feeling was more intense. It sat in my guts like a cold pot of stale broth.

I waited by the lake, sitting on the mound where I last saw her. A beautiful silence descended as if to calm me down. For a short breath or two, the hum of passing cars from the nearby highway was inaudible, and the occasional squawk of ducks ceased as though shushed by the lake itself. I was there for about twenty-five minutes. By then the sun was on its way out and silence had given way to the whir of cars and the odd echoes of voices in the distance. Dora was nowhere. I walked home in quick strides, overcome by fear, breaking into small trots without looking back.

Word came that night. Her bloated body was found on the other side of the lake. The night itself was animated by voices in pockets, everywhere, chattering about this discovery, with sighs and hisses so loud they became eerie additions to a night already fraught with an aura of tragedy. I blocked my ears with both palms, my face between my thighs.

"What's the matter?" Mama asked.

"I'm cold," I said.

She was standing behind me.

"Are your joints aching? Is your mouth bitter?"

"No."

"I'll make you pepper soup with uziza leaves, okay?"

I did not reply.

She walked around me, lifted my face, and placed her palm on my forehead.

"It looks like you are running temperature," she said. "You must have pepper soup with uziza leaves, okay?"

"Okay. Thanks, Mama."

There was a full moon, beaming and dispelling the blackness of night, offering false daylight to exuberant kids who, in spite of what was going on, were already in play mode around the blocks. I searched the moon and saw nothing but a ball suspended in vastness, ambivalently and menacingly beautiful. The frozen woman and her baby were still there, trapped in the moon for all eternity. I recalled the story we were told to warn us against breaking community rules. It was said that she had gone to market on a sacred day, knowing full well that women were to stay indoors while men communed with ancestral gods at the square. As punishment she was banished to the moon, with her daughter who, as the story goes, was strapped to her back when the gods passed their judgements on her case.

The shrubs between our block and the next shone. An ominous wind rustled their leaves, adding to my fright. Each jubilant leaf grew more grotesque with the whip of wind. The woman-in-the-moon seemed genuinely animated, her shape moving against the westward stream of thin smoke-like clouds. Her hair pointed in three directions like Dora's hair. Did Dora offend the gods? I touched the stone in my pocket. What is it about women and gods? Was it the gods that killed Dora? How did she offend the gods? Are there female gods that punish men for breaking community rules, for inflicting pain on young girls? Whose job is it to freeze Jide in the moon, or to whip his bare back like a woman in Iriebe was reportedly whipped for sleeping with her husband's friend?

"You are crying? I'll call Mama."

It was Ricia. She was standing in front of me, obscuring the moon, her body a silhouette against the light. I almost stood up to hug her, my sister, and beg her to stay away from whatever would land her in the moon or dead by the lake.

"I'm fine," I said in my finest masculine voice.

"Why are you crying then?"

"I'm not crying. I don't know why," I said, helpless as tears warmed my cheek.

"It's malaria," she said. "It makes people cry and shiver like small flowers."

"I'm not a flower."

"But is it malaria?"

"Yes, it's malaria."

"Mama is making you pepper soup. It will warm you up," she said.

"I know. And I'll share some with you."

"No. It's for you. I'm not shivering like small flowers."

"I'm not shivering like small flowers."

"I think you are."

"I'm not." And the tears streamed more.

Before bedtime I wrapped Dora's stone in paper, put it in an old sock, tied the sock into a knot and hid it at the bottom of my basket of clothes. It would live in that sock for another six years, untouched but often remembered as events, both in my dreams and in real life, triggered memories of its existence.

She appeared in my dream that night. We held hands and walked by the lake. Her eyes were the colour of the lake, shifting from amber to deep blue. Her young breasts, dark around the nipples, brushed my chest as she hugged me several times. Her hug lingered, calming, warm.

"Why did you run away?" I asked her. "They said you were everywhere? But you weren't. I waited here for you, because I believed you were somewhere in the bushes. Why did you run away?"

She released me from her embrace, looked away before replying in a whisper:

"I did not run away. I only walked away from trouble. See," she pointed at the blocks, "there is too much trouble over there. You should join me. We'll be happy."

She walked ahead, into the lake. The water reached her neck. She turned and beckoned. I took two steps in her direction. Her eyes were no longer the colour of the lake, but had turned red. I panicked, shivered like small flowers, and fled. I awoke to Mama's face staring down at me. had been kicking, talking and twitching in my sleep.

"What is it?" she asked, a jar of "blessed" olive oil in her hand.

"Nothing," I said, still panting.

She ignored my remark and went ahead to empty the "blessed" oil on my head.

8

The day after Dora's body was found was a Sunday. The blocks had snapped back to their normal rhythm as if nothing had happened. There had been a small burial the same night her body was found; she was too young for anything more. Ibe would later share how it went. How he was allowed there I do not know.

"They put her in a small box," he started, "a small, small box that was shorter than her real height. And then they carried her off to the lake."

"You mean they tossed her in the lake?"

"No. They buried her near the lake, since she died there."

"Who else was there?"

"Her parents, their pastor and a lot of women."

"Were they crying?"

"Not loud enough. I thought they would be falling in the grass and screaming her name. But they were not loud at all."

"Because she was a child?"

"I think so."

"Was the hole deep?"

"I think so. They say it must be six feet deep."

"Why?"

"Because, because... I don't know. Wait. I think it's because God created humans on the sixth day. Yes, I think that's why the hole must be six feet deep."

"What if it's five or seven? Or an inch above or under six?"

"Well, I think those mistakes are the reasons why ghosts walk around at night. Shallow holes make happy ghosts, while those that are too deep make wicked ghosts."

"That makes a lot of sense. I think Dora will be a happy ghost. I hope her hole was exactly six or some inches shallower. Were there any kids there?"

"None. It was too early."

"So where were you?"

"I watched from a distance. My mom was there. I knew she was going. I sneaked out and trailed her."

"I wish I had watched from a distance. Did you hear the preacher?"

"A little. He prayed. I think he said she was in heaven."

"So she's not here? I thought she would be here for awhile before moving on to heaven?"

"I think dead people go between heaven and here, or hell and here. But I don't think they go anywhere, to be honest. I think they just rot."

"How about ghosts? I thought you said something about happy and wicked ghosts?"

"I made that up. People rot in those holes they dig for them. It's simple. You bury them and they become food for ants."

"Ants?"

"Or worms."

"How about the soul? Isn't there supposed to be a soul, like the pastors say, that runs through a white tunnel towards heaven or hell?"

"That's what they say, but we don't know since there's no eye witness with a story from that other side."

"I believe there's a soul in everyone. And it jumps out and runs around when we die, the same way we run around in our dreams when our bodies are lying down."

"I don't agree."

"So you mean Dora is now in the hands of ants and worms?"

"In a day or two, yes."

"I don't believe you."

That Sunday, like every Sunday, bibles were clutched under arms, ironed shirts and toe-touching skirts were worn and polished shoes marched to various churches. The Catholics were often the first to leave. Their morning mass and the rooster's first alarm coincided. You could hear them shuffling between blocks as they hurried to church before everyone else was awake. Knowing how they loathed the Pentecostals, I believed they left early to establish a stronger rapport with God before the rambunctious Pentecostals showed up at the Lord's corridor. On a regular Sunday evening, after hours of sobriety at the lord's feet, the drinking would commence. It was not unusual to find two casual Christians, one Catholic and a Pentecostal, sharing a bottle of seaman's aromatic schnapps and merrily mocking their respective religious persuasion to the mortification of those who took such matters seriously.

The Sunday after Dora's death was different. There were no clusters of merriment. But this was not a sign of collective mourning for the departed girl. On the contrary, the absent clusters were due to the presence of an itinerant magician who had appeared. A crowd had formed around him, animated by an anticipation that cancelled whatever morsel of sadness Dora's death may have sprinkled on the blocks. You would expect the excitement to be tempered by drops of sadness.

The magician rolled out his mat, and emptied the

contents of his sack on to it: beads stringed together, cowries, leaves, twigs, seven bottles of Fanta, a small bell, a small cassette player, and a wooden box. Around him, eager faces stared. I was there too, unsure of what or how to feel but aware of the giddiness around me, spreading from the crowd like fire atop a stream of petrol. Someone asked if I was ready to make money. For a second I thought it was the magician, but he was busy walking around his mat, muttering things to himself, moving his items around as if to align them with the stars. Ibe had asked the question. He was right next to me, sitting on bare ground a few feet away from the magician's mat, with a fat grin on his face. Behind him were three girls chattering excitedly as they took turns pointing at the items on the mat. I had calculatedly planted myself next to Ibe, where I was sure to access all possible back-stories that might add flavour to the unfolding episode. There were always back-stories to all events at the blocks, and they were often juicier than the events themselves. Ibe was a purveyor of back-stories.

The faces around me bore no traces of collective sadness. Achu, who was there when Chisara pounced on Jide, was in the audience, huddled between two women, his face covered in a smile. Achu was one of those men who lingered around the blocks at noon when the others were away at work. He would stop to listen to whatever stories women had to share: an adulterous husband, a mean neighbour, an overbearing mother-in-law... He was their man, a listening ear. He played his nice-guy cards well. The husbands had their suspicions, but that was all they had— suspicions. Achu walked the blocks a free man, flirting his way around, receiving and offering free hugs wherever he went.

There were a few kids lined up at the feet of grownups. Some were still in their Sunday-only shirts and shorts, and were visibly thrilled by what was unfolding before them. They would run from one spot to another, chuckling, unable to contain themselves.

The prancing magician's first act began unexpectedly. The stringed beads were there, lying still on his mat; the cowries were there, idle—we knew they were used for divination but the fellow before us was neither diviner nor priest; the leaves and twigs were there too, untouched. After shuffling his items around he sat at a corner of the mat and picked up a bottle of Fanta. He gripped the crown cork with his teeth and it yielded and detached itself from the bottle. Then he sat crossed legged like a monk. His black trousers, much like what Pa Suku would wear, were tight. His black jazz shoes, unpolished for who knows how long, had gone from black to grey, with holes emerging at the tips. His white shirt, with an inscription that had faded into illegibility, was equally tight and jumped to the midriff—more to the thorax than the navel. He guzzled the Fanta, his head tilted up. We watched. He drank as if we were not there, an act that surprisingly doubled the suspense.

The girls were bending over to ask questions about the magician, and Ibe supplied them with succinct but well-crafted answers: he is from Akwa Ibom but lives somewhere in Port Harcourt; he is so powerful he could transform into whatever he wishes; they say he has travelled up to Lagos, and had wowed the crowds there before returning to the south; he is this and he is that. They believed Ibe. I believed him.

The magician stood up, empty Fanta bottle in hand,

and walked to the head of the mat. He tightened his grip on the bottle. The bottle's bottom, now pointing out to the cloudless sky, shivered as his arm, straight out, vibrated. The vibration became more dramatic as though the bottle, annoyed and revolting against the spectacle, was drawing electricity from the dry sky. In one bold move he swiftly lowered the poor bottle on his dreadlocked head. The bottle's bottom severed itself from the rest of its body, shot out sideways, and landed a few inches from Ibe's feet. Ibe had seen it coming and had frantically lurched back. The girls dispersed but quickly re-assembled behind Ibe. The crowd was already enjoying the show. The next act was no less spectacular. He picked up the butt of the bottle, jagged and menacingly sharp, and clasped it in both hands, squeezing tight. Then he majestically walked around the mat for his audience to see and acknowledge his feat. The crowd pushed forward, waiting for blood to gush from his grip. Not a single drop of blood. The bottle's butt was tossed aside. Several rounds of applause followed.

In-between claps, Ibe whispered in my ear, "You ready for the money magic?"

"What money magic?" I asked.

"See that box?" he asked and gestured with his head in the direction of the wooden box. "There is money in it, that box."

"Money?" I studied the box, squinting as though it might be transparent if I looked hard enough. It looked like a tree stump sawed and chiselled into shape. The diagonal, coin-size hole at the top showed that it was, indeed, a moneybox. Did he expect us to tip him? Or was he one of those money doublers? He was now clapping with the crowd, his face deadly serious. He did a few jumps in readiness for his next move. It was clear that his performance was not an on-the-spot improvisation but a calculated production, a scripted act tried and tested in various street theatres, a one-man show designed to electrify audience such as the one around him now. One move, they gasped and clapped. Another move, they fell quiet.

The cassette player was the next on his script. Bending over to push a button, almost ripping his tight trouser, his arse shot out in Ibe's direction. He pressed the play button. The beat and voice that followed was that of Majek Fashek, and the song, an anthemic household number, was Fashek's "Religion Na Politics". The dreadlocked magician clapped and marched to the beat like a soldier. Left, right, left, right, left, right. Then he broke into a hop, alternating the hopping leg from right to left. He continued faster and faster, almost out of time with Fashek's beat. His audience did not waste the music; they did not wait for a call to dance. Achu swayed like an okra plant whipped by an ominous July wind, and was rewarded with a flirtatious slap on the shoulder, to which he responded with a gushy grin and whispered something in the slapper's ear. Ibe moved his shoulders, slowly. One of the girls stooped to knead the moving shoulders. The girl's nails were well trimmed and covered in red nail polish. But I was more interested in Ibe's show of masculinity. He, the man, squaring his shoulder while the girl, standing behind, kneaded his shoulder. Why was it not the other way around?

The dance was over. The box was tapped several times and dramatically lifted to the heavens. A cheer rang out from all corners. He clamped it under his arm and organized us into three queues.

"Ready, ready?" he asked in a monstrous roar. It was the

first time he had spoken to his audience.

"Ready," they echoed.

He repeated his question. They screamed their answer with giggles and chuckles in-between. It became a singsong affair, going back and forth. He added a clap; someone else added a little staccato clap, offbeat but fitting oddly. He raised his hands like a conductor, the audience stood still. The box was tapped again, more of a drumming with the fingers. I followed his quivering muscles and contorting face. His locks swaggered about—a prominent part of the performance. His eyes, bloodshot and firm, bore a certainty. There were no traces of fear in them. But somewhere there, hiding in those eyes, I imagined a boy with a mother and a past, a boy with a wondering mind. I studied the boy in the man, but the man was too busy performing for his audience and his pocket. His eyes began to change, oscillating as he pranced. The whites were darkening like clouds before a torrential rain. Then they cleared, darkened again, and then moved between amber and dark blue, like the lake where Dora drowned herself. Each time he turned in my direction, I saw the change in his eyes. They finally turned ripe red. And were the eyes of Dora, the way I saw them in my dreams. They glowed, filled with anger, remonstrating with the nonchalant crowd. I felt my legs giving way. I fell back a step. I held still. I was dizzy. I left the queue and joined a small group of onlookers outside the queue.

Achu stepped forward to the box. He dipped his hands into the pockets of his shorts and brought out a few coins, all of which went into the box through the little coin hole. The dreadlocked one covered the box with a white cloth. Then he danced and clapped around the box. Achu was asked to sit on the mat. The cloth was dramatically lifted from the box, as though unveiling a bowl of fruit. The box was turned upside down. Several coins came out. Achu had won a few coins in excess of his initial investment. He leapt off the mat and hugged the woman next in line. Eager to reap her own coins, she slapped Achu off and hastily stepped forward to try her luck. Inspired by his win, Achu bribed his way back in queue and was next in line.

"What's wrong?" a familiar voice asked.

"Nothing," I answered and fell a further two steps back before holding up my pose.

It was Ma Ike's voice. She had seen me walking out of the queue.

"Is it malaria?" she asked.

Her voice was a faint flap of many butterflies. I felt the lake rising to my knees, my waist, my chest, my neck…

"Let's play here," said a different voice, the silky voice of a girl.

"Where?"

"Over there, next to the shrub," she said.

Her voice was one with the quack of floating ducks, a frightening laughter. Her skin was as smooth as glass, and her eyes shone like a colony of glow-worms.

"But see, I'm held here by the lake," I said.

"Swim," she urged me. "Swim out and join me."

I tried to flee but remained glued to the same spot. I woke up drenched in cold water with Ma Ike, Mama, and Ricia peering into my face.

"Thank God," Mama cried when I blinked. "Thank you, my sister," she said to Ma Ike.

"Thank God, my sister," said Ma Ike.

Ma Ike had rushed me home, hauling me on her shoulder like a sack of grain. The show had continued without me. I tried to imagine the bop of my head as Ma Ike raced my unconscious body home, and tried to picture my mother's initial reaction to the sight of her unconscious son on her enemy's shoulder.

The next day, now in good terms with Ma Ike, I asked her what had happened to me. We were in her open kitchen where her kettle whistled atop a green, kerosene stove. Ogoamaka loitered nearby.

"You fainted. Your mouth moved like you were talking to someone. It's malaria," she said, "it scatters the brain."

It is not malaria, I wanted to say. I had seen things and had heard voices. I was at the lake and was in it.

"What happened after I fainted?" I asked. "Did Ibe win any coins?"

The kettle whistled louder in bubbles. It was an aluminium kettle. The handle was gone. The cover was gone. Its colour and symmetry were not what they used to be.

"Ibe won a few coins," she said, "and ran off to celebrate."

"Did Achu win the second time"?

"He did," she answered. "But he wasn't lucky the third time. By the time I was carrying you out, the magician was on the ground with Achu and the crowd on top of him."

"Why?"

I also wanted to know if anyone had seen me slump, and if there had been any show of concern.

"They all wanted to win," Ma Ike said.

"Why?"

"Why? That is the way we are. We all want to win."

She turned down the stove. The kettle stopped whistling. Ogoamaka walked away, distracted by something else. I thanked her for being kind and strolled off to see Pa Suku.

9

Pa Suku's door was shut when I got there, but the window was slightly open. There were voices inside. One of the voices was asking a question. Another voice answered, and another voice added to the answer. The voices died into an echoing murmur, then the radio waves surged again and the lead voice posed another question. Pa Suku grunted, irritated. I peeped through the open window. He was there, hunched over the radio, with a small pile of paper on his desk. He looked distressed, and was writing frantically, almost at the same pace as the voices on his radio. The accents were Nigerian, except the one that was asking the questions. The words "military," "politics," "Africa," "election," and "Nigeria" were all over the place. Then there was a break, followed by the headlines: the Pope is in Spain, a church has been razed in Rwanda and refugees killed...

"For Christ sake," Pa Suku snapped, "what is wrong with the black man? Why the mindless killings?" He buried his face in both palms, took a long breath and lowered his head. Then he dropped his pen, turned off the radio and neatly folded his notes. I tried to tiptoe away but he had heard the light shuffle of my feet.

"How was the magic show yesterday?" he asked.

"Nice," I answered.

He unlocked the door and joined me outside. We took our usual positions on his veranda, from where we could look either ways and count the rooms on both side of his block and the block across. He was wearing shorts that used to be trousers. A shrouser as I called it then, a term that comes to mind ever since. The scissors had not done a good job of evening out the lengths of both legs; one length of shrouser hung below his left knee, the other was about an inch shorter, with drooping threads.

"I heard the roar," he said. "They must have enjoyed the show."

"He danced and played us Majek Fashek," I said.

"Good music. He was roping them in, like politicians do around here. What you witnessed yesterday is a mini-version of what happens in this country. Bones are dangled before the poor. They drool like starving dogs. But as they nibble on bones, their souls are wrenched from them, their destinies chopped and discarded."

"They beat him up later," I said.

"At least they had the courage to revolt against the street performer. The real thieves are out there, deceiving, plundering, and walking free. Did you listen to the interview just now?" he asked rhetorically. "They were talking about us—you and I, and that child over there." He pointed to a toddler playing in the dirt with an older boy about my age. "We are Nigeria. Whatever those political magicians do rubs off on us. Whatever shame they plant and cultivate is ours to bear. Anyway, did you win any money?"

"No. I fainted," I said, studying my feet.

"Fainted? What happened?"

"I was dizzy."

"Dizzy?"

He was not as dramatic as my mother. Papa had not been around. If he had, perhaps he would have been more dramatic than Mama, shivering and calculating the cost of treating the alleged malaria.

"Dizzy like Dizzy Gillespie," he said in a singsong.

"Dizzy Gillespie, who is that?"

"An American jazz trumpeter and composer. Great musician," he said. "He died last year."

He was beginning to shake both knees, a sign of memory surge, like the radio waves returning.

"It was Isodje who introduced me to jazz—Gillespie, Charlie Parker, Dave Brubeck, and many more. He had their records and would share them with me. Anyway, why were you Dizzy Gillespie?"

"I saw Dora," I said.

"The dead girl?"

"Yes."

"Were you friends?"

"No."

"Have you been thinking about her and what happened to her?"

His voice was straight and blank. No emotions.

"I was…"

I tried to say that I had seen her walking into the lake that morning but could not bring myself to do so. I felt strangely light and could not feel the weight of my own head. It was as though my words, as they were about to come out, drained the contents of my bowels, forcing weightlessness upon me. I started rubbing my palms together.

"Are you alright?"

"I am," I answered, "just a little Dizzy Gillespie."

"Good one, my boy. Dizzy Gillespie. One second."

He went inside and came out a few moments later with a cup of water. A plastic cup with a crack at the rim. He handed it to me. My firm grip widened the crack, spilling half the contents.

"Drink, my boy," he said.

It was the first time he had offered me water, anything for that matter, beyond the routine dose of knowledge shared.

I handed him the cup, rubbed my palms again, and turned to watch the toddler and his older playmate gathering sand. It appeared they were erecting a sand wall around them. The toddler was rather more interested in building and destroying at once, gathering and flattening at the same time. Then, as if inspired by the sand itself, he began to rain fistfuls on his head, giggling. His older playmate tried to stop him but soon gave up. I looked away only to swiftly return my stare when the toddler released a loud cry, a piercing shriek as though a needle had found its way under his fingernails. His playmate, puzzled, dashed off and disappeared into one of the rooms nearby, re-appeared with a slender woman, who ran ahead, reached for the toddler, and began to blow his face as though killing a small fire. It turned out the toddler had grains of sand in his eyes. So the woman blew at his face, then held his eyelids apart and blew straight into his eyes. The kid howled even more, thrashing his little hands against the wind. Confused, the playmate stood at a distance, perhaps anticipating what was coming next—a hot smack on the cheek from the woman as they walked away from the scene. It was the playmate's cry that lingered in my head when the toddler had long stopped crying.

Dizzy Gillespie. But I was not dizzy anymore. Pa Suku squeezed the cup.

"What is it like to die?" I asked.

"Well, I'll tell you when I die and wake up to preach about death."

"Will you go to heaven?"

"Heaven?" He looked up. I followed his gaze. "Do you think it's up there, covered by those clouds?"

I nodded.

"And you think it's all white, with a bearded God, angels, big buildings, wide streets?"

"And white horses," I added.

"And gold everywhere?"

I nodded, picturing the image of heaven as painted by the resident pastor at our church: palatial, opulent, a perpetual feeling of warmth and elegance.

Pa Suku excused himself, walked inside, and came out later with a thick hardback. He handed it to me and asked me to flip through. It was a catalogue of historic European architecture. There, on the first few pages, were pictures of palaces and castles around the UK: Kensington, Windsor, Eltham, Hampton, and more. The Diocletian's Palace was present, its peristyle displayed as a spread between two pages. More palaces: Turin, Schönbrunn, The Doge's, Oslo, Brussels, Nymphenburg… I pronounced these words with great difficulty, which, to a great extent, shrank the beauty of the buildings they marked.

"What do you think?"

I was not thinking. I was distracted by the stiff sounding names and landscapes that I could not identify with. I flipped to the last pages. More imposing structures, white and grey and gold coloured, with wide columns. Beautiful yet aloof, like shrines that must be revered and never approached nor touched. It did not help that there were no humans seen in the vicinities where these buildings were planted like timeless baobab trees. The publisher had not thought it wise to include humans anywhere.

I closed the book and handed it back. What do I think?

"They are big, big houses," I said.

"True. And they are all important, with a long list of important people that have gone through their walls. Big, big names. Heaven must be like one of those, or a collection of important houses, yes?"

"Maybe."

I pictured Dora in those European palaces, running between columns here, rolling and laughing through the gardens there. She seemed happy, like I believed the dead who made it to heaven would be. Years later, in one of my dreams, she was a fuller girl, with pronounced breasts and hips, lying flat on her back by the entrance to a gated palace. I could see Jide's face in one of the windows, high enough to almost obscure his features. Then it was no longer his face, but that of a bearded white man.

"Are you alright?" Pa Suku asked again.

"I am," I answered, "Just a bit Dizzy Gillespie."

PART TWO

Of all the books I rescued from the street bookseller whose stand consisted of a mat and a short bench for two, *The Palace of Dreams* holds the most important place in my heart. This, to be frank, has nothing to do with the book itself. It simply happened to be the book in my hands when I first met Professor Ojo, who would eventually lead me to Osagie.

I was sitting on a log by the entrance to Adam Hall, reading Kadare's *The Palace of Dreams*, when Professor Ojo emerged from his flat. I was surprised to see him there but thanked my stars, for I had been hoping to meet him, this noted scholar whose latest collection of essays on West African literature I had read from cover to cover. He came out and stood still, contemplating the line of palm trees outside. Then he looked left, where small shops and shacks hugged the campus fence. He studied the shops, hands on hips as though preparing to make a pronouncement. After this brief contemplation he turned right, and walked towards the main gate, which opened to a small cluster of bars.

I closed *The Palace of Dreams*, cleared dirt from my trousers and followed him. He stayed on the right side of the road. I gave him a few yards and stayed on the left. Nearing the university health centre, he stopped as though there was a red light ahead, pulled out a small writing pad from the breast pocket of his collarless shirt, and scribbled furiously. Then he paused to study the dying flowers at the entrance to the health centre.

I turned into the narrow street leading to the administrative building and sat under an almond tree, waiting. He returned to his pen and pad, wrote for two to three minutes and walked on. I trailed him. He reached the main gate and lingered there. I turned right, towards the university library and stopped at the sculpture garden where twenty years' worth of sculptures lay unenjoyed. Snuggled between the library's west wing and two mango trees were my favourite pieces in this abandoned collection: a man and a woman as one sculpted piece. Her headgear is neatly tied into an upright knot; she is holding a child to her bare breast, and with the free hand she is grabbing the man by the crotch; his eyes are distended disproportionally, his mouth agape, his tongue falling out.

There was an artist next to the sculpted couple, facing the gate, his easel stationed before him. I walked closer to steal a glance and was glad I did. He had included Professor Ojo in his drawing. I complimented his work. He turned and asked if I knew "the man over there."

"Not personally," I answered, "but I know he's visiting from Ife."

"Ife! Great university."

"So I hear," I said, admiring the way he tilted Professor Ojo's face in the drawing, making it seem as though he was studying the skyline. Also positioned in the painting were motorbikes and the silhouette of a car.

A busy sketch. But every stroke had a place, a purpose. It did seem, looking closely at the work, that he started with an imaginary line, from left to right, and then ensured that each figure was on that line, branching out or falling in; and it appeared he was enforcing a sense of movement, a procession from left to right, from right to left.

I wanted to ask if he had looked up, read, or seen anything by Norman Lewis, but was not sure if the two or three pieces of Lewis I once saw online were sufficient to draw connections. Nonetheless, the painting, though at its infant stage, perhaps days or months away from completion, had a rhythmic resonance that is unmistakably connected to music.

"There's something jazzy about your work," I said.

"Interesting," he said, "I never thought of it that way." He drew back, looked at the work admiringly and went for his pack of cigarettes. "Jazz. Well, I suppose my interest in jazz seeps into my works; it's not intentional, though. I suppose it happens in the subconscious… I suppose these things just happen."

His repeated use of "I suppose" was a bit distracting. I ignored it and concentrated on the work-in-progress. He was now looking at the picture, a grin over his face, as though seeing it for the first time, his mouth ajar. One could conclude he perhaps was encouraged, or had his ego puffed by my interest. I almost offered to buy the piece, to collect it whenever he was done. But the idea of *collecting* art, of being the one who *encouraged* him to stick to his art, to his career, struck me as pretentious, delusional, an overestimation of my worth. I nearly laughed at the idea, at how easily I slipped into a place where I thought I could drop an opinion on art, on life itself. I however ventured to ask what he intended to do with the work.

"No idea," he said slowly, carelessly, and I was disappointed. How could he not know what he wanted to do with his work. But he did have a plan, I corrected myself, and the plan was to do nothing.

The professor was now moving, heading for the first bar

outside the gate.

"Well," I began, "if you're holding a show anywhere, anytime, do let me know. I'm in room 97, Adam Hall."

"Okay, okay," he said. "I'm in 65. I'll let you know. In fact, there's a group show next week, at the faculty of arts, I'll be showing six pieces connected to this one. Not sure I'll have this ready by then."

"I'll try to be there. Anyway, good luck to you." I said, and left.

The evening sun was now a thin layer of loitering light above rooftops. A thin cloud, dispersing, assured me there was a near zero chance it was going to rain. I walked into the bar. The professor was at the far left corner, close to the wall. There was no one else. I sat next to the door. The ceiling fan wailed and hauled heat at us. The wobbly zinc walls, barely nailed to the beams, clattered annoyingly as though a maniac was kicking from the outside. The bar owner, doubling as our server, brought him a bottle of Star. His eyes swayed with the shake of her baggy trousers, which did exaggerate her hips, especially since the large floral patterns were unflatteringly placed on the sides, creating an illusion that delighted the professor. I caught the flicker of her earrings: silver, modest, dangling.

"How are you today, Prof.?" she asked in a disarmingly rusty voice.

"Not bad," he answered, both palms spread out on the table. He examined the thick froth on his glass, waiting.

His phone rang. He ignored it. A text came in. He ignored it. He went for his beer, sipped.

"And the new book?" she was asking, cleaning the table next to him.

"It's coming along, thank you." He inserted the phone

in his pocket.

"All the best," she said, "let me know when it comes out."

"I will personally deliver your copy," he said with a wink.

She moved closer to him, brushed off an idle drop of dust from his greying hair, patted his shoulder, and strutted away to the counter. I went to her and thoughtlessly ordered a bottle of Heineken, expecting a change from the conviviality I had just witnessed to the usual nonchalance of customer services around here. She asked how I was doing, her teeth an ambivalent milky-white. I mumbled an answer, quite unprepared for her familiar friendliness. My drink appeared. I scuttled off to accomplish my mission.

There were two empty chairs at the professor's table. I decided to make my presence known and be done with it. He had picked a random point on the wall, upon which his gaze fell.

"May I join you, sir?" I asked. My hands were already at the shoulder of the chair on the other side of his table, pulling it out.

"Yes you may," he replied, "and may I ask why you have been following me?"

His eyes fell from their heights and landed on me, before moving quickly to Kadare.

"I met your Kadare in Paris," he randomly said. "The year was '94, and the world was covered in blood."

I looked at the book then back at him. His cheekbones were evenly cut, sharp, like those of a regular runner. But then his eyes, dull and wandering, and the subtly collapsed shoulders, all countered the impression of athleticism. He must have shaved not long before; his brow and the skin underneath his chin were unusually smooth. I began to have this strange feeling that I had met him somewhere before. But I knew this was a trick of memory. I tugged my mind to see where and how this sense of familiarity came about. No response. It then occurred to me that he bore a striking resemblance to the man who once visited Pa Suku at the blocks, the only person I saw pay him a visit. Pa Suku's visitor had the same face, but must have been taller, more muscular, in a sky blue shirt, with upper buttons left to bare a hairless chest, pure white trousers tight and immaculately trimmed. He had walked straight to Pa Suku's door, hands in pockets. I was there, sitting outside with Pa Suku. Both men had hugged for what seemed like a lifetime, and I was dismissed to go home. It must have been the dismissal, the abrupt closure of a hitherto warm conversation, that made me remember the incident which planted this stranger's face in my memory.

"It was Rwanda," the professor was saying." You know what I mean?"

I nodded.

"After our meeting," he continued, speaking as if we were reviving an old conversation, "which was not planned, as I simply happened on him at a friend's house, I bought his books."

"I like his style," I said, hazarding a line of thought.

"Right. His opening lines have the effect of ten blows. Please read me the opening lines in chapter one."

I read:

The Curtains were letting in the uncertain lights of dawn, and as usual he pulled up the blanket in the hope of dozing on a while longer. But he soon realized he wouldn't be able to. He'd remembered that this sunlight heralded no ordinary day...

"What a perfect opening," he beamed. "I read those same lines in France. I'd been following the situation in Rwanda and could not reconcile it with the view from my hotel room in Paris. The contrast was lacerating. I imagined the streets of Rwanda, a place I'd never seen in real life. My mind yielded nothing but the horrors I read in the papers."

He recited a few lines from an Albanian poet he had read after discovering Kadare.

> May the day dawn
> That will bestow upon us
> A great light,
> Giving birth to:
> Civilization,
> Prosperity.

"Naim Frashëri," he announced.

Naim Frashëri. It did not ring a bell.

"Pardon my little unplanned lecture," he said, his facial muscles tightened by the sour surge of memory. "*The Palace of Dreams*," he mused, "how random. I mean, it's rare to spot Kadare around here."

I saw the circle of stress around his eyes, the shadowy hollow that marks the onset of something more troubling. I introduced myself. Double major in English and History. Fledgling poet with a few publications in obscure journals edited by obscure poets for obscure poets.

"I read your latest book of criticism," I added, "and thought it was interesting that you—"

"I'm working on a new book," he cut in, suddenly animated. "It's my most ambitious work to date, and it does not in any way pay attention to the big names in African literature. On the contrary, it seeks out and centralizes writers who, sadly, are almost forgotten today."

The zinc walls clattered more, giving one the idea that the imaginary lunatic outside had gone crazier, or had miraculously grown two extra legs with which he kicked the zinc wall.

"Have you read anything by Aniebo?" he asked.

"I haven't. I've heard the name, but haven't seen or read any of his novels."

"It's a shame," he said calmly, meditatively. "It's shame that a writer of such merit is largely ignored today. He wrote novels and short stories, some of which, to me, are among the greatest texts to come out of this country. You should read *The Journey Within*, a work that announces a writer dedicated to style and aware of the cadence of language. Anyway, I will send you a copy of my book when it's done. It's a project that's entirely devoted to forgotten or nearly forgotten writers like Palangyo, the Tanzanian writer whose only novel, *Dying in the Sun*, is no longer talked about. There's also Serumaga, the Ugandan whose plays and only novel are nearly forgotten. I don't know, I'm just generally drawn to neglected writers, and I dig to know why they are neglected: the nature of their works, or a fallout of a system that picks who and what to promote."

He pushed back his chair, and folded his hands. A fly landed on the brim of his glass of beer. He left it there, staring as though expecting a performance from the restless creature.

"*Mapping the Margins of African Literature: A Critical Survey of Writers Outside the Canon.* That's the working title of the book. I'm hoping it will draw attention to these writers, and facilitate a re-reading of their texts for what they are, with an eye for style and language."

There was so much passion in his voice, so much concern for the texts he had chosen to promote, that one did imagine a bigger motivating factor. It was not long before I began to see the real reason for his passion. It turned out, as he eventually shared, that he had lost his wife three year before, the primary reason why he left Ife, the sabbatical was a mere cover. Championing the cause of forgotten writers was one way he distracted himself. It struck me as ironic, this idea of distracting one's self, forcing the mind to forget a tragedy, by digging up something else that is on its way out of collective memory.

"She killed herself," he said over his third beer, "and I blame myself for it."

For a second I was tempted to ask for more, to know what might have caused her suicide. But I realized it would be completely inappropriate to do so; I thought the whole conversation was inappropriate.

"She was dealing with depression for so many years," he continued, satisfying my unspoken curiosity, "and I ignored it. I thought she would snap out of it, that she would one day escape the dark clouds above her head. You know," he looked up to meet my eyes, "I was, like many people in this country, unaware of how depression works. We don't believe one can be depressed. Depression itself is not a word, or an experience, that has a place in our culture. We don't discuss it. We don't even know it when we see it, when it appears and takes hold of us. We are not interested in understanding it.

"In fact," he continued, "any form of mental illness is considered a curse from the gods or the work of an evil spirit, a sign one has been shat on by the devil, hence an object that must be despised, locked away, left to rot."

"We should probably start by educating people," I said eagerly, "I know very little about mental illnesses. Who knows, I may be dealing with one as we speak."

"I've only now started reading up myself. Isn't that sad?"

"Quite unfortunate."

"Well, I don't want to take all your time, young man. I'm glad you are interested in my work. Let's meet again. Stop by my office, it's around the corner, behind the administrative building over there, or come to my flat for tea or beer."

I said I would and stood to go. He invited me to *Opia*, the monthly reading he started when he moved here from Ife. He shook my hand again. This time the handshake was firm, as though he had been energized by our conversation. I picked up my empty bottle, walked to the corner of the bar where crates were stacked, and inserted the bottle into an empty crate.

It was unusually cold outside, the temperature had dropped dramatically. I almost ran back inside, but thought otherwise. I walked on towards Adam Hall, hugging myself, the cold wind threatened to peel my skin.

Near the university health centre, I turned to see the dying flowers. They seemed content in their pathetic state. I began to hum a piece I had recently heard on a BBC broadcast, a piece by Rubinstein performed by some group somewhere. *The Piano Concerto No. 2 in F major, Op. 35.* If I remember correctly, it was the first movement, and I recall trotting as I repeatedly hummed the opening, the first two and a half minutes or thereabouts, which was the only part I remembered. A water delivery truck passed, blaring its horn as though a herd of cattle was in its way. It turned right towards the Vice-Chancellor's quarters, to deliver clean drinking water to the venerated household of his holiness the vice chancellor. I turned left towards Adam Hall, where our tap water was not only contaminated but frequently packed up, leaving us with no choice but to trek off campus for water.

The weather waxed colder, and it occurred to me that I was indeed not prepared for the change of season that had crept up without notice. It was the dry season already, and my skin had gone ashy from not using the right lotion; the days were now greyer, colder at dawn and at dusk.

As I stepped into Adam Hall, I began to wonder what kind of conversation the professor had with the bartender. They were, obviously, from different intellectual backgrounds. But she had asked about his forthcoming book, which gave one the impression that they there could be a shared interest in literature, or culture in general. One would not be surprised, I thought, to walk in and see them holding an intense conversation about the cultural significance of beer in Nigeria, perhaps a comparative analysis of beer culture by region. "Considering the fact that Muslims do not consume alcohol," the Prof. would possibly say, "beer might not essentially be part of the socio-cultural fabric up North. However, the secret consumption of beer, one could further imagine, would not be unheard of. Hence, beer is no longer beer as we know it in the South, but a symbol of rebellion, the very juice of a thriving underground culture. You know, there could, in fact, be a Marxist angle to this beer thing, I mean the possible consumption of beer by the working class up North…" The bartender, perhaps more practical than her learned companion, would ponder what brand of beer circulated up there, and how much of it was consumed by Southern Christians up North.

Perhaps they did not engage in this sort of conversation. One could walk in and find her on his lap, or the other way around, doing whatever it was that got their canoes rocking. There was no doubt that they both had something going, which made me wonder if she paid him a visit, or if he was the one who did the visiting. If he did, which was completely possible, considering the fact that he did not strike me as too arrogant to explore the low income flats around town (I am, again, assuming she lived in a low income flat); if he did, what did they do out there? I know these are pointless ponderings, but I found myself giving them room in my head. To what end, I did not know.

What if she was the one that paid him visits, which is very likely, one could see her walking in for the first time, wondering whose picture was on the wall, "is that your wife? She's beautiful." And then setting down the basket of fruit, or the cooler of beer (or food) she had brought with her... wild thoughts, wild thoughts.

There are no photographs on his wall. I know this from the time I paid him a visit, two weeks after the bar conversation. He, however, had large prints of paintings on all sides of his wall. "That," he said as I lingered before a print that housed an assemblage of almost surreal shapes, "is a painting by Le Corbusier. They are all prints." He had written short descriptions and posted them next to each work on his walls. "Le Corbusier," he continued, standing next to me like an enthusiastic young dealer making a first impression on a collector, "we know and have been enormously influenced by his architectural designs, but sadly not his extraordinary paintings, which I believe are more beautiful than his buildings." On the wall adjacent to his bookshelf, three Alix Aymé prints were posted side by side. 'Portrait of a Young African Woman Holding Her Head in Both Hands', 'Portrait of a Young Man Lost in Thought', and 'Michel/Christ.'

"Alix Aymé is almost forgotten today," he said. His voice had thickened at this point, as though a lump had formed in his throat. I could not take my eyes off 'Portrait of a Young Man Lost in Thought', the slender body, the visceral innocence almost punctuated by the emerging teenage beard, the overall nakedness and vulnerability. I nearly broke down in tears when I was told how the Young Man died, in an internment camp in Indochina, where Alix Aymé's husband was commander of the French Army during World War II. The Japanese had rounded up the family and carted them off to a camp, where the Young Man, Michel, Aymé's son, passed away. He was also the subject of 'Michel/Christ', drawn after his death.

I did not linger much before 'Portrait of a Young African Woman Holding Her Head in Both Hands', a charcoal drawing that, as Professor Ojo announced, was done in the Congo shortly after it gained its independence from France.

"Alix Aymé was there," he added, "and one is forced to wonder what was crossing her mind as she met and drew her subject. There, in that space, was the ex-colonizer, as represented by Aymé herself; and the colonized, the black woman, her face registering what we cannot say. Contempt? Fear? Ambivalence? So much history is articulated in that drawing. Did Aymé intend her to symbol the moods of her new country? Well, someone has to dig for more."

A black and white photo of what seemed to be a petrol station was by the door to his kitchen. I walked over and it was indeed a petrol station. 'The R. W. Lindholm Service Station,' it said on the note, 'situated at 202 Cloquet Avenue, Cloquet, Minnesota.'

"The only petrol station designed by Frank Lloyd Wright," Professor Ojo declared. "Not as popular as the houses he designed across America."

On the other side of the door hung a poem, framed, Max Ehrmann's "Desiderata": *Beyond a wholesome discipline, be gentle with yourself. / You are a child of the universe no less than the trees/ and the stars; you have a right to be here.* Underneath was another poem, Nikolay Nekrasov's "Farewell": *We went separate ways midway,* it read, *We parted long before we parted, / Having thought: no more misery, / In that last and fateful "forgive,"/ Even to cry we've no more strength...*

Outside both poems, everything I saw hinted at his attempt to centralize items that are lodged in the periphery—in the case of Wright and Le Corbusier, on the periphery of their own lives and work. What draws a man to the periphery? In his case, it was obvious that he was bent on forgetting a personal tragedy, hence the passion for the already forgotten, a rather absurd way to trade one thing for another.

He offered me beer, and said half-heartedly, more to himself, "I just don't understand wine drinkers..." and was about to take his seat when electricity was cut off. "Bastards," he cussed and started looking for a candle. A cat purred in the kitchen, in the dark, a long drawn purr. And I could hear its footsteps... I stood where I was, waiting for his candle...

*

I finally stepped into my room on the 3rd floor. Rubinstein had long disappeared from my head thanks to the stupid water truck. I tossed *The Palace of Dreams* on my bed, and stretched out beside it like a snake measuring itself against a log.

My bed is by the window and at night, when my roommates are asleep, I open the window and listen to the gentle hiss of the Ethiope River as it wound its way from Umuaja to the great Niger. There are nights I look out and see small lamp lights atop the water, a sign that local fishermen are at work.

But as I stretched out on my bed that day, I did not think of the river as I usually did. Professor Ojo's fleeting but disturbing comment on suicide was on my mind. He had mentioned how a friend of his in Paris found it "rather fascinating that Africans are not as prone to suicide as Europeans," an observation Professor Ojo thought was fundamentally racist for what it implied; that Africans do not share the same spectrum of psychological states as people of European descent. "It was completely condescending," he said, "and basically goes to show that after many centuries of contact with Africa, the West is yet to penetrate the very core of our humanity; they've not, I can say for sure, entered the centre of our existence, not as if they tried in the first instance. We too are susceptible to suicidal thoughts."

Could it then be said that Professor Ojo's own death—two months after our meeting at the bar, after visiting his flat, after seeing him happy and vibrant at the reading he hosted—was an attempt to disprove the Frenchman, to prove that Africans were capable of taking their own lives like Okonkwo in Achebe's *Things Fall Apart*, not as ultimate resistance but a sign of intrinsic connection to humans elsewhere?

"Suicide," he had said, "is the one common denominator, though the lowest, that tethers us to our collective, primitive nature."

I recall feeling numb inside as he said those words, trying to reject and unhear them. They stuck, and replayed themselves when I saw his body where it was found by the Ethiope River on a rather peaceful Sunday. Those who saw him had released a scream at the sight of what was left of his body. The fish and crabs of the Ethiope had done their duty.

I was there when the police arrived, two hours after the first scream and phone call. There was a bulge in the left pocket of his trouser. A slim pamphlet, rolled up like a scroll, was peeping out. The more I looked at the body, which the police were tragically hesitating to touch or carry away, the more I thought of his obsession with the peripheral, though it seemed he never quite forgot his personal loss by seeking out the peripheral and forgotten. He chose to erase memory itself, to die by drowning, to be defaced by river creatures and the elements; his mutilated body constituting an ultimate metaphor for the erasure of memory. I could not but recall Kay Sage's "Small Portrait," the face without a face. I became nauseous and turned to leave.

In the end I chose to see him the way I saw him last, at *Opia*, surrounded the by university literati, where he seemed so happy his suicide would have been unthinkable. It was at *Opia* that I met Osagie.

2

Opia was held at the arts auditorium, a chapel-like structure perched on the west end of our university. Designed to hold two hundred people, the poor turnout gave it a hollow look, conjuring the image of a crater in the middle of nowhere. The pew-like seats looked up apologetically to the dome. If you were in the back row, you would see a lake of learned heads shimmering in their greyness: over there, an old professor of classics; there, an emeritus professor of African history. The air hung tight and mouldy.

A band from the music department performed between readings. Osagie was on the piano. Perhaps it was the way he shut his eyes and looked away from his fingers that attracted me. Or was it how he bounced on his seat, visibly thrilled at his own performance? When he opened his eyes, he connected with the cellist, a petite girl with dreamy eyes. She would pretend to look away only to return with a quick glance at Osagie; I felt an inexplicable pang of jealousy. From a distance he looked my age, young and promising. His fingers rippled, working together like the claws of young crabs, filling the dome with waves and waves of melody.

Tombara Clarke was leading the band and working the trumpet. Trained at the Royal College of Music, he had returned three years ago after teaching at universities on both sides of the Atlantic. The loitering smile that patted his beard, I realized, was that of pride in his contribution to music education in these parts. He was proud of his students and their performance was indeed spectacular.

The first piece was a ripped and reassembled Afro-Cuban version of 'My Grandfather's Clock'. The drums and bass started and slowed down for Clarke to blast a call, which he did with swollen cheeks. The band responded with a friendly attack on the piece. Clarke called again. They responded and exploded into an improvised conflagration, after which they slowed down and Clarke beamed and bowed to the greying crowd.

The day's special guest, Alex Ochuko, a renowned poet and memoirist, was visiting from far away North Carolina, where he occupied an endowed positioned in the humanities. He read a couple of poems from his collection, *Looking Back to Look No More*, published by an independent press in New York to great critical acclaim. In one poem a river calls him at night, inviting him home to swim and fish in her waters; another was about a market in rural Ughelli, his hometown, where he once hawked smoked fish with his mother. There were suspirations from all corners of the auditorium. At one point I wondered if the sighs were dropping from the dome like punctured parachutes, or rising from the dusty, concrete floor.

Then came the short break after his reading. Professor Ojo tapped my shoulder. I turned to see him holding out a bottle of cold water. "Are you having a great time?" he asked. I said I was. He invited me to meet the guest. He led the way, the split in his suit clapping as he walked down the aisle, flinging chummy grins at guests. Then we got to the exit, from where I sighted the day's special guest cooling off in the shade of an almond tree. There were two other guests with him, a short, bald man with the jolly face of men whose nights were split between bookshelves and bottles of Jim Beam, and a tall woman in ankara trousers, holding a brown tote bag.

Ochuko needed no introduction; a whole session was dedicated to reading his profile: this fellowship here, that grant there,... monographs, articles, honorary degrees. Professor Ojo introduced the rest: "Ms. Uchi Emene, who's making us proud in London. One of our diaspora voices." He winked at her conspiratorially. "Kalu Nduka, the recent winner of the Common Prize, a colleague at Ife." The conversation ran from a recent reading in London to the life of a certain Nigerian-British actor who, as I would later learn, was Ms Emene's ex-lover, and who now—having found fame in America—jumps from one Eastern European model to another. It was at that juncture, before things became more awkward than they already were, that I sneaked out and returned to the auditorium.

Osagie was talking to the cellist. I walked up to them and introduced myself and I expressed my admiration for his performance. He shrugged his shoulder, perhaps suggesting he had not done his best at this particular show. He introduced the cellist, Cynthia, a fellow music major. She avoided my eyes.

"You should come to our rehearsals," he said. To *his* rehearsals, that is. "The studio is not far from Adam Hall," he added

"I live in Adam Hall," I announced.

"How come I've not seen you?" he asked.

"I'm a bit of a hermit," I said.

"Well, let's see if we can change that," he said. "There're several events going on in this tiny town. I'll make sure to invite you."

After the event, on the way out, I saw Osagie waiting for me at the door, with two tickets to see a production of

Soyinka's play at the Harlequin Theatre. He had changed into a fitted jacket and had an umbrella, which came in handy since the evening clouds were set to unburden their contents. The cellist was gone. He handed me a ticket with the following inscription on the reverse side:

THE ROAD.
A play by Wole Soyinka
Directed by Leonora Chuka
Gates at 7:30

It began to drizzle. The evening withdrew at once and darkness, as though waiting in the shadows, descended. The drizzle became a downpour, releasing the fresh smell of wet earth. He opened the umbrella and asked if I had plans for the night, or would like to go see the play with him.

I inhaled the fragrance of wet soil, pondering what to say in reply.

"We don't have time," he added, "it starts in twenty minutes."

I nodded.

"Is that a yes?"

I nodded again.

The downpour intensified. We defied it with Osagie's small umbrella and arrived at the Harlequin only a little drenched.

From the entrance we could hear someone reciting 'Alagemo', the prefatory poem to the play. Perhaps it was the boom of the reader's voice, or the dramatic way in which it was read, that made me reread it the next day. I read it more than once afterwards but could not understand what it meant: "Rain-reeds, unbend me, Quench/ The burn of cartwheels at my waist!" I still do not get it.

*

I began to accompany Osagie to his rehearsals. The studio, or the shithole that called itself a studio, was located behind Professor Ojo's flat, on a small northward incline. Looking out the window, you could see his flat, beyond which, across the road, was the entrance to Adam Hall. In a sense, the bungalow was at the base of the incline, in a line of buildings that ran up to the university gate, constituting an upward slant that is not noticeable until you were at the gate and turned around to see Adam Hall where it hung desperately, down there, at the edge of the Ethiope River. This view, from the river looking up, would have been a wonder if not for the pseudo-brutal library that crowned it at the very top, next to the university gate.

Osagie had what he called his "rehearsal ritual," which was another term for a warm-up before the plunge into whatever piece he had scheduled to rehearse. "I start by playing a piece of *razz*," he said the first time I went there with him, "something I enjoy for its sake, not because I am obliged to. Razz, know what that means? Rag blurring into jazz, or jazz blurring into rag. Got it?" If I had any doubts about our blooming friendship, his comment cleared them there and then. Rag. Razz. Jazz. Not quite jazz. It did not matter.

That first day, while he was introducing me to the idea behind his rehearsal rituals, someone walked in with a trumpet, a rather bulky boy, our age, perhaps a year or two older, twenty-four at most. Osagie introduced him as his rehearsal mate, Charles. He shot me a curious look before assuming his position behind the grand piano. The piano itself, pounded senseless and left to rot, occupied half the space, the pedals as weak as overused brakes.

Charles, or Charlie, as Osagie called him, blew into the window, "clearing his pipes", and one could practically picture the roar of his trumpet descending, cascading down the slope towards the Ethiope River. Another guy walked in with a trombone and also went for the window. I had not expected company, at least on that first day; later on it would not bother me. But in that first instance I did not know what to say to these strangers, especially since I was only beginning to lower my guard around Osagie.

"What are we doing today?" Osagie asked Charlie, and fingered the piano.

"How about some Jelly?" asked the trombonist, picking his nose. "Some Jelly Roll Morton."

"Why not," said Charlie, now wiping his otherwise clean trumpet with a blue handkerchief.

The trombonist, after staring blankly into the window, suddenly began to click his fingers. Osagie tapped two keys and nodded. An agreement was reached. What agreement? I was in the dark. But they knew where they were going with the piece. What piece? I did not know, but soon enough Charlie and the trombonist were releasing joint blares that shook the room. The rest was, as they say, jazz. I was assigned a minor role, to clap and sway, to be the audience, for "there is no music without an audience."

When the piece was done, Charlie and the trombonist left, leaving a vast silence in their wake. Osagie fished out several sheets from his grey folder. I knew it was rehearsal time. I had a novel with me, Gertrude Stein's *Ida*, the 1971 Copper Square Publishers edition. I opened to where the page was folded to serve as place marker, on page 30:

> *Ida when she had a dog had often stood by a gate and she would hold the dog by the hand and in this way would stand.*
>
> *But that was long ago and Ida did not think of anything except now. Why indeed was she always alone if there could be anything to remember. Why indeed.*
>
> *And so nothing happened to her yet. Not yet.*

I read on. The studio was getting dim, as the evening swung the rays of sunlight elsewhere. I glanced at the sheets in Osagie's hands, some left to lie on the piano keys, and saw who he was planning to play, to add to his repertoire: Akin Euba.

We left around six-thirty, stepping out to an evening that was neither cold nor warm, simply dry and humid. He suggested dinner, and was quick to announce that it was all on him. We walked down to Sizzle Pot, a shack restaurant near Ethiope Hall, the all-female dormitory to the far right of Adam Hall. Tables were set outside, but Osagie picked a spot inside. Our server, a lanky fellow with exaggerated hips and lips he would not stop licking (as though each sentence dropped was a squeeze of honey), kept making small talk with Osagie. We placed our orders. I went for eba and okra soup with stock fish. It came with a complimentary bottle of beer, courtesy of the server. I still do not know why he offered me free beer.

When we stepped out of the Sizzle Pot, and headed for the lawn across Ethiope Hall, the night had descended, and the street lights, flickering like near-dead glow-worms, revealed smatterings of students sitting and lying in the grass. We picked a spot near the path that ran up to the university staff club, where, as it turned out, a party in honour of the Deputy Vice Chancellor was going on. The music was mild, but loud enough to tumble down the lawn outside.

Osagie stretched out on the lawn, his legs spread out in a V shape. I sat next to him, hugging my knees. The poor street light revealed the figures of girls walking to and from Ethiope Hall. I followed them with my eyes, suddenly curious to know what their dorm looked like. The building itself is an exact copy of Adam Hall, and both are on the banks of the river, forming the campus's eastern border, beyond which the tropical rain forest ran all the way through Agbor, Sapele, the small riverine towns in-between, to Benin-City. And just to be fair, the planners of the university campus had some sense of aesthetics, at least they felt the need to situate dorms at the slope of the hill, from where students could enjoy the pleasure of seeing the river at sunrise and, looking up, towards sunset, the rows of university houses that hugged the hill all the way to the main gate. Be that as it may, ignoring the state of the dorm—decaying ceilings, erratic water and electricity supply, community kitchens and bathrooms with disease infested puddles—to concentrate and enjoy the beauty around, requires enormous mental muscles.

Osagie was saying something, speaking into the sky as though in a coded conversation with the beings up there. And then, to draw me into the conversation, he rolled on his side, facing me. The darkness had covered his face, but I could sense the intensity in his eyes. I turned to face him.

"It's unusually quiet this evening," he said. "Normally, you'd hear those girls hauling laughter into the void, from the windows over there. Sometimes I want to go up and laugh with them, make small jokes… it feels like I belong there." He sighed and fell quiet.

As if to counter his remark on how "unusually quiet" the night was, a cheer rang out from the Deputy Vice-Chancellor's party, followed by a burst of fireworks. The music resumed, louder this time. A street lamp died in the distance, distorting an already set picture of the area. I felt Osagie's fingers tracing a shape on my forehead, progressing down to my neck, my chest, where – lingering – he began to scribble words, pretending to erase each word once it was done, asking me to guess what it was. A group of girls settled a few paces away from us, and soon enough there was laughter and loud chatter.

A week later, he would repeat that line, "it feels like I belong there," while showing me some of his writings, his manifestoes on life, culture, and society. He had them in different headings: 'On Masculinity', 'On Sex and Music', 'On Freedom and Control'. They were, to me, radical thoughts for these parts

"Someday," he said, "I'll publish these thoughts and that will be the end of me. But I'll rather die than watch them lie dormant without a place in the world."

I picked up the notebook. His handwriting was almost perfect, as though he had studied the art of calligraphy for years. 'On Sex and Music', he drew a comparison between lovemaking and the various tempos in music, arguing that we would enjoy the process better if we consciously aligned each stage with two or more tempos, picking from the whole spectrum: larghissimo, lento, adagio, etc. I confess to not understanding where he was going with his thoughts.

"I have alternativeiivenge viewsay through Agbor, c.meant:April, 2017.l work views on everything," Osagie would frequently say, and that was evident at the secret party he organized off campus, at an isolated house near the Turf Club. He was a member of the club and I would later learn that the house, fully furnished, was his maternal uncle's vacation home. At the party, attended by his close friends, freedom was celebrated like nothing I had witnessed in my young life: a girl, a second year physics student, with eyes glittering like red candles, sucking off a shirtless guy at a corner, while the party proceeded as though nothing was happening; Charlie, who was also present, shoving his hands into the trousers of the server with exaggerated hips, who was—to my surprise—also present. Osagie was calm, a small mound of marijuana on the table before him. I woke up the next day, in bed, naked, with Osagie and the second year physics student, my head a whirlwind of blurring recollections I would rather not recount here.

3

To write a memoir is to paint the past. Each drop of memory is a brush stroke, the paint making intended and unintended patterns on canvas; the result a presumed replica of the past.

Those were my assumptions when I started working on this book. I also assumed that memory would always be there to scoop from. It would always be available, abundant, and waiting to be laid on my canvas. And the final piece must, to be worth the effort, form an aesthetically coherent whole, a text that one can explore. I am thinking of texts like Hemmingway's *A Moveable Feast* here, where scenes evoke and historicize streets and faces, making them touchable, making them leap from the page and assume presence. Now you are at Place Contrescape; and there, on the page—no, at a corner—is the Café des Amateurs, and you are a breath away from 'the drunkards of the quarter' who congregate there, whose collective stench is that 'of dirty bodies and the sour smell of drunkenness'. You are moving through the book and can feel your feet moving about the city, beholding it as though through a gallery, each street and café carefully accounted for on canvas.

Edward Burra. His Paris paintings. His Harlem paintings. You look at his works and do not see the images but the places they immortalize, the moods therein, the moments captured as they are, not exact reality but approximations that ring familiar bells, that draw you in… That, I believe, is what good writing should also do. Burra's own life is what good writing should read like: elusive but looming somewhere on the horizon, rejecting conventions yet aware of their existence, gathering and documenting the dark side of society, alive but always dying, in the moment yet retrospective and forward looking.

Confident that I would fetch words to reconstruct my childhood, to historicize the faces and places that have shaped my worldview, I slammed a deadline on myself. The goal was to celebrate a first draft in December. A first draft! How lovely. The idea of holding that draft, a thick collection of loose leafs containing my young life, made me giddy and conjured images of renowned writers hunched over a bunch of papers—Wole Soyinka over the manuscript of *Aké*, Amos Tutuola over a draft of *The Palm-Wine Drinkard*—grinning and drinking to the fruit of their labour.

I imagined Georges Perec, a cigarette in hand, admiring loose leafs containing the first draft of *W, or the Memory of Childhood*. Smiling, he randomly picks a leaf and reads aloud, 'From this point on, there are memories—fleeting, persistent, trivial, burdensome—but there is nothing that binds them together.' He picks up a pen, cancels a line down the page and returns it to the pile.

The first draft! How did Italo Calvino react to the first draft of *Invisible City*? Well, they all do the same thing: push back on their chairs, stare intently at the resting pile, and then randomly snatch and read out a page. 'When a man rides a long time through wild regions', Calvino reads, 'he feels the desire for a city.' He likes what he hears. And down the page he adds a line: 'Desires are already memories.' He drops the page, walks to the window, cracks it open and draws a lung-full of air. He deserves it. Years later, commenting on his writing process, he would let us in on the difficulty of reaching that place of deep satisfaction:

I write by hand, making many, many corrections. I would say I cross out more than I write. I have to hunt for words when I speak, and I have the same difficulty when writing.

How about our beloved Jean Genet? The first draft of *Our Lady of the Flowers*. Written in that prison. On sheets that were not for writing. Uneven and savage. Raw. Like the story they would later bear. And Genet, assuming his position, perhaps lying belly-down, the sheets spread out before him on the dirty floor, reads from a random page: 'I shall speak to you about Divine, mixing masculine and feminine as my mood dictates, and if, in the course of the tale, I shall have to refer to a woman, I shall manage, I shall find an expedient, a good device, so that there may be no confusion.'

That first draft. How grand. How feasible. I could see it. It was as real as the idea itself. I drank myself full with this image, the bulk of loose leaves bulging as I heft them from place to place, reading and re-reading, crossing out lines and scribbling between and over lines of texts, *'cancelling lines and revisions'* like Italo Calvino. Intoxicated by this picture, which I lived as though it was my reality, I assumed the story would write itself. I had, in fact, enthused myself into the future, reaping that sublime thread of satisfaction that comes with a finished work—the first draft. After all it was my story, my memory. Would it not be a piece of cake to whip up the puzzled look on Jide's face the day a crowd gathered at his door, curious to know if he had indeed sexually molested a child? How hard would it be to share Ma Ike's story, how we went from passive enemies to public friends? It was my story and would not be a pain to reconstruct.

I am in my early twenties, I said to myself. In other words, my childhood was still at my feet, close enough to recall every inch of it. When July came, six months after the day I swore to start, there was nothing to show, nothing but a stack of loose leafs waiting for ink. I remember frantically scribbling rubbish in response to a frail voice that seemed to blurt as though in mockery, "It's been six months and you are less than a page into your book."

*

If the past was a block that awaits the sculptor's chisel, did I want it chiselled into recognizable shapes? Recognition itself destroys storytelling, eliminating all elements of surprise and spontaneity. Contemplating recognition as an ultimate goal gave me the shivers, making me see the act of narrating my life as trite and vain, as predictable as swatting flies off a plate of soup. Damn recognition, I said to myself.

What if my childhood was polished out of context, perhaps super-imposed on imagined experiences and on distant realities? What if it was a corrupted version of the original—trips abroad to visit uncles at Cambridge and aunties at the Sorbonne, breakfasts at dawn with eggs and strawberries, houseboys to run the laundry, Alsatian dogs chained by day and left to pounce on strangers at night?

What if Old Jumbo was a young man, perhaps cutting the pose and shape of Uzo Egonu's *Man with Pipe*: an orange hat tilted to the left, a white pipe tilted to the left, his face abstracted against recognition? What if I plucked narratives from elsewhere, from the books I read, revising memory as though it were a deck of cards shuffled and passed from hand to hand? What if I rewrote my neck of history at whim, with the liberties of uncontested authority? What if I cut up the past *a la* Williams Burroughs and created 'A certain juxtaposition of word and image' randomly assembled from unrelated events yet internally coherent?

To strive for recognisability is to impose limits on the imagination, in the same way that emplotment—the assumption that history is singular and linear—entraps and stagnates, reducing life to a set of numbers logged into a formula, unsurprising as an ordinary line graph plotted on paper: begin at 0, progress east and regress west on x; progress north and regress south on y; and then insert an uncertain flight of a decorous straight line from top left down.

*

I made some progress in August: two sentences separated by a semicolon. A month later I crossed out both sentences and fell into despair.

An untold story is cancerous. It consumes from within and will somehow find a vent, whether one likes it or not: in sudden outbursts of anger, in resentments, in nightmares that bite to the bone, leaving the dreamer bitter at the break of dawn

While I despaired, my untold story continued to animate itself, snarling and snapping. Characters from my childhood would convene, converse, disperse and reassemble. I heard voices and saw images. I saw Dora running into the lake where I last saw her. I saw Pa Suku fanning himself with a folded newspaper, impatient with himself and the blocks. "Here, bodies rot like dead trees," I heard him saying, his voice a faint chime obscured by the scream of wandering children.

*

Duplicates are never the same as originals. Memory is ice, vulnerable to changes in temperature. It is the inevitable oscillation between states—water to ice, ice to water—that displaces and compromises.

Recollections are the fleeting spread a breath leaves on a clear mirror—air disguised as foggy essence, ethereal and transient, masking the observer's reflection only to disappear as temperature rises. The observer—the reader—who takes that fleeting spread for real is deceived and disappointed by its slow but sure disappearance.

Old Jumbo's flowers were not as unkempt as I now remember them. In fact, he was reasonably young back then, and was always in the company of a light-skinned woman and a little boy with curly hair. "Is she oyinbo, that woman?" I once asked Ricia. "No," she answered in a snap, "she's black. Her nose is flat." State School One was east of the blocks. But in my head, in my recollection, it is positioned west. What else do I misremember? Yes, the coffin maker. He never said he took naps in coffins. Or did he? It does not matter any more. I remember what I remember, or what I have consistently made myself remember.

We are, indeed, wired to remember in twos: duplicates superimposed on originals. The original loses its composition the farther away we are from it.

Recollections themselves are inevitable, at times

untriggered. In many instances, however, they are spurred by sights and smells: the fragrance of a harsh perfume, the kiss of a lover, the clamour of waiting passengers at a station, a child that resembles an old classmate, the sneeze of an infant at a public park, the sight of egrets defacing a peaceful evening cloud. We are, in a way, objects of memory and helpless victims of the things we remember, how we remember and eventually how we are remembered when we are no more.

*

Misrememberances. I have always wondered whether we know why and how it happens. "It's a sub-conscious process," declared Uzo, my roommate and nerdy psychology major. Uzo is warmer than the rest, and he frequently seizes every chance to inject psych jargon into conversations.

"Why do we misremember the past?" I wondered aloud, knowing Uzo would jump on this golden opportunity to school me on the complex workings of the subconscious.

"It might interest you to know," he started, throwing on a v-neck t-shirt and bouncing into his bunk. The slim mattress, warily lying atop the narrow metal frame, was almost concealed by his bulky person, a bulge visible underneath, close to the floor. "It might interest you to know that we misremember for some important reason." He sprang up enthusiastically, ready to launch his lecture.

I shifted in my bunk, turning away from the window to face him, "How do you mean?" I bet he heard the excitement in my voice, not because I was expecting an expert answer—I mean, they read out-dated books and theories in that department—but because I wanted to hear someone else's take, whether crude or refined, on the issue that bothered me.

"Ever heard of BTT?" he asked.

"BTT?"

"Betrayal Trauma Theory?"

"Not at all."

"Well, I've only recently read about it." He turned to face me. His bunk creaked. "Let's start from there. BTT. Betrayal Trauma Theory. Coined and propounded by Jennifer Freyd. She's American. I like Americans, by the way. They know how to discuss difficult subjects with a kind of informality that baffles the rest of us. I digress. So, BTT. It basically says we figure out a way to forget traumatic experiences, like sexual molestation, perpetrated by those we trust, our caregivers for instance. We forget, or somehow choose to remember those incidents differently, because we want to maintain the relationship we have with them, even when we know our trust has been betrayed."

Silence.

He was grinning from ear to ear, as if he had just swallowed a cupful of vanilla ice cream. Betrayal. Trauma. Sexual assault. Memory. Uzo's little lecture sounded alright, and I was left to appropriate it to my experience, to plug my past into the formula he had spread out before me, and to see how my misrememberances were tied to a traumatic past.

"Were you sexually assaulted?" he asked.

"What?"

"Never mind, just trying out my thoughts. Any major traumas?"

Silence.

Time to change the subject before the Uzo, already in

his element, drew me into his shrink's corner.

Trauma. The death of Dora, and the drama surrounding that death, was painful and could pass as traumatic. But I do not see the betrayal, if there was any in her death. Be that as it may, if the blocks were personified and robed as a person, it could pass as the one individual that betrayed me back to back. That fucker of a space. The gloom that it was, the collective realities of impoverishment, that staggering distance from whatever counts as progress, be it material or otherwise—

"Sometimes," Uzo droned on in his high-pitched voice, before I had a chance to swerve the subject away from traumas and sexual molestations. "Sometimes you really don't know you've been betrayed until you are years removed from the traumatic experience. I call it the privilege of distance."

The privilege of distance. There are a few events that I look back upon and can sincerely see that they left scars on my memory.

Let us begin with the day Papa returned after a week away from home, with a gaping cut on his forehead, his whole body reeking of stale piss, like he had spent the previous night napping at a public toilet. He came back at night. And all we could hear were sobs from their side of the divide. Mama had turned into a wall while he was gone, and would not say where he went, even when Ricia asked through tears.

I still do not know what happened to Papa, nor do I know why Mama was sobbing that night. I had a few guesses: that he had been in a fight and was carted off to the police station, locked up for a week; that he was accused of stealing stuff from his place of work (what work? I do not know) and was carted off to jail; that he was ambushed and kidnapped by rogues on his way home, and was whisked to an unknown destination, left to find his own way back. Ricia had her own speculations. But then, all that mattered to me then, what broke my heart in that moment, was the silence from Mama, followed by her sobs through the night.

Speaking of sobs, I also recall the day I saw Ibe moving his waist on top a girl from block q. I had sighted them from a considerable distance, on the path to the lake, and had paused to study what they were up to. It was her 'sob,' which was not particularly a sob, since there were no accompanying tears, that made me walk closer, concealing my presence behind a cluster of elephant grass. There they were, in a small clearing, 'sobbing.' Ibe's breath was heavy, as if he was being crushed by an invisible weight. At first I thought he was beating her up, hammering her to the ground, so I thought of running up to push him away from her. But he could not possible be hammering her to the ground with his waist moving up and down, with her legs stretched and hanging free for him. And why was he hammering without his shorts? Why was she grabbing his bare buttocks? Why was he grunting like she was doing the hammering?

Her sob doubled, sustained itself for a fierce second or two, and was gone. Just like that. And Ibe, as if punched in the lower belly, groaned deeply, and collapsed like airless balloon. Just like that. They both sprang up immediately. I could see Ibe's lizard standing stiff like a spatula. It seemed to speak to me in a language that rang in my guts, sending mixed signals throughout my body. How did he, not much older than I was, manage to grow s spatula almost two times my index finger, and nearly trice in diameter? I tried to sneak back to the path, but it was too late. She saw me and gasped. Ibe turned and there I was, not sure if I should run off or linger to study them for another second.

"Hey, Ibe," I said awkwardly, forcing a confused smile.

A startled flock of weaver birds scattered behind them, taking with them the comforting chirps that surprisingly kept me sane while Ibe hammered the girl from block q. Then, regaining his mental balance, Ibe shot me a stern stare, and rushed forward to grab me by the shoulder. I had not seen him this way before, angry and violent. He shook me several times without a word, and when he spoke his voice was shaky.

"You did not see anything. You hear me? You did not see anything." He pushed me away from him. "Now run."

I was too confused to run. I stood there. He went back to her. His lizard had shrunk into the size of a worm. She had put on her skirt. He picked up and put on his shorts. Holding her hands he slowly walked past me.

I had almost forgotten this bizarre incident until Uzo stuffed my head with BTT; and even at that, my recollection started with the event after that encounter, from where I slowly peeled back to the "hammering" scene I had partially erased from memory. What I recalled was the string of sharp pain that engulfed my legs when Ibe left and I was too shocked to leave. It turned out that I had been standing on a track of fire ants. They had climbed up my trousers, and were biting away without care, making their way towards my essential organ. This is Ibe's fault, I thought, stamping my feet and pulling down my trousers.

I ran home naked like a lunatic, and endured the pain until it subsided several hours later. I cannot tell if there were curious eyes that followed my naked frame around, as I dashed for block o, my trousers waving in my hands like the tattered flag of a defeated army.

I think it is strange that I remember the fire ants and not the scene with Ibe. If I were to re-write Uzo's argument, I would add that betrayal might not be the only reason why we selectively remember or subconsciously forget.

4

After announcing that I had six months to finish the first draft, I went in search of the perfect writer's desk. A writer without a desk, I mused, or a pile of books against which he or she leans to contemplate the work-in-progress, is like a car without wheels. It is not the desk nor the pile of books that does the writing, but the "zone" that is created by both objects; the feeling that one is indeed prepared to do the job. So I told myself. Near the university gate, an elderly man had set up a stand, a weak table and a straight stool on which he perched watching and waiting for customers. There were uneven dents on his cheek, which conferred him the pious look of a famished pilgrim. On his table lay a tray of kola nuts. He smiled as I approached his stand, his eyes dim but alert. When he saw that I was not interested in the nuts, he glowered. "What you want?" he asked, irritated by my strange presence and stare.

"The table," I answered.

He made no reply. His neighbour, a woman of about forty-six, in a black blouse and a green wrapper, chuckled and shook her head. She moved her tray of boiled groundnuts and swatted a team of flies tap-dancing on them. She was an itinerant hawker and had stopped to rest for an hour or so. Her feet bore marks of her status as itinerant trader: dust and hard veins. As she tittered, I noticed the black stud earrings matching her black blouse. Her hair tie, worked into a dovetail, was also black. Who was she mourning? Death was visible in the dark bags beneath her eyes. But those eyes darted, robust and alive, leading the body through whatever must be borne for the dead to pass in peace. She reminded me of Ma Ike when she first moved to the blocks. She had worn black clothes for a whole year. At first I was not sure why Ma Ike wore black all the time, but I always stole glances at the impervious dark wrapper she wore.

"Why is she always in black?" I once asked Mama.

She sighed and said "the woman had just lost her husband to armed robbers."

Ma Ike had just moved in but the story of her husband's death could be freely plucked from rooftops ten blocks away, and if you were keen enough to pursue details, you would find someone who knew her late husband's name, his job, his whereabouts when he met his untimely death, where he met his wife… It was not long before more stories emerged that she was born to a polygamous family in Igbo Etche and had eloped with a casual oil worker who was temporarily stationed there. Then she eloped again, this time with the janitor at a commercial bank near Ogbunabali in the heart of Port Harcourt. It was this last husband, as the story goes, who was shot by bandits.

"It will pass," Mama added, "she will return to normal clothes."

It did pass. And out came the ankara blouses with zippers that ran to the waist.

The rachitic table stood there, almost swinging like a gangling dancer. The owner's eyes scanned me. His white kaftan and lush white beard contradicted his neighbour's black outfit. After several minutes of silence he managed to speak through his glare.

"You want the table?"

"Yes." "Why you want the table?" he asked, cocking his

153

head to the right, towards the woman in black. I suppose he was more dumbstruck than insulted. How could I be interested in an item that was that worthless?

"I like the table," I answered.

He flinched. "You no want kola nut? I get many kola nut here," he said, wagging a finger at the kola nuts I stayed calm but secretly feared he was going to dismiss me.

"How much for the table?" I asked

"I no sell the table," he replied curtly and looked away.

The street was getting busier in the falling evening. The woman in black chuckled again and turned in my direction. Our eyes met. She suddenly looked younger than I had thought. In the lucent black of her eyes was a faraway charm shredded by the sun. Her hair, poking out from the sides of the hair tie, was half braided and half loose, neither black nor grey.

"I no sell the table," the trader was saying, "if you want kola nut I got plenty." More serious wags were directed at the poor bundle of lobes.

"What if I gave you something for the table?" I suggested.

"Something like what?" he asked, not as curtly as before.

I pulled out a Casio calculator from my back pocket and wagged it at him:

"I give you this calculator, you give me the table."

He took the calculator and looked at it suspiciously. He flipped it. I waited. He punched away without saying a word. He leaned towards the groundnut seller, whispered something and rose with a smile. She also had a smile on her face. I sensed something between them. He was Muslim, and to me she looked Christian.

"Now we do business, yes?" He was all face and cheer.

"Yes," I answered, surprised at this swift turnaround.

"Wait here," he instructed and crossed to the other side of the street in long strides. He was a tall man. I followed him with my eyes and saw that he was talking animatedly with a fellow who, but for a few strands of black beard, could be his twin. The fellow nodded several times and returned to fiddling his beads.

"Sit," said the groundnut woman. I declined politely.

While I waited the sun began to fade. There were students everywhere, trudging under the weight of academic labour. On both sides of the street were shops that stocked student necessities, from condoms to ready-to-go noodles. At the far end of the street, where it narrowed into a track cuddled on both sides by private hostels, I saw a crowd gathering, and I assumed there was a fight or a quarrel of sorts. There was always a fight or a quarrel of sorts.

"Okay, five minutes you take the table," the kola nut man was saying. He was back and was holding a folded mat, which he had obviously borrowed from one of his brethren. He rolled it out, pushed his stool aside, and moved his tray onto the mat. Then he sat on one end, his legs folded. The woman in black joined him.

"The table, take it," he said, as if invigorated by her proximity. Then he looked away, rubbed his palms together, and returned to sprinkling his kola nuts with water from an aluminium kettle.

*

"You are on the verge of schizophrenia," Osagie said in September, pointing out how I repeated the same scenes to myself until I "no longer made sense." He had used the word schizophrenia as a joke but I was certainly not amused. I was not offended either. "Writing eliminates the repetitious vocalization of internalized narratives," he said. "You write to move on, to heal from the inside."

That morning, like most Saturday mornings, we were in his room, positioned on either side of the window where I had planted my desk. His room is the same size as mine but shared by four students. He calls their side of Adam Hall Belgravia, after "a certain part of London." He and his roommates pay a higher rent and had arranged a weekly cleaning service. The walls are smooth and newly painted. The ceiling fans work. I had asked if I could move my desk into his room, since he had more space He agreed but was particular about where he wanted it, between his bunk bed and the window. I like windows that open to nature. Osagie's window—to my distress—opens to a disorienting cluster of unfinished bungalows cramped into a few acres of land.

That Saturday morning, I was on the left side of the window, at my desk, with blank sheets blinking and waiting for ink. He was on the right side of the window, four feet to my right, pinching a zit on his cheek. He adjusted the small mirror-on-a-ledge for a better view, pursed and whipped his lips to the right for a better pinch. The screened window lay flat between us, facing the mattress. The window itself emptied into the fragile morning and the clunky display of roofless bungalows two storeys below, outside the walls of Adam Hall.

"Writing is progressive," he had said.

I had nodded absent-mindedly, and after several minutes of silence, made an off-hand announcement, "I figured out a way to write without writing." He robbed his right cheek with the tip of his manicured fingers, and left the mirror for the foot of the mattress. I joined him. Our shoulders touched. He leaned into me, his skin as warm as the hours before sunset. I put my left arm around his neck, a gesture that was only possible when his roommates were not around. He asked how I intended to write without writing. I contemplated the window.

"I'm going to hire someone," I began.

"And who's this person?" he asked.

I launched another line of conversation.

"Do you think there is a connection between the protagonist of Paul West's *Rat Man of Paris* and Lucien Freud's *Naked Man with Rat*? I know this is random but hear me out. Freud's family flees Germany to escape the Holocaust after one of his cousins is killed in Berlin. Forty-four years later he begins work on *Naked Man with Rat*. I don't know where this is going. Bear with me. Freud pairs Man with Rat, the rodent placed next to Man's genitalia. Have you seen the painting I'm talking about? I looked it up at the Internet café. The man looks dead, death itself dispelled by his physicality—sensual, almost erotic— with his legs spread into a love-shaped V. How does this remind me of Paul West's book? Well, *Rat Man* came eight years after Freud's painting was finished. The man himself, Etienne Poulsifer, is from an Alsatian village in France. The word Alsatian reminds one of Alsatian dogs or German Shepherds as some are called. Like Freud, Rat Man is scarred by Nazis-era atrocities. Years later, *Rat Man* would entertain—or scare—the world with rats and Freud would strip man naked and pair him with Rat. I must also remind you that Freud's grandfather had conducted an experiment in which a patient was nicknamed Rat Man—"

"I do see the connection you are trying to make," Osagie interrupted, "but I don't see how it applies to the matter at hand."

"Neither do I," I said, "but I think there is something to be said about the way rats handle memory and the way we do."

An uncertain silence fell. I stood up. Went to the window. The day was young. I returned to the mattress and left my palm on his lap.

"Let's cut to the chase. What do you have in mind?" he asked.

"To make you a proposal."

"Go on."

"Is there any chance that you would write while I talked?"

"And?"

"We become co-authors."

"I prefer not to," he said, laughing.

I did not get the joke. I despaired. He saved me.

"Bartleby? Remember that Melville story?"

"Ah," I cried, relieved, yet unsure of where this was going. "It's interesting that you should bring Melville into this conversation," I drew from his remark, "Melville, in a strange sense, is a metaphor for memory: once forgotten, as we are wont to forget the past, later rediscovered and immortalized."

"Right. So, what's this new arrangement? You talk, I write?"

"Yes. I need to regain my sanity; these recollections are tormenting me."

"True that."

He stood up and went to the window where a spider,

trapped in the screen, was struggling to break free.

"You sound sure of my services," he said in a calm voice, watching the spider.

"I can't think of anyone else," I said.

"I have other commitments, as you well know."

He returned to the edge of the mattress. I did not know what to feel and could not press my plea. I felt the mattress caving under my modest weight. The spider had stopped moving. I declared it dead. I was wrong. It was beginning to writhe. I refused to believe it was alive. It may have simply resurrected from the dead. All things are possible. Osagie held my knees and kneaded them. Then, as if in an attempt to salvage a lump of dough, he kneaded harder and said in a near-whisper: "I prefer not to, but..." he paused dramatically, "... I will."

I leapt off the mattress, freed myself from his kneading hands and broke into dance, my face burning with an uncontrollable grin. I danced in measured plods to the window, where the spider was no longer stationed against its will, but was webbing its way down. After the celebratory dance, I returned to my desk. The blank sheets, waiting for ink, stared. I ignored them and moved closer to the window. For the first time in a long time, I noticed that there were clusters of unwanted grass between the ugly bungalows outside.

I have been spending time in Osagie's room, three to four nights a week in his bed, the warmth and softness of which words cannot describe. After the first night in his room, I woke up the next morning with a stubborn erection that refused to budge.

Erections at dawn are normal, but are known to back down when one hit the toilet, or when one's imagination strays into absurd territories, or when one consciously contemplates a piece of serious literature.

That morning, Beckett's "Text," a short story he wrote in 1932, came to mind. I pictured the taut and opaque story, the way it sits centralized on the page, angrily daring the reader to decipher what the author's intentions or non-intentions are. I recited the first line, "Come come and cull me bonny bony doublebed cony swiftly…"

The erection did not back down. Osagie's cigarette pack was on the mattress. I picked it up and read everything on the label, reading it like poetry: "Luxury Length St. Moritz/ By Appointment to/ His Royal Highness The Prince/ of the Netherlands…"

Nothing happened. I pretended the label was a complex assertion, the type Coetzee parcelled out in *Elizabeth Costello*: "I take seriously the claim that the artist risks a great deal by venturing into forbidden places: risks, specifically, himself; risks, perhaps, all…"

Nothing happened. I turned to John Ashbery, whose *April Galleons* I had rescued from the wild streets a week before, and pretended the third stanza of "Ostensibly" was printed on the cigarette pack: "A rigidity that may well be permanent/ Seems to have taken over. The pendulum/ Is stilled…"

Nothing happened. I was not alarmed but amused by this event. It reminded me of a certain story from the blocks, one of the countless far-fetched accounts that stuck to my memory. It was about a man who was said to have died while making love to his wife. The frightened wife, having fled to call neighbours, returned to see the dead man's penis still as erect as the horn of a black rhinoceros.

I left the cigarette pack and began to wonder what could have triggered my erection. Nothing came to mind. Then I began to recollect a dream I had that night.

The more I pieced the scenes of that dream, the more I remotely saw possible connections, albeit vague and, to be honest, contrived. It was a strange dream, no doubt, and it left me with the burden of a participant as against the detached, passive recollections of an observer.

In that dream, I was at a poorly lit bar on Souzey Street. If such a bar existed, it would be so clandestine that only a few would know anything about it. But there it was in my dream, barely illuminated by a light bulb attached to a thin holder that dangled above a low, round mahogany table. The only guests or patrons or whatever they were called sat in a semi-circle around the table, adjacent to the counter where bottles of cognac and whiskey gave off their glitter. The smell of marijuana was as present as the fragrance of perfumes; an absurd mix I enjoyed.

At the centre of the semi-circle was a clean-shaved man in a fitted black suit, a plain white shirt, and a slim tie. He looked thirty-five or thereabouts. His tie was loose and the shirt was equally loose to the third button. He was holding court. Legs crossed, wine glass on one hand, cigarette on the other, he spoke and swayed, cutting for himself a pose from the jazz age. His eyes flickered with excitement like the thin thread holding the bulb. In-between words, he would pause to grin, a grin that floated between the table and the bulb, like the cigarette smoke he puffed, which hung lazily like artificial clouds at a disco.

To his left was a broad-shouldered fellow of about forty, with a receding hairline, a hollow cheek, in a tight, black t-shirt that blended with the room, and faded-black jeans that distantly complemented the grey sofa on which they all sat. His right shoulder was mildly brushing against that of the man in black suit, who was still talking and pantomiming with his glass and cigarette. "There are times you have to knock things over just to be yourself," he was saying, crossing his legs, pouring more wine. "We huddle here like bats, like midnight gutter rats, just for a chance to talk about what we are." The semi-circle was quiet. He gestured with the cigarette hand, grinned and raised his glass. The broad-shouldered man hesitated but clinked anyway before announcing he was "getting married in two months."

There was silence. A mellow music drifted through invisible speakers. The broad-shouldered man emptied his glass in one gulp, pursed his lips and sighed deeply. He looked up, briefly studied the light bulb and spoke into that silence.

"My whole family has been on my neck for ten years. My younger brothers are married and settled. They think I'm irresponsible."

"Nonsense," the guy in suit cried. "Nonsense."

"You know how it works around here," said the broad-shouldered guy.

"I leave for Germany in a week," said a third member of the group.

"Whereabouts in Germany?" asked the guy in suit, who was now fiddling the cigarette pack on the table.

"Hamburg," answered the third member, "my favourite city in Europe, after Paris."

Then he cocked his head, and with a little upward tilt puffed his weed and smiled the breezy smile of one who has seen many airports and sniffed the salted air of beachfront hotels.

"Ah Paris," exclaimed the be-suited fellow. "You know what John Berger said of Paris?" he asked. "Paris, Berger says, '… is a man in his twenties in love with an older woman.'" They laughed. "I have never been to Paris," he added, "neither have I lived in Hamburg. But I spent three years in Munich."

"What were you doing in Munich?" the third man asked.

"I taught briefly at Ludwig Maximilian and worked as an independent curator." Here, like his friend, the be-suited man exuded the airs of a relentless globetrotter. "So, when will you be back from Germany?"

"I don't know. I don't have any return plans yet."

Another silence fell. The be-suited guy punctured the silence.

"Is this our last night together?"

"You think so?" asked the Hamburg-bound man.

"Well, I've been offered a job in Austria," said the suited man. "I haven't accepted the offer. But with everyone leaving or getting married, I may as well…"

The bulb held still, briefly. From the invisible speakers

a familiar song wafted. The wavy voice was unmistakable. Ella Fitzgerald singing 'They Can't Take That Away From Me' with Louis Armstrong trumpeting and husking himself in and out of the chorus. I hummed along from my perch on a stool by the counter.

Drawn into the baritone embrace of Louis's voice, I looked around for the hidden speakers, as if Satchmo would emerge from where they lay hidden, eyes alert in excitement, trumpeting the night. I gave up my futile search and focused on the faces around me. They were enduring another silence, more of a consensual non-speak by all, including me. The man in the suit leaned back on the sofa and crossed his legs, his Markowski pointing at me. The broad-shouldered man buried his face in his palm. The third man stood up and, to my surprise, walked towards me. I had thought myself invisible. I felt invisible. He came to me and in a crisp metallic voice asked what my story was. Then he sat on the stool next to me. I could smell a musky fragrance rising from his pores.

"What story?" I asked.

"You heard us…" He paused, turned, and looked into my eyes. He squinted and stared hard, saying quietly, "You heard our stories."

"What stories?" I turned to see his friends looking at us. It was then clear that I was at an exclusive spot, a space where stories were shared for mutual comfort.

He retreated to the sofa. And like all dreams, the bar fizzled into nothingness, "received up… into heaven" like the vessel of clean and unclean creatures in St. Peter's dream. By the time I was done replaying the whole conversation in that dream, my erection was gone. I was relieved.

6

One morning, after making tea for himself, Osagie randomly mourned how much he missed a particular type of cheese. This special cheese was shipped every weekend to his family in Benin City from Lagos, a standing order by his mother, the daughter of a serial entrepreneur and investor who—up to this minute—sits on the board of five major companies, including the local franchise of an international beer brand.

Several days later, going through his photographs, I saw his family around a breakfast table, with cups and cutlery and jars of I-do-not-know-what in a circle at the centre, huddled shoulder-to-shoulder as they waited to render their services to his family. Osagie must have been ten or twelve, and was rather busy away from the table, near the electric stove with four visible burners. He was almost cut out of the picture, as was the towering fridge beside the stove, on which postcards—like garlands—perched from top to middle. There was a sister with short braids leaning back on her chair, her slice of bread half-finished and resting on a plate. She looked older than Osagie, so I knew she was the "big sister" he was so fond of, the one "pursuing a degree in biology at a small liberal arts college in Connecticut."

The matron of the family was absent in this photo. Osagie did not remember why but thought she may have been on the phone with her sister in Milan, "Auntie Osas," a fashion designer with her own label." This sister was now back in Nigeria, settled in Lagos with a high-end boutique in Lekki. But as at the time the photo was taken, his mother rang her almost every weekend, mostly at breakfast time, which I thought was odd—but what do I know about breakfasts and international phone calls?

There is a toddler on his father's lap. Both father and toddler have their hands in the air, as though waving at the camera. The toddler is shirtless, and so is the father whose bulging stomach seems to push the baby away. The toddler's cheeks are chunky, with dimples. There is a flower vase at the centre of the table, with yellow, red and green petals erect, looking well fed. I cannot tell if this flower is artificial or real. The vase itself sits on a flat white disc.

There are three empty chairs detached from the table: one for Osagie, one for his mother, and the third for the photographer. Osagie does not remember who took the photo. A visiting cousin? A neighbour invited up to join the family? He does not remember.

I spent a great deal of time deconstructing that photograph, what it represented, what it was that I was not, the line it drew that clearly marked our difference. This tickled and disgusted me at once. I tried not to feel the latter but it came in gusts, disfiguring every single face in the photograph, turning them from what they were to what I thought they were: fat and not starved enough to be beautiful.

There is beauty in hunger, I said to myself. How absurd, that statement. Beauty and hunger should never be placed side-by-side. Or should they? I do know that poverty holds the capacity to rid one of the inner eyes that see beauty, since it plunges one into a perpetual state of survival, at which one becomes too busy—scraping by—to see what is left of clouds after rainfall, to listen to the giggle of children running in the rain.

That hunger shields the eyes from beauty does not, though I may argue otherwise, erase the beauty inherent in hunger itself, perhaps the reason why religious people fast, denying the body of food in other to *enter* that type of beauty only present *in* hunger. Maybe, maybe not. I really was thrown off balance by the picture I was gathering of Osagie's background. There was another photo of his family standing behind a maroon Peugeot 504, next to a sign that screamed at me for no reason: Benin Airport. "We were on our way to Lagos," Osagie said, "and off to our first tour of major European cities: Milan, Paris, Munich,…"

These discoveries about his family put a hole in my chest. I did not expect the reaction that flowed from me. I saw myself wedged between admiration and envy. I suppose both go hand in hand. Perhaps not. But in my case they did and it began to show in small withdrawals, in small accusations unvoiced, as though he was responsible for my grim childhood. It happened involuntarily, this repulsion. I would wince when he talked about his family. And then the guilt came. Why was I doing this? His innocence, the freedom with which he revealed himself to me, made it even worse. The guilt, that is.

Seeing those photos and listening to his highlights of a rosy childhood made me recall a certain day in '91, when Mama was a 'guest' at her boss' birthday party. Ricia and I were hauled along to this party, decked in our best. Mama was not as thrilled as we were. I reckon she knew what awaited her. We were ignorant, so we jumped around like intoxicated fauns.

As it turned out, though we did not care as kids, Mama had been 'invited' to work in the kitchen—a space as wide as three rooms at the blocks. Ricia and I were confined to a corner in the kitchen, on the floor, following Mama and the other kitchen hands with our eyes, as they walked back and forth like soldier ants in the service of a mean queen. The boss' wife would occasionally walk in, pass a few instructions: how much of this or that spice must be added; the need to wipe down the counter as cooking progressed, since guests would be given a tour of the kitchen as they arrived.

Ricia and I, in the company of other miserable kids, watched. There was this kid, Obinna, who kept creeping away from the kitchen into the wider space, into the sitting area where guests in clusters chatted and drank from transparent glasses. He would be dragged back only to return there soon after. Frustrated, the young rebel nursed and hatched a plan. Holding his crotch, he announced that he needed to pee, more of an anguished cry, so loud that there was a momentary hush everywhere. His mother ignored him. Ricia and I watched. He called again and was ignored. Having failed to gain attention, he improved on his plan. Standing at the edge of the kitchen island, he unzipped his fly and began to urinate, drawing a liquid line from the kitchen to the open area with guests and all.

After the rebel was led home by his mother, Ricia and I got stern looks from Mama, warning us to suppress whatever shenanigans we were conceiving or find our way home. We were rather too confused to think or gather the thoughts that sprang up in our heads. From where we were, we could hear guests laughing and could hear their children giggling, chirruping, crying, nagging; being children. I never forgot that incident. Neither did I forget the Christmas we all silently stared at our plates of rice, traumatized by the absence of chicken thighs from the tomato stew.

Rice and chicken stew on Christmas was a yearly ritual for everyone at the blocks. I do not know how it came to be, this bizarre ritual, but it certainly was what happened on Christmas. For as long as I could remember, everyone I knew ate rice on Christmas day. Families would swap bowls of rice to show goodwill, celebrate the birth of Christ, and also celebrate year's end. The poorest amongst us would be fed. Churches would fling their doors open for all. Kids would go from room to room, garbed in their Christmas-only outfits, consuming rice and chicken stew and candy, returning home with bulging stomachs and greasy lips, their pockets heavy with coins received from hosts around the blocks. Those days are long gone. Nowadays, parents guard their kids like hyenas on crack.

On the eve of Christmas, or what we called 'wash night', the air would be dense and saturated with varied fragrances of steaming tomato stew. And if you have a keen nose for spices, you would surely sniff the wild mix of local herbs, the harsh smell of smoke rising from make-shift fireplaces with boiling pots of rice and, of course, the nauseating smell of chicken flesh shrinking in hot water, having had its innocent blood spilled to celebrate the birth of Christ, its wings plucked until the bird is reduced to a shadow of what it used to be.

There was also the drama that came with slaughtering these chickens. You begin by identifying the free-range cock that will die. You ambush it at a corner. It sees you and scampers for dear life, and makes it way to the bushes. You recruit your friends to join the chase. There it is, crouched next to a shrub! You tiptoe from an angle. Your friends take adjacent angles. You lunge and miss. It leaps away, cackling devilishly. You rise and dive again. This time you have it by the tail. But that is all you have: a fistful of feathers. Now it is in pain and is gradually losing speed. It makes a wrong move by re-entering the blocks. Soon it is encircled, and eventually pounced upon by a lucky lad. The cheer is raucous. Everyone is happy. The wailing cock in their hands is nothing but a roasted thigh atop a bowl of rice, a robust breast grilled with hot spices, a set of wings fried and served to visiting uncles.

Mama did not raise her own chickens. Not that she hated them or thought they were worthless. She simply was not a chicken person, the way some are not dog or cat people. But a day or two before Christmas, she would go and source her cock from a pop-up chicken stand around the blocks. These temporary shops, set up for the season, had giant crates for cocks of all breeds and sizes. Buyers would ogle them from all corners, pointing and shamelessly haggling prices until deals were sealed, and life would go on as usual.

Seeing Mama approaching with her cock would always trigger celebration. My brothers would go mad as they hurried to snatch the doomed creature and show it to its quarters—a small cage near the goat pen. We, however, did not enjoy the privilege of chasing our own rooster. This was a tragedy, since it denied us the stories that followed the chase, and the very thrill of seeing our victim, realizing its death was nigh and inevitable, slow down and yield to us.

There came a year that our tragedy was doubled. No purchased cock, in addition to the usual absence of the chase. A month before that Christmas, Mama had received word that a relative was terminally ill. It was cancer. Well, it was only later that we knew that it was cancer. But when the news came, it was believed that he had been 'sent' this incurable illness—in other words bewitched—by an envious co-worker at the garage where he was head of stickers. Head of stickers, a glorified garage thug. Mama was devastated. She wept. She prayed. What could be done? She asked. "Well," the messenger cleared her throat and began, "we have tried native doctors. No solution. But there's hope. We know a great healer in Benin City. It will cost us money. They say this healer does wonders. And can dispel evil at one glance." Money. That was the gist of her visit. She was going round and asking for contributions from near and distant relatives. Mama was a distant relative, so far removed from the dying relative that a clear line of connection was nearly absent.

Mama was so moved, or rather burdened by this sad news that she gave more than she should, emptying three months' worth of savings into this "project." It was an investment that was doomed from the start. Not because the relative was nearing death, but because the messenger had her own agenda. As it turned out, the money did not reach the ill relative. We never saw that messenger again. We nonetheless remember the absence of chicken from our Christmas rice.

It was from these memories that I drew to interrogate Osagie's photos. A part of me saw him as one of those privileged children at the party Mama was invited to. I allowed myself to see the difference posed by our backgrounds. It was a subconscious process. It started small—from wincing when he told a childhood story to countering those happy stories with my repertoire of mood-sinking memories—and matured into coldness towards him. I shrank away from him. Was it really our social and economic differences that tore us apart? I am rather inclined to believe there was something more that pushed me away from him, that put a hole in the intimacy we shared. Whatever it was, Osagie was not at fault. I take full responsibility. He had been himself, flamboyant, spoilt, honest. And he had lived the way he wanted. I, on the other hand, was trapped between the past and the present, a liminal being unsure of his place in the present, unable to move on, to see memory for what it was—a part of life.

Memory or no memory, the real deal, as I now believe, was a struggle with the brewing intimacy between us. Recoiling from him was a stone to scare two birds: avoiding the painful past he made evident; and escaping the person I was gradually revealing to myself, that I liked but had not quite accepted. Would I have acted differently, let go and yielded completely to what was happening to me, to us? I am not sure. I was not prepared.

PART THREE

An A4 print of Van Gogh's "Sorrow" sat on my desk, next to the poem it had inspired, a piece I had abandoned for months. Margaret did not like Van Gogh. At first I thought I knew why, but would later realize that her stand was personal and more complicated than I had assumed. As I revised the poem, looking at Clasina Maria Hoornik's stooped frame on the A4 paper, I began to recollect how, six months earlier, the operator at the Internet Café on No.3 Pele had winced when he saw what I sent to the printer. It was an automatic shudder, a repulsion, after which he called me up for "a little talk."

"My good friend," he started, "this material is quite interesting."

His voice was the mild buzz of bees basking in communal honey, happy but poised to sting. I observed him, this fellow with the physical structure of a teenager. Many thoughts crossed my mind. I sorted an appropriate reply since I was not sure where he was headed: a sting or an ordinary flutter.

"Indeed," I said, "It's an interesting piece." I stood back, staring at Clasina Maria's curves, tapping my chin. "In fact," I continued, "it's one of my, um, my…" I stopped myself when he started shaking his head like a priest chastising an adulterous parishioner. It was then clear that there was something wrong. He looked up from his computer.

"This picture," he whined, "is a little too much for our policy here." He pointed to a sticker on the wall: No

Porn Here, Try Another Café. Next to the slogan was the crossed and fade-out image of a topless blond woman, an image I found ironic and bizarre on two counts: first, it displays nudity, a crime the café abhors; second, it assumes all pornographic contents start and end with white, and specifically, blonde women. Why not a Yoruba woman with two tribal marks on each cheek? I did not voice my concern.

He looked from Clasina Maria's breasts to my face, shrugged, gave me an oblique smile and tapped his computer screen, his puritan fingers circling Clasina Maria upper body. "Sorry, my friend," he said regretfully, "I can't print this one."

Earlier on, he had printed three non-nudes without problems. He had neatly clipped them together, placed them in-between a white folder and handed them over with a brotherly smile. I stood wondering how to change his mind. Then I sputtered a case for myself.

"My brother," I began, "it's just a piece of art…" Clasina Maria's vibrant breasts and thighs seemed to interfere with whatever progress I was making. On a closer look, they seemed to jiggle and jeer, daring him to do his worst. I waited patiently. The piece had to be printed there. There were three other Internet cafés in town, but none was as fast, with a functioning printer, as the one on No. 3 Pele.

His boss walked in, a muscular man with bloodshot eyes, who fancied the idea of himself as 'a learned fellow'. He greeted us and disappeared into his office, emerging few minutes later with a pack of Rothmans and a matchbox. I was still at the operator's counter, persuading him to print the piece. A foot outside the door, a lighted cigarette swaying on his lips, the owner watched what was going on.

Between robust puffs and a cheek-to-cheek shuffling of candy, he asked if "anything was the matter?"

"Oh no," I answered.

The operator was not pleased by my euphemism, which I thought was in his favour, knowing that the owner's opinion would not be as extreme as his.

"He wants to print a nude sketch but I told him we don't do such things here," he said.

"It's a Van Gogh," I cried.

"Sam, have you joined the porn panders?" the boss teased.

I was not amused but hopeful. The puritan operator shrugged and pulled a face. He did not see the joke crashing down on him. The boss puffed his last, tossed the cigarette butt in the street and walked back to his office. I noticed his blue polo shirt and how it matched the sea-blue walls, distantly complementing the dark, red rug.

"Over here," he called from his office.

A copy of Sun Tzu's *The Art of War*, with a red page-marker sticking out on the side, was sitting on his sickle-shaped desk. On the left side of his office was a thin bookshelf, about six feet high, not wider than the stretch of my arm. I ran through his small collection. Among others, there was a copy of Dostoyevsky's *The Idiot* hugged on one side by Sartre's *The Age of Reason* and on the other side by Armah's *The Beautiful Ones are Not Yet Born*. The walls were grey and blank, except for the black and white framed photo of a man staring into the abyss.

Sitting behind his formica-top desk, curiously peering into his Toshiba Satellite, the boss looked nothing like the revolutionary ambience of his office: the books, the existential air… There was one window behind him, barely open. The alleyway outside the window was shaded. And I could sniff stale urine and decaying garbage wafting in from that direction. "I googled the piece and I perfectly understand why Lazarus would not print it."

"Why?" I asked.

"Two things: ignorance and religion."

He moved his mouse and clicked several times.

"Don't get me wrong," he continued, "I don't have anything against religion, and I don't care what people do with their brains. As for Laz, his views are somewhat extreme. But I keep him here for other reasons. First, he's trustworthy. Second, he somehow manages to drive profits up by attracting the church crowd." He shook and unplugged the mouse from the laptop. "As you know," he resumed, "the churches are upon us, including student-run churches. Laz is well connected in that world. We don't necessarily agree but it's all about the numbers."

"Right, numbers matter," I said, helping myself into the only empty seat—a black, leather chair that swallowed my buttocks in its soft depths. "I wish he had a more balanced grey matter."

"I don't care what he has up there, brains or mashed potatoes. I really don't care. I'm a businessman."

"Right. I still think he needs a balanced grey matter, else—"

"You better keep that matter to yourself and watch what you say around him. Ever heard of political correctness? That's how to play and win in today's world. Stay here."

He walked over to the open area and returned a short while later with the print. On the way out I saw Laz walking in with a bottle of Pepsi and doughnuts wrapped in newspapers. The boss had carefully sent him on an errand before printing the sinful image. He offered me a lavish smile; I broke into a little run and disappeared through the door.

When I got to my new hostel and narrated this ordeal to Margaret, she looked at me and wondered why I was obsessed with Van Gogh.

"You won't understand," I answered. "We go a long way back."

2

I see him standing at the door like the shape of a tree leaning over, about to fall, struggling with the feral rush of oncoming wind. His face is marked by an unreadable expression, a mysterious expression abandoned lovers know how to draw.

I can tell he had been stabbed by my absence. I walk to the door. He does not move an inch. I offer him a hug. He pushes me back and steps into the dark corridor. The doors are shut on all sides. The neighbours are either in their rooms or away in some class. I extend my hand. He declines. Our eyes are still glued to each other. I can see the blood in his eyes boiling with questions I cannot decode.

I try to see him differently, young and beautiful. I also wonder, in spite of myself, what it is that makes him feel what he feels towards me, and what it is that has moved him to find me here, in this hovel, my new abode away from Adam Hall.

The longer we lock eyes, the more he transforms from a beautiful man to a vulnerable figure, weak and hollow, an empty gong. The corridor lightens up. A student walks in. Osagie is no longer there. I am now awake, sitting on the edge of the mattress, studying Margaret's face as she sleeps. I return to my Gogh-inspired poem but cannot concentrate; the image of Osagie continues to haunt my imagination.

*

"Why are you obsessed with this Van Gogh?" Margaret asked when she woke up.

"You won't understand," I answered, "we go a long way back…"

And that was the truth. I met Van Gogh in the art segment of the *Weekend Globe*. That was before I met Margaret, before I left Adam Hall. The article was a short piece on a Nigerian artist whose sound installation was gaining serious attention in Amsterdam. His installations, as the writer reports, simply transported Dutch audiences to the mad streets of Lagos, where they could hear bus conductors calling for passengers and street hawkers announcing their wares in screams. The reporter had mentioned Van Gogh's name in connection to Amsterdam, in passing, but I was captivated by the little allusion to his life and career. So I ripped the page and headed straight to the internet café at No. 3 Pele, where I looked him up and was instantly hooked. It was in that same week that I dropped out of university and left Adam Hall without notice.

Osagie did not know my whereabouts. I left before he returned from the term break we were supposed to spend together. I had lied my way out of the planned road trip, and moved to a different part of town to hide from my own fear, from the uncertainties that were beginning to drive me mad. I relocated to hide until I was sure of where next to go. My disappearance must have scared him. I, too, was frightened by my action. It appeared there was an inner tug that resisted reason, that drove me further and further away from common sense. At a deeper level I felt a need to run away from Osagie. He was too much of a mirror. In him I saw my past contrasted with his past and present, and with him I saw a longing I did not wish to cultivate. In choosing to run from him, I lost touch with everything else, including the desire to complete my studies.

I moved into a private hostel on Pele Street, No. 24, an old three storey building. The bottom floor was occupied by families, mostly local townies; the top by students, mostly undergraduates. My room was halfway down the hallway, sandwiched between two rooms. In those first months at the new place, I hid in my empty room, peering at the world through the window, avoiding neighbours though I listened to their voices, their steps, the rustle of textbook pages in their rooms... I followed every sound and extrapolated what each motion meant. I knew when they left for class and when they returned. I knew the room with the most traffic, where I believed the occasional smell of marijuana came from. At first I assumed I was the only hermit around, but I was wrong. There was another hermit next to my room. I would later learn that she also eavesdropped and had also mastered my routine. She knew when I scuttled to the shared bathroom down the hallway, when I bolted and unbolted my window, when I sneaked out at night to buy a loaf of bread. I had mapped her moves and knew she hardly left the building during the day, only at night. I called her the Owl-next-door. I do not remember how I came to suspect that the owl was a she, but my suspicion was spot on. One night, on the way to get bread, we ran into each other. I knew she was the one; she was on her way out at the same time as always. She winked. I hurried into my room. The next day, at about eight in the morning, there was a knock on my door. I unlocked to see who it was, and it was the owl.

"I know you," she said, "and I've read your book reviews

in *The Ethiope*. My name is Margaret."

Too stunned to speak, I smiled an awkward smile. Her face glowed with stale make-up, her hair hung high, carelessly erect but alluring. Our neighbours were gone. The hallway, dim and vaguely ominous, transported her voice from the entry door to the bathroom at the other end. Something skipped in my guts, an involuntary caper that made me self-conscious and suddenly aware of my racing pulses. I introduced myself in a near-whimper, holding out my hand in pretend courage.

"Nice to meet you," I said. "Thanks for taking the pain to read my reviews."

Realizing I had said "pain" instead of "time," I followed with a question:

"Which of them did you like the most?"

"I thought your review of *Our Only War* was great. Chinda is a good writer, and she handled that subject the way one would expect of any serious writer."

"How do you mean?"

"I mean, she revisited a war we've chosen to forget, and did so without apportioning blames." Her eyes seemed to repeat every word, unblinking.

"She writes well," I said but did not pursue the subject.

I could not place her accent. She did not sound Igbo, Ukwuani, or Yoruba, the usual suspects around here. We were still at the door. I was in my morning boxers, shirtless, and aware of my concave, unmanly chest.

I did not invite her inside. My room was a hovel of used books, with a tattered suitcase and the stiff smell of a space closed to traffic. Her light-blue nightgown hung down in a V-shape between her breasts. The tight outline of her underwear was visible, glaring at me suspiciously. She knew

I was probing.

"There's hot water for tea in my room," she announced, "and I have a fresh loaf of Tea Mate bread. Feel free to knock on my door."

She turned to go. As an after-thought, she added, "It was nice meeting you."

Two steps later, she turned right and disappeared into the next room.

The Owl-next-door now had a name and a face. She had been friendly but aloof, her warmth coming in small chunks, which I interpreted as an attempt to open up yet draw the line. That line would always be there, albeit blurred by time, fizzling into an undefined relationship that was unnamed and untamed. Her introduction was a seed that eventually sprouted into a longing—not the usual longing for the frivolities of intimacy but a fancy to know her, to know and appreciate the way she talked, to master the movements of her eyes, the workings of her mind, to see and know the sources of her.

That swish to transcend our first handshake, to embark on a journey to friendship, was—I suppose—a direct consequence of my loneliness. At first I did not see it that way, because loneliness did not manifest itself as loneliness, but paraded itself as some kind of objective detachment from the world without, a variant of solitude, elevating itself beyond what it actually was. I convinced myself I was undergoing an introspective stage, a time to be alone, to draw from the essence within, to see the world without the obfuscation of distracting views.

A week later, having rehearsed several opening sentences, I knocked on her door. The rap was as weak as the feeble thud of my heart that morning. What would she say? What if she saw through me and stumbled on the uncertain person within? I knocked again. Silence. I could hear the movement of her feet inside. She was there. I knocked. Silence. She was ignoring me, I concluded. I replayed our first encounter. She had been polite and I had also been polite. Could I have betrayed any off-putting anxieties? Were there cues that I missed? Were there ways I could have been more elegant, perhaps asked her inside for tea? Was I wrong in not returning her courtesy the next day and the day after? No, it was certainly the way I looked at her, devouring her with my wretched eyes. That was it. She saw me picking her shape and impressing it upon my lascivious mind. Silly me. I should have been more cautious with the dart of my eyes.

I made to go but decided to knock once more. Another neighbour appeared, walking down the hallway, the collars of his t-shirt raised, his jeans folded to reveal read polka dot socks lodged between his jeans and brown boat shoes. I almost melted into Margaret's door trying to avoid his curious glance. He stopped by the door before mine, and offered me a smile. I turned away quickly, he said hello, deliberately ignoring my dismissal.

"Hi," I greeted.

He came forward and repeated his hello, that mischievous smile on his face, as though to warn me that I could no longer escape the tentacles of my neighbours, having wandered out of my closet.

He said his name was Nkem, he was from Enugu State, and he was studying Business Management.

I suppose he anticipated an equal introduction from me, a warm reception and reciprocation of his chumminess, but I was not forthcoming and was rather hoping the earth would cave and swallow us both.

He dropped another bait, hoping I would trail him into that realm of neighbourliness expected of me. He liked living around here, in this little hostel, he declared. Living here afforded him the pleasure of knowing other students at a more personal level. Then he asked if I was aware they had weekly dinners? That he "ensured everyone was well fed."

Apparently, every weekend, they all gathered in his room where they were provisioned with drinks and food at his expense.

"Nothing much," he went on, "Just an old family habit I inherited from my grandmother. Before she passed away three years ago, her house constantly buzzed with parties—politicians, business owners, celebrities—you know what I mean."

I grunted something to the effect that I appreciated his invitation. But I sincerely wished to tell him how much I would rather have him turn around, head back to his room and leave me to the Herculean task of re-introducing myself to Margaret, who I imagined was eavesdropping. Picturing her passing judgments on me, I decided to return Nkem's warmth. I was born in O., outside Port Harcourt...

"Ah," he beamed and said he once visited Port Harcourt with his parents, "a long time ago, and spent a whole day in Bori Camp" where his cousin served as a cadet officer. Then he wondered why I travelled all the way here for university when there is a great university there. He had applied there but was turned down.

"I wanted to get away," I answered, more for the benefit of Margaret who I believed was listening.

"I also wanted to get away from Enugu," he said

and launched a long spiel about his family, about his grandfather—a politician, journalist, editor and early nationalist—who raised his father to be blah and blah, and his father in turn wanted him to be so and so and so. He chose not study at the University of Nigeria, where his father went and his grandfather was a major donor, and applied to schools in the south.

"You should come for dinner this weekend," he said.

I said I would—but never went, and made no attempt to see him or any of my neighbours afterwards. He said something about forgetting his keys at a shop outside, shook hands again, and went away. I sighed, contemplating my next move: to knock on the closed door before me or wait until nightfall when Margaret would step out? As if reading my mind, she spoke, obviously aware of my indecisive presence at her door. "Come inside," she called. I could hear a giggle, which added to my paranoia. The closed door had filtered her voice into teasing fragments. Unsure of myself and what would happen next, I held the doorknob with the utmost care. I was glad there was no peephole; she could have seen the forced grin on my face. I opened the door with a gentle twist but stepped back when I saw her clad in nothing.

"I'm sorry," I stuttered and drew back.

"For what?"

I stood at the door, holding it ajar. Struggling not to stare at her, my eyes roved up to the ceiling and the window next to where she was neatly folding her clothes, making a pile on the mattress on the floor.

"Come on in," she said. "And do feel free." She folded a green camisole and started another pile. "The body is just a piece of art, mine and yours. That's the way I see it. Nothing more, nothing less." She grabbed a handful of panties and bunched them in a corner of the mattress. I swallowed hard and reminded myself that I only wanted to *know* her, perhaps a bit beyond the usual friendly banter. That idea—of merely seeking to *know* her—was rapidly fading the moment I walked into her room. I was not, however, certain of what it was evolving into.

"Pretend I am a piece of art," she was saying without looking at me, "a Gustav Klimt, for instance. If that fails, just go ahead and look at me. I don't care." All this she said without raising her face from the pile of clothes. I felt she was denying me that gaze. I wanted her to offer me a glance; as though she owed me a flirtatious stare.

She picked up another camisole and threw it on. I hesitantly stepped into the room. A faint lavender fragrance hovered. There was an empty cup atop a plastic table, with two plastic chairs pushing in on either side. The only window was directly opposite the door. I pulled out one of the plastic chairs. She took the other one and asked if I was in the mood for tea.

"No, thanks." I said.

"You're up early," she said and folded her hands across her breast.

"I go to bed at 2 a.m. and wake up at 6."

"That's insane."

"I've been insane all my life."

"You don't look it," she said, "you look innocent."

"Innocence is insanity and insanity is innocence. Both are overrated."

"Where did you get that from?" she asked, raising her eyebrows.

"From being innocent and insane. The former became

the latter." I could hear Pa Suku's voice in my head.

We both fell silent.

Knowing that I had dropped an improvised statement, for which I had no substance to pursue, I clasped and unclasped my hands and tried to maintain eye contact.

"What is innocence?"

She stood up, walked to the window, and looked out to the cloudy morning, her camisole ebbing at the waistline where it formed a fine flutter that seemed to sway in the windless room.

She turned and revised her question. "How would you define innocence?"

"It is hard to define," I started, "but it sure isn't the absence of guilt." "You confuse innocence for ignorance," she said.

"Both are bedfellows and sometimes indistinguishable."

"Well, I think one is either innocent or ignorant," she said, "I doubt we could be both innocent and ignorant. No?"

"It's a question of context and perspective."

"Would you say a child is innocent or ignorant?"

"I think ignorance comes with age. We are presumed innocent as children. With age comes ignorance. It therefore is a question of responsibility, the responsibility to seek knowledge. When one ignores that responsibility, the gift of innocence dissipates. Remember those lines from Paul the apostle to the Corinthians? 'When I was a child, I spake as a child, I understood as a child, I thought as a child: but when I became a man, I put away childish things.' It's our job to do the putting away of innocence and then go forth to embrace knowledge."

"I don't read the Bible. Good idea, though."

She returned to her chair and sank into its dry hold. "Why did you come here if not to take advantage of my breakfast offer?" she asked.

"To have a conversation like the one we are having," I said.

"And you think I'm a good conversationalist? Or you just need a sounding board?"

"You are an intelligent woman," I said, unsure of the implication of my comment, which I immediately thought was somewhat condescending.

"You sound like my dad."

"How?"

"Well, you know," she looked away, sat up straight and folded her arms, "he's one of those charming thinkers."

"Interesting," I said. "Hope he does not smoke a pipe, wear thick-rimmed glasses, and pound an old Olympia while sipping whisky before sunrise."

"Do you smoke a pipe and pound an old typewriter? Tell me you don't."

"I wish I did, perhaps that would make me more of a confident writer."

"I think it'd make you a pretentious young man, or better still, a denier of the present, which is what all nostalgic people are—sufferers of UAS."

"UAS? What's that?"

"Unconscious Anti-Present Syndrome. When the mind resists contemporariness, privileging the past over the present and gloriously doing so to the distress of everyone in the present."

"Wow."

"By the way," she said, changing the subject, "I know a lot about you, my reclusive neighbour. I've seen you at several readings and art shows around this town. But you always seem to slip through the crowd, to disappear. I saw you at Chike's first show at Kenny's Gallery. You know he died a week after that show, right?"

I was not aware and had not known Chike that well. I remembered his art: collages of found objects. I had hastily dismissed them as impulsive and had jumped from one piece to the other looking for what would reinforce my idea of beauty and artistic coherence. In the wake of her revelation—that the young man was dead—I thought more of his assemblages. There was a self-portrait, an abstract interconnection of threads held in various places by corroded pins, with dry leaves glued at odd corners. It struck me as revealing more than a portrait. I recalled leaving it at that and progressed to the next piece, a black canvas with a fired chicken bone glued to the centre. If the circumstances were different, I would have told her the chicken bone caused my early exit from the show. Its state—hopelessly alone and confined to that colourless expanse—was stabbing and sad. I still have not forgotten that image. I suppose that is the function of art, to shake us up as Kafka said of books, "the axe for the frozen sea inside us." "Sad," I finally responded. "How did he die?"

"Suicide," she said. "He was found dead at the studio space he shared with two other artists."

"Sad."

"We were childhood friends, you know. We both learned how to paint from his father, who taught visual arts here."

She stood up, went over to a black handbag on the side of the mattress and fished out a pack of St. Moritz.

"Cigarette?"

"No, thanks. I don't smoke."

"Never tried?"

"Not between my lips. I've only sniffed at close range."

"Good for you," she said. "I hope you don't mind."

"I don't." I said. "It must have been hard for you after Chike's death."

She lit a stick and walked over to the window. She ran her fingers over the window screen and peered outside.

"It was hard for me. But that was several months ago. He left me a note in a sealed envelope. It's somewhere in this room, unopened."

"Why unopened?"

"I don't know. I thought I would read it after his parents left for the United States. But I could not bring myself to do so. I prefer to let it lie, unread, a mystery that I would someday unveil."

After a second or two of profound silence, I collected myself and cautiously asked if they were 'involved'.

"Chike was gay," she said. "We loved each other, though. In a sense we were a couple without the stupid encumbrances of sex. Frankly, ours was a relationship like no other. He was always there for me and I for him. I was the only one he came out to."

"So his parents moved?"

"Yes, they left for the US after a hasty funeral. His dad picked up a teaching position at Columbia."

"Quite a transition," I said.

"Well, he did his PhD there and had taught for a year before returning to teach here, like my dad who was at NYU but also made the journey home to teach."

She stepped to the mattress and picked a pair of khaki shorts. Her cigarette swung on her lips as she pulled the shorts up her hairless calves, up her thighs, and finally her hips were covered.

"I'm doing all the talking," she said.

"You talk so well, Margaret."

"If you say so."

"I could listen to you all day." "Are you flattering me?"

"I'm being honest," I said.

"Don't push it. Honesty is overrated. No?"

"I agree, it is overrated. Blame it on the human condition."

"The human condition," she repeated. "Well, I see we agree on a lot of things and we are especially similar in one regard."

"And what might that be?"

"We both are running away from society, for reasons we are yet to discover. You are here in this room because the *thing* in you is attracted to the *thing* in me."

"What *thing*?"

"I don't know. The moment I know, or you know, we'll no longer enjoy each other's company. I dropped out of art school last September, a month before Chike's death, breaking my father's heart. I moved out of his flat to be free, and to come to terms with my decision. In a way, we're like stowaways surreptitiously sailing to where we don't know."

"I did the same a few weeks ago," I said. "I dropped out, too."

"I know, and was about to point that out."

"How did you know?"

"Because you've been hiding in that room since you moved here. You don't attend classes like the rest."

"I wish I knew more about you."

"You will know me and may not like me anymore, but I doubt it. You are different."

"How do you mean?"

She raised her eyes to the ceiling where a 60-watt light bulb hung, starved of electricity. She took a deep breath and continued, "See, I live alone, I walk alone, I eat alone, but at night, two to three nights a week, I'm in the company of strangers."

"I don't understand."

"I will explain more, for one reason and on one condition. Reason: you are a free spirit like me. Condition: don't try to make sense of what I'll say, just keep an open mind."

"I don't know if I'm strong enough to handle it," I said. "But I'll listen."

"Good. That's all I'm asking for: a listening ear, an open mind"

"You can talk to me."

"I'm an artist of the flesh and have been for three months."

"What does that mean?" I asked, genuinely confused.

"Ever read anything about Dirck van Baburen's 'The Procuress,' Or seen Jan Vermeer's painting of the same title?"

"No. Do they explain what you mean by artist of the flesh?"

"Sort of. It's my euphemism for the oldest trade." She returned to the table and stood behind the plastic chair, one arm across her chest, the other outstretched, holding the cigarette. "It's not the money," she continued, "it does pay well, but it's not the money."

I sat still. Grains of ash fell from the tip of her cigarette.

Its smoke eddied in ascending curves, almost obscuring her face. Then, as though roused from a sleep, she pointed to an oil painting hanging at the back of the door. I turned to see a naked woman lying face down on the floor, hands clasped to her side, legs stretched apart. Next to her were four pairs of men shoes in various sizes.

"That's one of my paintings," she said. "The only one I keep in my room. The rest are in my father's flat on campus."

"Why this one?"

"Because I'm that woman, and it reminds me that all men fall before their birth, hence are forever face-flat as they make their way through this world."

We went on our first walk that evening, my head spinning with what she had shared. The walk was my idea. She chose the route.

In the days that followed—before I moved in with her a month later, sub-leasing my room to a student who claimed he was an Igbo-Jew—we spent time discussing art and literature. She introduced me to Muldoon and Heaney, Brodsky and Walcott, Breytenbach and Coetzee. She was a world unto herself, awash with curiosities. We held private readings, which was her idea. I would read her my poems and she would read from poetry books, mostly gifts from her father, a literary scholar himself. Walcott was her favourite. The day she read me "As John to Patmos," her eyes were as misty as collected vapour. She repeated the third stanza until that vapour became a downpour:

This island is heaven—away from the dustblown blood of cities;

See the curves of bay, watch the struggling flower, pretty is

The wing'd sound of trees, the sparse-powdered sky, when lit is
The night. For beauty has surrounded
Its black children, and freed them of homeless ditties.

She would later share why she was that attached to Walcott's work: her mother was from Saint Lucia.

"She was born there but moved to New York in the seventies, where she met this young, handsome bloke from Nigeria. He was a PhD student at NYU at the time."

"Neat," I said, expecting more.

She indulged me.

"She worked at a bar on West 3rd Street. Don't worry about where that is."

"Well, I know it's certainly not here in Abraka."

We both laughed.

"He lived down the same street," she continued, "and would show up several times a week for beer at the bar. He made several moves. They fell in love that spring. I was born in '82. She died in '94, the same year my father returned to teach here. I was twelve."

She lit another cigarette.

"I remember the look on my father's face when we landed at the airport in Lagos. I cannot really say what it was but it betrayed shock, as though he had been hit by an unforeseen reality. Beside the unbearable heat, everything else looked cool to me. My dad, who had always told me beautiful stories of 'our homeland', didn't look pleased. 'We are the giant of Africa,' he used to say back in New York, especially when his friends, African scholars like himself, came to our place for drinks and jazz. A week before we left, the group convened to wish him well. I overheard one of his friends saying to him, 'Phillip, you might want to think twice. Our colleagues at home are leaving in their numbers. It's hostile down there. Wait awhile.'

"We left anyway. I think the fear of losing me to my mother's family was behind his move. I also think my mother's death forced him to mentally sever ties with America. A friend of his, a former adjunct at the City College in New York, who had returned several years earlier to start and run the *National Daily*, picked us from the airport. A bespectacled bald man with a large face, he chain-smoked all the way to his residence and spoke very little. My dad did not speak much either. I remember wondering if I'd see a group of white people on either side of the road, or signs announcing familiar gas stations. It wasn't long before I fell asleep. At dinnertime both men were quiet. I was too exhausted to look at their faces or read their moods.

"After dinner, Lucas—that was his name—showed me to my room, an empty space with a bed and a rug. The bed sheets were blue. The rug was floral red, with patches of leaf-green and wood-yellow. The bathroom was simple: no bathtub, but the shower worked. There was a single bar of soap. No shampoo. I couldn't sleep. I walked to the door, sat and leaned on it without pushing it open. I could hear their voices on the other side,

"'Why did you return, Phillip?' Lucas was asking. My dad was silent. I heard the click of a lighter. 'I commend your courage, but it does not make sense, my friend.'

"'This is home, Lucas,' my dad answered, 'I want to raise my daughter here, I want her to see her country.'

"'There's nothing to see, Phillip. What were you

thinking? It is '94 and we have a maniac in power.'

"'I'm not interested in politics. I'm not an activist, Lucas. I'm a teacher,' my dad said, his voice shaking. I leaned closer to the door. 'I just want to teach at a college and raise my daughter.' The lighter clicked again. 'No offence,' said Lucas, 'but when was the last time you saw a Nigerian university? I don't mean to dampen your spirits. I'm only concerned that you are no longer in touch. You've been away for a long time my friend.'

"Someone coughed. The lighter clicked for the third time. 'I may leave the country soon,' said Lucas, his accent as American as my dad's.

"'What?'" Dad asked.

"'It's no longer safe to oppose the regime from within,' Lucas said.

"I fell asleep by the door. A week later we ended up in this small university town. Lucas never left."

"It must have been a shock for you, moving from New York to Abraka."

"It was a big shock. I never got over the shock. My father didn't help matters. As soon as we got here he threw himself into his teaching and didn't spend much time with me. He taught several classes a week and organized several academic events. He edited books, journals—too many things. His secretary, Vuakpor, used to plead with him to slow down, but he wouldn't hear that. Meanwhile I struggled to adapt to life here. At the university staff school where he enrolled me, the girls avoided me. They spoke to me in questions. 'Where are you from?' 'Who's your father?' They didn't believe I was Nigerian. Can you imagine that? I looked like them—"

"But your accent was different."

"True, and for the first time I was conscious of my own presence. When I spoke, I heard the strangeness of my voice. 'You are like them,' my dad would say when I raised the topic, 'don't be intimidated.' I tried, but it was hard. Kids are mean. While the girls kept their distance, the boys cautiously warmed up to me. They wanted to know about America. One asked me where Texas was and said his dad had studied there, in a city called Austin. They thought I knew every dot on the map of America.

"I was surprised that they all wanted to move there for university. These were children of professors and administrators. I didn't understand why they would leave for a university far away from home. To me, the US was just a place, a space like every other, although I secretly considered it home.

"Having lived here for ten years, it is safe to say that I now completely understand why their parents would want to send them abroad."

3

The night faded into the past, and the morning twittered with weaver finches. Their voices, a sad-sweet chime in the bushes outside the window, mocked the Sunday school bells of my childhood.

Margaret was still pulp in the embrace of sleep. I had been awake since six, reading and re-working my Van Gogh-inspired poem. From time to time I would be fed mini-gusts of screen-sifted morning breeze, and a repeated helping of the weaver finches' calls.

The serenity of that morning put me at ease, and I decided to read Margaret the poem later that morning.

Her response, which I should have anticipated, was far from my assumption that she would enjoy the piece for its sake. I should have known better. We had been through a similar experience before, and I did understand that Van Gogh was not the problem; we were the problem.

She had spotted, as I had, the parallel between herself and Clasina Maria Hoornik, and how that placed me in Van Gogh's shoes, a near-truth that troubled me as much as it did her. I chose to see it differently, as a sign.

After I finished reading her the poem, she looked at me and said how uncomfortable it made her. "Perhaps it's because I don't like your 'Gogh'," she said. "In fact, I'm bothered by your look into his mind."

Her response ripped the serenity of the morning. The birds without, as if offended, hushed in mid-twitter. A silence fell. She should have pretended not to care, I thought. She added that it was "not a personal attack," and went back to sleep.

An hour later she woke up and returned to the matter. "Let's talk about this Gogh for a minute."

"I'm ready," I said, still at my desk, the same desk I had placed in Osagie's room, which I took along with me when I escaped Adam Hall. "What do you want to know?"

Clasina Maria's trade mirrored hers, and she knew that I saw that parallel. What she did not know was that I would not go beyond that resemblance, neither would I become Van Gogh, which seemed to be her greatest fear: that I may end up with a mind adrift. The yip of a dog rang outside the window. A stray dog, I thought. There were dozens of them roaming the streets of Abraka, scavenging and snarling at passers-by. I thought of looking outside to see if it was within sight. But I ignored the idea, as everyone else ignored stray dogs. I was, however, reminded of a time when I looked out and saw a toad on the heels of a snake. I had hastily applauded the toad but stopped when it was swallowed and became a peristaltic spiral down the snake's tube.

"It isn't what I want to know," Margaret said, "but what I already know, and would like you to take seriously. I think you need to understand a few things before you slip into the same stream that drowned your insane hero."

Her concern was clear. Nonetheless, as always, she tiptoed around the parallels, avoiding a direct confrontation with the connections we both saw. I did wonder if she thought I was passively protesting her night shifts by reading her a poem inspired by the portrait of a prostitute.

"You have my ears," I said. "I'm listening."

"I don't want your ears, silly. I want to stop you from chopping them off." She rubbed her eyes and sneezed.

"Well then, my spirit and soul are yours."

In an attempt to further defuse the growing tension, I turned from my desk to face her and forced a grin. "Be serious," she cautioned and slid out of the sheets. She sat up and leaned back on the wall. There was a prominent speck in her left eye. I disregarded it and returned to my bid to lighten the mood.

"I'm as serious as Jackson Pollock," I said.

The tension lessened a little.

"I hope you are not making fun of my Pollock-mania," she said. "I still think the moon museum should have only picked abstract expressionists and excluded Warhol's inverted penis."

"It was not Warhol's penis," I said. "It was his initials, artistically fashioned to depict a rocket ship and a penis, depending on how you look at it, or how perverted you are. Rauschenberg had a place. What did he do? He drew a straight line."

"But have you thought of the significance of that single stroke?"

"What? Was he implying that aliens, at least those in his days, were too unsophisticated for the complexities of earth-made art? Was that why he gave them a simple stroke?"

"Maybe, maybe not. At least the New York Times published an image of the chip with that single stroke, which suggests how significant it was. What happened to your Warhol? I mean, his inverted 'thing'? It was covered with a thumb," she said triumphantly.

"Speaking of aliens," I said, swerving further away from Van Gogh, "isn't there something out there in space named after a Nigerian artist?"

"Enwonwu," she answered. "An impact crater on Mercury was named after Ben Enwonwu."

"That's something to be proud of, I mean, it's not like anyone remembers or talks about it."

"Who cares about prominent artists and Mercury around here?"

"I do," I said.

"You don't count."

Just when I thought we were miles away from Van Gogh, she exhumed the subject.

"On a more serious note," she started. "Why this Van Gogh? And of all his pieces, this one of a faceless whore?"

"There's a lot to this piece. Here was an artist who faced the reality of his choices. He didn't sneak around with this woman and pretend to be a saint the next day. He loved her and immortalized her in several paintings. Isn't that touching?"

She raised an eyebrow.

"I'm inspired by his sincerity and humanity," I added.

"What insane humanity?"

The dog's voice, sounding like the shriek of a distressed lad, rang again.

"She was homeless and needed help," I said. "He didn't take advantage of her. He rather provided help and shared his meagre income. I don't care what you think about Van Gogh, I seriously think he should be a saint somewhere. Saint Vincent of something, somewhere—"

"There are several Saint Vincents out there."

"The world is large enough to house more saints named Vincent."

"Saint Vincent de Paul was Catholic and was canonized by the church. He was known for helping the poor. There was also Vincent Ferrer, the friar and logician who was equally canonized by the church. Where does your Vincent stand?"

"He mustn't be Catholic or a Catholic saint. A saint is a saint. Coltrane is a saint of the African Orthodox Church. William Blake is the patron saint of thousands out there. Sainthood is like the OBE, you don't have to be born next to the Queen's front porch to appear on the list."

She rolled her eyes.

"It doesn't have to make sense now," I pressed, "Give it some time."

"And you hope to be the first Vincentian of the new order?"

"Of course. You may want to join me before we hit the roof."

"In ten thousand years?"

"Maybe less."

"No, thanks," she said with finality.

We listened to the fading yap of the stray dog outside. A wasp appeared from nowhere, buzzing between us, as though on an urgent errand, perhaps to help us find a common ground; and if that was its mission, it is safe to say that it failed colossally, since we simply let the conversation fade into silence without a resolution, stashing it away for another day.

She took another nap, a sign that she intended to work that night. Her work: another term for a bizarre reality we never discussed. Strangely, the fact that we did not talk about her work reminded me of my father's own work that I knew nothing about, that I still do not know anything about. It does feel like I am doomed to a life surrounded by mysterious people. Pa Suku said he was a freelance writer and a full-time thinker, but never did break those down for me. I cannot, after all the years I spent with him, place my finger on the exact nature of his freelance and full-time engagements.

I cooked lunch and ate in silence, intermittently turning to look at Margaret. Her lips were slightly open, and I felt like kissing her. "Kisses are statements," she once said, and I pretended I knew what she meant. "A well planted kiss, at the right time, on the right lips, with the perfect intention, could stand for a full page of love notes written by the greatest poet alive." I could write a book of aphorisms based on her random one-liners. I looked at her bare shoulders, and suddenly the thought of her in the arms of other men filled my head. I pictured her in her little black dress, dazzling them with her brilliance, charming them with her knowledge of the world. I imagined a satisfied old man, ugly and disgusting, pulling out his wallet, counting and peeling out crisp notes while she slid into her dress and touched up her make-up. She never talked about the pay. I did not ask. It was part of our silent pact.

Unable to make sense of the whole situation, and aware of the absurdity of our own relationship, I began to wonder why I moved in with her. I knew I was attracted to her, but that attraction was in itself absurd, and didn't follow the routines and expectations of a boy-girl attraction as told in the movies. It just happened. Besides, I was not sure the attraction was mutual. If she was attracted to me, she neither said so nor betrayed it in the tiniest way.

The decision to share a room had been sudden: there was not a single pause to contemplate what the details were, the possible outcomes, the consequences. That decision, I must say, tops the list of all the spontaneous decisions I had made up to that time. Two days after the idea was born, I was in her room with my belongings—a suitcase full of shirts (mostly second-hand plaids) and chino trousers, four boxes of books, a pair of leather sandals, two pairs of shoes (a pure leather boat and a worn tennis shoe), a half empty pack of black bic pens, a plastic bag with five boxers (all grey in colour), two tooth brushes, a pack of candles.

I remember what we had for dinner that first night, fried yam with tomato sauce. And what we drank that night, a mix she made and called cocktails. Cocktails. It was my first sip of that hard mix. "We'll do it without ice," she said as she pulled out two small bottles from one of her work bags. "I call it pretend cocktail, since it does not resemble or taste anything like the real thing." I drank with care, paying attention to the burning sensation on my lips, listening to her speech between sips: "I go through these bottles each night I go out for work. I like the kick, and how it goes from the gut to the brain and down the spine to the waist."

I was feeling the kick as she spoke, and secretly wishing it would confer me the courage to conceal the anxiety that enveloped me. I ate dinner with caution, which prompted her to ask, with her fork heavenward, if there was something wrong. "You look like a child under the watchful eyes of fierce parents."

"Nothing," I said, still eating slowly.

I cannot say if I was shy, nervous, or betraying the identity crisis that lay underneath, that displayed the image of Osagie each time I sipped the cocktail, that reminded me that I owed myself a rest.

"Are you trying to play the gentleman? I mean, is this your version of being a gentleman? Pinching your food like a child? Please, eat," she said, prodding me the way you would prod a kid to finish its vegetables. "This might be the last time I beg you to eat," she added. "Well, I'm sure you'll snap out of it after this night."

A few days later I staggered back to what one might consider normal: lying on the mattress without bothering to cover my man parts, holding conversations without averting my eyes... But at that first dinner, as her roommate, I tried to hold still and smile, to fork and dip my fried yam in tomato sauce without shivering. I offered to do the dishes afterwards. She looked at me, and gave a short laugh. "You are trying too hard to be a nice man. Be yourself. Don't try to impress me. There will be more dishes around here, and it would be great if you saved your energy for those. You are my guest tonight. But it's only for this night. Your guest status expires at dawn. So, relax and unpack your stuff."

She did the dishes. I unpacked and sat on the mattress, waiting, confused. Leaning next to the window, she smoked two sticks, quietly. The hostel was quiet, except for the occasional door opening or shutting to mark someone's entry or exit from the bathroom we all shared. She came to bed but was not ready to sleep.

"I want to get a few things out of the way," she announced. "I guess I should have said them before you moved in." I listened. "First, there will be a lot of nudity in this room, as you may have noticed. I'm either scantily clad or naked here. It's just the way it is. And I'm sure you will do the same when you return to your comfortable self. Second, as you already know, I smoke and I'm fully aware of the consequences. I know you don't mind. And I'm hoping it stays that way. Keep your judgements to yourself, if there are any. Third, don't try to impress me, please." She stubbed out her cigarette butt on the empty pack.

An hour later we were shaking like adults are wired to shake, sweating and sighing and gasping, after which she asked to recite me a poem she knew by heart. I held her tight as she ran through the words, releasing each line as though she was making a point. I wept like a helpless child at the end of her reading, tearing up like a punctured bag of water. She would later return to those tears and dig to find their source. I would evade her questions, perhaps too embarrassed to tell her what I considered the truth, that what I felt for her—which she may or may not have noticed—may in fact be inauthentic or just as authentic as what I felt for Osagie.

4

We arrived at The Delta Bar on Souzey Street around seven. The sun was long dead, leaving a moon that hung shyly behind thin clouds. It was our first time at The Delta Bar, which was only a street away from us. We usually explored bars away from where we lived, to avoid running into neighbours.

The Delta had a tricky layout. Once you walked through the door, you would see a small space with two tables and a closed red door beside the counter. The red door, as we found out, led to another space with more tables and another red door at the right corner. We walked through the last door. It opened into another space with more tables.

We took a table for two at the far right, near a screened window. The music was mild but bouncy. Highlife music. The other rooms had R & B and hip-hop respectively. "The song sounds familiar," said Margaret, slowly swaying to the bounce.

"'Onuigbo' by Chief Osita Osadebe," I announced.

A couple walked in, a bulky man in sunglasses and a fair skinned girl who could be his daughter. I wondered why he was wearing sunglasses in a badly lit bar after sunset. The server took our orders.

"We should do this more often. I think I like this bar."

"I do too," she said. "It's not as crowded as a typical bar on Souzey Street, and we have not run into anyone we know."

Our drinks arrived. Onuigbo gave way to Rex Lawson's

'Abasi Ye Enye'. I drank my Heineken from the bottle. She poured herself a glass of Guinness. Inyang Henshaw upstaged Rex Lawson with 'Ebonjo Ekididem Iban'. I stole a glance at the odd pair. The man in glasses had two bottles of Star beer in front of him. One was already half-empty. The girl stared at her orange juice, visibly shy. "You know how I feel about these things," he was saying in a loud whisper. She lifted her face from the juice to meet his eyes and wriggled a grin. He leaned back heavily on his chair and attacked the half-empty bottle of beer. The red door opened. Two men walked in. One had a brown briefcase; the other had a blue folder. They took the table next to the man in sunglasses.

"Let's get out of here," said Margaret in a sharp whisper. Her drink was nowhere near half. I turned around to scan the room. She was calm and her voice was firm. "Let's leave now," she commanded. I looked from her to the drinks before us, confused but trusting her abrupt decision. She stood first and headed for the red door. I followed sheepishly. "I know that man," she said as we shuffled our way through the first two rooms that were now crowded with students. "I think he recognized me. The man with the briefcase." We pushed through the stench of beer belch and sweat. "He was a client several months ago." Now her voice bore traces of distress.

"I thought your agent ensured there were no run-ins like this?"

"Theoretically, yes, but you know how unpredictable things are. He lives in Lagos and was visiting an associate here when we met."

We were now out in the windless night. Souzey was wild and teeming with activities: street restaurants and bars with loud customers, honking cars and motorbikes, idlers flooding back and forth like waves on a lake .

We headed for the Souzey-Pele intersection. She lit a cigarette, held it out between her left fingers and squeezed my hand with her right. I felt the panic and anxiety in her squeeze. Having lived with her for a while, I knew she did not smoke for smoking's sake. She smoked to something, the way one danced to music. She smoked to poetry, for instance, and smoked to the violent thrust of memory the same way she smoked in reaction to a sudden surge of emotion.

She leaned into me and we wobbled along slowly without words through the thickening night. At the Souzey-Pele intersection she stopped and asked me to follow her. I was led to a narrow backstreet between two shops. The shops were already closed for the night, barred by display tables rolled over and jammed to the door. The backstreet seemed darker than the night: we could see the street but the street could not see us. "Let's watch the world from here," she said and tossed her cigarette butt, crushing it with her sneakers.

We rested our backs on the wall, holding hands and looking into the dark space before us. The street was just visible to our left, but our immediate surroundings were not. There could have been a snake between our legs, or a pack of rats frolicking around the bend. We did not care. She heaved and, out of the blue, said she "once did drugs" and it made her paranoid, so she stopped for good. I asked what type of drugs she did. "Coke," she answered.

"Coke," I repeated, nodding as though I knew what she was talking about.

"Have you done drugs before?"

"I haven't."

"What's the wildest thing you've done?" she asked.

"I don't remember. That's another way of saying I haven't done anything wild, like drugs for instance. I suppose growing up the way I did was wild in its own way, since we were constantly at the mercy of ailments and poverty."

"Lucky you. Those of us who grew up in middleclass families were left to explore the dark side. It's not as if our parents rang a bell and asked us to go hunt for sex and drugs in the garage. But they were too busy building careers, making money to secure our futures. So we figured out ways to fuck ourselves up."

Lucky me? I thought of the rich kids I knew, how they gently walked home from school like sweet lilacs, too fragile to swat flies away from a fruit. They were the lucky ones. Were they? I also had an absent father and sincerely wished he made more money and had more time to spend with us.

She turned to face me. I could feel the heat of her breath. She slid her hands into my side pockets and pulled me closer. I yielded and reciprocated by driving my hands into her back pockets. Her lavender fragrance covered me. Her hands worked and so did mine, our hearts pounding. The sound of wild laughter, coming from the other end of the backstreet, startled us back to earth. We saw the silhouette of an approaching figure. The voice was masculine. His steps were unbalanced and difficult. He cackled again and mumbled words to himself. We watched to see if he had company. He was by himself. He smashed a bottle against the wall and laughed again, cussing the wall and the bottle. We held still.

"Motherfucking fucker you," he yelled at the wall. "Fuck off, motherfucker you." He staggered, fell and picked himself up and broke into song: *Could you be loved and be loved? / Could you be loved and be loved?* HAHAHAHA, he laughed: *Don't let them fool ya, / Or even try to school ya! Oh, no!* He knelt and pulled his trousers down. "Motherfucking fucking you," he screamed louder and slapped his palm on the wall. Then came the splash of piss against the wall and an accompanying loud moan. When that was over he began to pleasure himself right there. He apparently had not sensed our presence; it was not as if his senses were still intact.

"Madness," Margaret whispered.

The silhouette stood up and trudged towards us. We leaned into the wall. He passed and disappeared down the street, leaving the backstreet with a pungent mix of liquor and piss. A stick of St. Moritz emerged in response to the scene. We resumed our walk home but halted at another strange scene: the beer-drinking and herb-smoking groups were all climbing into a lorry. There was excitement in the airy. A male student was helping a girl into the lorry, practically pushing her ass as she struggled with her tight mini skirt. Another lorry arrived. The hauling continued. Where were they going? We decided to find out. So we headed towards the bar and asked a girl whose face was smeared in oily substances, with disc-like earrings jingling on both sides of her head.

"A new club is opening tonight," she answered without looking at us.

"Where?" She looked at us, irritated by our ignorance.

"It's in Abi," she replied, "two towns away. The owner sent out flyers and arranged for transportation. Are you coming?"

A third lorry arrived. She did not wait for our answer, which of course did not matter to her. A tipsy boy pushed her into the lorry. We continued our walk home, holding hands. Margaret squeezed my hand, I missed a step and almost fell. A maroon Mercedes pulled up in front of us. The window glass came down. It was the man from the bar, the one with the brown briefcase.

"Excuse me miss," he said to Margaret, his voice bearing the politeness of a modest but desperate salesman, "You look familiar. Did you work for Olu & Olu Associates, the law firm in Warri?"

"Not at all, sir," said Margaret, forcing a lose smile that hung dry like a blank placard.

"Sorry then. You look like someone I know."

They drove off. We headed home, huddling as we walked without a word.

5

The room was unusually stuffy when we got back. I was struck by how it felt abandoned, almost hideous in its stiff, airless state. For a second my childhood home, the room I shared with Ricia and the rest, flashed before me, which was rather strange since I vigorously fight to forget that space and all it represented.

Margaret went to the window, and cracked it open. A murmur, a mix of fading music and violent laughter, eased in and then was off again. The darkness without was almost total, broken here and there by a flicker of faraway headlights and the thin moon that occasionally parted the curtain-clouds.

I lit a candle. And, for the first time since the maroon Mercedes pulled up, I saw her eyes. She must have shed a few tears, I thought, looking at how red they were. She had her back to the window, both arms crossed just underneath her breasts which, for a fading minute, fired up a desire in me. It then occurred to me that I had never initiated love making between us, that I had not so much as drawn her to me for a long, intimate hug. She, on the other hand, would often start the kissing, working her way down to where, hard as wood, I ached hesitantly. But this, as we both knew, was merely a consequence of proximity, for we never considered ourselves a couple.

Sometimes I felt a pang of guilt, not because she cared whether I was or was not in love with her, but because I frequently replaced her face with Osagie's; her touch and kisses became his. Was she aware that it really was not her that stirred the beast in my trousers? There were days the beast would not rise at all, reluctant to carry on with the pretend passion I courted.

She turned to face the night, leaning into the window as though to sniff the air outside.

"What's on your mind?" I asked.

She shrugged and said nothing.

"Are you thinking about the maroon Mercedes guy?"

"Kind of," she answered. "Remember that passage you read me about memory a few days ago?"

"From Bachelard?"

"Yes, what was that fancy word?"

She turned around and gently sat on the floor, stretching out her legs.

"Topoanalysis," I said, taking a spot in front of her, at the edge of the mattress, on the floor. "Topoanalysis," I repeated. "Why?"

"I think it might explain how I feel at the moment."

Gaston Bachelard's *The Poetics of Space* was my most recent rescue from the streets. I recall reading her the passage where Bachelard introduced the term 'Topoanalysis' to which she responded with a simple nod, as though it had made sense to her. 'Topoanalysis,' says Bachelard, 'would be the systematic psychological study of the sites of our intimate lives.'

I did not quite get how it explained her mood, but then there was no way I could be in her shoes.

"It feels like there're small bits of me everywhere, in hotels and private homes. I know your Gaston Bachelard is talking about the home, as in our childhood homes, as the one place where memories and localized. But I do think the same is the case with the places we bare our most intimate parts, be it our hearts our bodies."

She fell asleep before midnight, right there on the floor. I sat where I was, studying her soft shape in the dying candlelight.

6

Father and daughter hugged. I stood at the door, hands in pocket, studying the living room. The flat was not too far from Adam Hall, on the same hill that rises to the main gate. From the front porch—about twenty yards from the grim-looking, algae-coated fence—you could see the entrance to Adam Hall, the broad, grey doors and the exhausted bodies walking through and disappearing into drab rooms where they would open wooden lockers and empty noodles into small pots.

The walls of Margaret's father's living room were eggshell white, interrupted here and there by framed photographs of him with various people. There was one with Margaret as a toddler in the arms of a woman. The woman was visible in the girl; the girl, now an adult, carried the woman in her eyes. I lingered before this photo, and thought, "Where is the man in the girl?" There was no resemblance between man and daughter, except for the height. The photos all had clear blue skies, brick buildings and neatly parked cars. There was one with the man as a younger version of himself, in a blue graduation gown, waving his mortarboard while another young man applauded a few feet behind him. The other photos lapped the wall around this one.

"Lucas and my humble self. NYU, 1980. A good year for the boys." He was standing behind me, shoulder to shoulder with his daughter. "That is a memento of the day we momentarily escaped the confines of the library, the classroom, the familiar smell of old books, and leapt to kiss the bouncy bosom of liberty."

"Dad," Margaret cautioned.

"What?"

"Your remark."

"Ah, I forget you're a feminist, or is it a womanist?"

She turned to face him and ran the introductions, efficient and elegant. First names were mentioned. A few things were said about my poetry and the memoir-in-progress. I was now an official presence in the flat. Seats were picked, he by the bookshelf, crossed-legged with both hands clasped and cupped on the knee, while I went for the spot under the photo. Margaret, after foraging in the mini-fridge for who knows what, joined us.

"To what do I owe this sudden intrusion, this interruption of my weekend serenity?" he asked, half-jokingly.

"I came to see you, father," she said.

"Wine or whiskey?" he asked the room, his voice flat but congenial. "Tea and coffee not allowed," he added.

"You must be asking him, not me. I don't suppose you've forgotten my favourite."

It was as though nothing had happened, as though she had not been out of touch for a few months. If they had missed one another, they did not show it. The initial hug was tight and lasted for a minute, but that was that.

"The question was to all," said the professor. "But now I must speak and act for myself. I'll do wine. Young man, feel free. I will fetch the wine. Do you smoke? No? Good for you."

Margaret did the pouring. I sipped first, nodded, and made an approving noise that may well have been the purr of a homeless cat. He grinned approvingly. I grinned in response, the way civilized people are supposed to grin at the sip of wine. Father and daughter held their glasses delicately. I wondered if there was more to wine than the red liquid before me. If there was any, my slum ass was yet to figure it out. Wine is wine to me, a red liquid that one consumes to loosen the tongue as the occasion demands.

He clipped his glass with his index and middle finger. The top bowl resting on his palm, he would occasionally shake the glass and watch the red liquid wrestle in its transparent confines. Her style was completely different but equally elegant. The stem was trapped between the tips of her thumb and index finger, leaving the rest of her fingers pointing out. I attempted what I thought was a civilized hold but quickly returned to grabbing the glass like a savage. He studied me. The residual smell of cigarette was present; there was stale ash in the black oyster-shaped ashtray on the glass-top table; a gold-coloured pack of Benson & Hedges waited next to the ashtray.

"How's Lucas?" she asked between slow sips.

"Lucas? He passed away three months ago. I thought you knew that?"

"Oh, no. What happened?"

"Cardiac arrest, they said. He was rushed to one of the hospitals in Ikeja. He died on arrival. Sad."

He stared at the restless red liquid in his glass.

"Are you okay?" she asked.

"I am. It is not his death that makes me sad, but his overall state before death took him away. He died a pauper, in pain and alone." He turned to me, "This was a man who spent all his life telling the story of this nation." He pointed to the photograph of himself and the late Lucas. "He was the first among my Diaspora friends to return at a time when this country was still in the hands of hooligans. He wrote like mad, and with his pen he fought the bastards here. He ran *The National Daily*, my friend Lucas, and turned that paper into a major force in this country. He was a humble man. But, you know, he was also human, and feared for his life in those days. At one point he considered leaving the country. But when I returned, he changed his mind and stayed."

The waiting pack of cigarette was picked up and a stick was pulled out. The pack was passed to Margaret, whose legs were now crossed—right leg on left, in the direction of her father. Out came a silver lighter from the professor's front pocket. Both sticks came alive. They both puffed at once. The cigarettes, as the wine glasses that were now left to wait on the table, were held gingerly. He trapped his between the right thumb and the index, so that it pointed at me. Hers nestled between the index and the middle finger pointing up to the roof.

"Lucas and I celebrated here in this room," Phillip was saying, making a 'here' sign with the cigarette pointing to the floor. "The occasion was the return to democracy. And our argument, more his than mine, was simple: the worst democracy is better than any form of dictatorship. How to start is to start somewhere, right? So we were optimistic. How much progress have we made? I'll let you decide." He paused for a puff. "I'll tell you a story." Margaret looked at me. "After the transition to democracy," Phillip said, "Lucas was offered a job as the press secretary to a minister. He moved to Abuja but soon resigned and returned to Lagos. He could not stand the nightly feasts on our collective wealth. My friend Lucas was heartbroken as he saw his romantic idea of a democracy crumbling before him. He returned to writing. I tried to lure him back to the classroom. There was an opening here which he was qualified for, but Lucas had become too radical for the classroom. The rot and lack of drive in this university would have driven him mad, anyway.

"Only six months ago, he got an invitation to head the Nigeria office of The Coalition of Global Activists, a network of freedom fighters, environmentalists, conservationists, reformers, feminists, human rights activists, and all the ists you can imagine. It was a buoyant list of rascals with a cause. Lucas jumped on it. He too was a radical with a large heart for progress. Meetings were held in the four geo-political zones. Issues were raised, discussed and implementations proposed. The Niger Delta was a prominent agenda on their plate. Lucas knew Ken Saro-Wiwa. So he took up the Niger Delta cause. A regional office of The Coalition was setup in Port Harcourt. Headquarters wired funds from DC. Rallies and advocacy meetings were held here and there. I was invited to the one in Warri. The oil companies, local Chiefs, interest groups, government functionaries and everyone that mattered in the Delta showed up. This is democracy, the mingling of the poor and the rich, the oppressed and the oppressor. Oil-suckers and their political appendages were well represented.

"Lucas spoke. The company representatives spoke. Chiefs spoke. You should see the Chiefs in their glory, all dressed up. Youth leaders spoke with passion. It seemed they all understood the problems: the roads were bad and inaccessible, more schools were needed and old ones must be renovated, unemployment was on the rise, more jobs must be created. Everyone who had a mouth prattled. A call for action was raised. The companies conferred among themselves. Agreements were reached. Two months later, Lucas resigned."

"Interesting," said Margaret, stretching out her glass for more wine.

"You sure need more wine for this part of the story," he said to her. "And young man," he turned to me, "hope I'm not boring you with this sad story?"

"He can handle it," she said.

"Lucas' story and experience is our collective story," I said. "And it is important for us, the younger ones, to know these things, and possibly anticipate them."

"Well said," he beamed. "After the Warri meeting," he continued, "the companies disbursed funds to towns and villages in the Delta, through the good offices of their Chiefs. The Coalition also received funding for community development projects. That was the beginning of the problem. News got to Lucas that a Chief in one of the villages was renovating his old house, had added a car to his fleet, and had sent his youngest son abroad. Well, he could do all that if he had the means, said Lucas to his source. What's the real news? It turned out that the Chief, the ancestral head of the clan, had halved the fund: a part for himself, the rest for the village. The lesser Chiefs pounced on the other half. A little clan war ensued. The money trickled away in rivulets. Meanwhile, Lucas' officers from around the country were pelting him with budgets for all sorts of frivolous ideas. Why, there were funds waiting to be used. The fact that there were existing projects that needed funds did not matter. The worst of all was that they all wanted to attend conferences abroad, and wanted Lucas to sponsor them with project funds. Lucas did not know how these things worked. His officers knew how to play the game. Unable to play the politics of activism, he resigned."

"Poor thing" said Margaret.

"I know. Now he is gone. Anyway, I will stop talking about Lucas. Young man, how did you get into poetry? It's not a likely passion for your generation."

"I had a neighbour who read me poems and encouraged me to write," I said. "He was my first influence."

"Interesting. I wish I could influence at least one student in my class." He chuckled. "But there are few with real interest. The others simply want to graduate and go out to do anything the world offers them. It's as bad as that."

"It's sad," I said.

"Indeed. In our days we were proud to be English majors. Today we are nothing but a nation of bankers and oil workers. The rest of us are mere onlookers." His face said more. He tapped out his ash and, on second thought, stubbed the unfinished stick. "Talking about poetry," he turned to his daughter, "I started a new seminar on twentieth century poetry, with a focus on poets from Nigeria and the United States."

Margaret gave me a quick look before responding to her father, "Sounds like fun."

"It is fun," he said. "I started with Hass and Okigbo."

"Hass? Now that's a leap from the known to the unknown."

"How do you mean?" He adjusted his sitting position.

"I mean it's Robert Hass. I bet they've not read him."

"Neither have they read Walcott nor Simic. Okigbo they know from secondary school. But it ends there. Yes, Hass is a leap but a necessary one. Partly because I want to shake them up a bit, and partly for a selfish reason: Hass was an early influence."

"You never mentioned that."

"His work was instrumental to my robust but short-lived experience as a poet." He turned to me. "I started writing poetry in '73, the same year Hass' first book was published. He and Milosz, whom he translated, were early influences. I read them night and day. I was young and full of ideas. Poetic ideas you may say." He reached for the glass of red liquid and asked how old I was. "I was about your age in '73. *Field Guide* was indeed a guide to me. I shook it upside down, cracking it for hidden meanings. And there were a ton of those. Hass, in my opinion, is a master at concealing stories within stories. I will show you something." He got up and walked into one of the two adjoining rooms.

"What do you think?" Margaret asked.

"Well, I like your dad. He's got a ton of stories—"

"You can have him. I grew up listening to stories after stories of meeting famous writers in New York and Boston and Providence. We have to stop him somewhere. Else he will go from Robert Hass to Günter Grass. We should probably leave in a bit and return some other day."

"That's fine. Does he really know about it?" I asked in a whisper.

"About what?"

"Your night shifts."

"Of course he does."

"You two are not of this world."

"It is what it is."

"I see."

He appeared with a book in hand. He fetched his reading glasses from the small bookshelf and returned to his seat. One of the temples was gone and the rims had several cracks.

"Looks like you need new glasses," she said.

"I sure do. It's on my list of things to do." He tossed her a reassuring smile, crossed and uncrossed his legs. His socks were not identical. One matched his charcoal black trousers, the other was red.

She returned his smile but hers was enveloped in a sudden sense of concern and worry. Just above, at the edges of the wall, a thick spider's web ran across like a zip-line. In Philip's hands politeness became an instrument of separation, with which he drew lines she was not permitted to cross. I caught him, once or twice, shooting her a look that seemed to express a deeper anger, a frustration concealed by the type of civility educated people parade.

"Here's Hass for you," he boomed. "Listen for words with dualities," he warned.

"I'll be back in a bit," Margaret said, leaving for the room behind her dad

Standing at the door, safely behind him, she waved, caught my eyes and tapped her wrist. I read her lips. He was so consumed in Hass's *Field Guide* that he did not see me nod.

"Here are the first three lines of 'Fall,'" he announced: *Amateurs, we gathered mushrooms/ near shaggy eucalyptus groves/ which smelled of camphor and the fog-soaked earth.* He paused, beaming, looked up and saw me nodding in agreement, more of a performance to keep the conversation going, since I was yet to catch the duality he instructed me to look out for.

"Mushrooms," he said, and repeated it for emphasis, the way one would read and repeat a street sign that vaguely reminded one of a place or a thing or a person.

"Mushrooms," I said, nodding.

"We'll be leaving now," Margaret said as she rejoined us. "It's been a great evening with you, dad."

" I'm trying to… anyway, thanks for stopping by. I will drop you off, if you don't mind."

"Don't worry. We'll walk. It's only a fifteen minutes' walk from here. The sun is down and the evening is mild. A walk would be splendid."

"Come on, Margaret. Do you really have to walk? I'm going out, anyway. So I might as well drop you off on the way."

"Where are you going to?"

"To dinner with Vuakpor."

"Vuakpor, your secretary?"

"Right. She's been of great help and support lately."

"Support? How do you mean?"

"It's been a difficult month, my dear. The doctor says I need to rest more, and Vuakpor has been extremely supportive."

"Supportive at the office?"

"No, here."

"Here? Vuakpor comes here now? I guess a lot has changed in the last couple of months."

"Should I drop you off on the way to Vuakpor's? It's a small town. I bet your place is not a mile away from hers."

"I assumed you were taking her to some nice restaurant. Do you still eat at the Upscale?"

"Yes, we went there three nights ago. Still as good as when you and I used to go there."

"How about the Borderline? You should take her there."

"Well, we're cooking at her place," he said flatly

"Nice," she said.

He shifted his attention to his antiquated glasses,

cleaning them with the edge of his shirt.

She was the loser in their little game. He enjoyed it. He had stuffed stories between sentences, leaving her high for more, an indirect way to show her how far she was from him, and how much he controlled that distance. This was how he punished her. I wondered what her mother would have done if she were alive and in that living room. Would she have extinguished the hidden war between father and daughter? Did they, the duelling duo, miss her? Did they wish she were there to take sides or play the neutral mother?

"Sure you don't want a ride?" he asked.

"Fine," she said.

"Oh, before I forget. I have a package for you."

"A package? From who?"

"From Peter."

"Peter?"

"Your uncle in Boston. Remember? He's your mother's brother and used to visit us in New York."

"I vaguely remember the name but the face I cannot place."

"He sent you a package."

"How did he get your address?"

"A colleague was at a conference in Boston and needed a place to stay. So I looked up your uncle and contacted him. I'll go get the package."

"When did it arrive?"

"About four months ago."

"You did not tell me."

"You were not here."

"You could have reached me by email."

"That's still new for old folks like us. We ring or mail friends."

"You use the internet."

"Only for research."

"Fine. Any idea what's in the package?"

"No idea. I'll go get the box."

Off he went to his half of the flat. I wondered if he occasionally poked his head into her room or walked in and wished his little girl were still there. What did her room look like? I tried to imagine her as a child occupying a room in Phillip's flat but my imagination was grossly limited. It thus occurred to me that I had never known a girl like Margaret, a girl who had her own room as a child; a room that, I suppose, was decorated to reflect her identity, with colours she liked, with toys she brought with her from New York, from the first space she called home, that must also hold some of her earliest memories.

He returned with a brown envelope the size of a book. "Here." He handed it over.

She flipped it.

"Shall we?" he said.

"Sure."

She led me to the front door while he took the back door to his garage. Soon the white Peugeot 504 pulled up in front of us, and I went for the backseat.

"Your car is unusually tidy. Where are the files and books and newspapers?"

"Vuakpor had it all organized. She's made life a lot easier for me."

"But you liked it the way it was, didn't you?"

The car died. He grunted and re-started it. It wheezed and started. And we were off.

"Vuakpor likes it tidy," he said, shifting gears.

She looked at the brown envelop on her lap as we passed

a line of bungalows with trimmed front yards and carefully manicured flowers.

"Looks like the Okupes are back from London," he said to himself, looking at a BMW convertible that was pulling into one of the garages in the neighbourhood. "That husband and wife are always on the road, it's either this conference in San Francisco or that fellowship in Chicago. I don't know if they teach here or just hold office for the sake of it. You know their daughter is married, right?"

"Efe is married?"

"Yes, two months ago. Big wedding at the university chapel. It was madness."

"Isn't she in her first year?"

"Second year, I think."

"That's still two young."

"We marry young in this country."

He pushed the radio button and a loud music ended the conversation. We passed the unpainted university chapel, curved left, and the main gate appeared. A guard in an oversize, grey uniform sprang from his plastic chair, unlocked the gate. "How the weekend sah," he greeted through a beggarly grin. Phillip ignored him. We hit the main street.

We were at the Souzey intersection in eight minutes. Margaret asked to stop there, saying "We live nearby." He pulled up by the side of Kenny's, the only barber's shop in the area.

"You live around here?"

"Not on this street but around here."

"Where?" he asked. The alarm in his voice was startling.

"Over there, on Pele Street."

"Isn't that where those ruffians lived?"

"What ruffians?"

"The ones that kidnapped the Vice-Chancellor?"

"That was ten years ago, dad."

"But still…"

"I like it there. It's safe and quiet." She hugged him quickly, "I'm fine, dad. I'll come see you next week."

"Safe?" he asked, staring ahead to where a shirtless boy was burning a mound of garbage.

She never went, and it was not long before she began to act as though he no longer existed. I did not ask.

7

I introduced Margaret to the kola nut seller. He greeted her but his eyes were on the other side of the street, near the bookseller's stand, where a small group of men in neatly ironed shirts and smart trousers conversed excitedly with the traders.

"Every month they come here for money. This sticker and that sticker," the kola nut seller was murmuring to himself.

The leader of the group—it was hard not to notice that he was in charge—was pacing back and forth. His phone was ringing so loud his team paused for him to answer. After handing his files to one of his men, an assistant, he walked farther from the group. "Who is this?" he yelled into the cell phone, gesticulating. The group would occasionally pause to listen. The call came to an end. He returned to the group and quickly retrieved his files. "Who's next?" he demanded.

"This man," said the assistant, pointing to the trader next to the bookseller. The man in question looked like he might cry if poked on the cheek. He was a small man. The boss' phone shrieked again, interrupting business for the second time. The files returned to the assistant. Margaret and I walked over to the bookseller's stand, just in time to hear the boss roaring into the Nokia. "Hello!" he bellowed in the middle of the street. "Hello, who is this?" He paused in mid-strut, pulled up his trousers and scratched his crotch. "I say who is this?" he snapped. "Can you hear me? Ah, okay. Tom. Is that you? Ah, okay. I'm busy now.

Don't do anything until I return to the office. You hear me? Good."

"What's going on?" I asked the bookseller.

"They are collecting taxes and the usual monthly fees," he said. "Those council bastards."

"Taxes and monthly fees?"

"Yes," he said, and sighed.

The street on which the taxed and the taxer stood was unpaved, with prominent puddles and mounds of garbage at various spots. The boss's starched and ironed shirt, sharply in contrast with the bland-looking traders on both sides of the street, glittered in the sun.

"It appears the tax is not collected without some fanfare," I said.

"My brother, it's always as dramatic as this. They have been going from one stand to another."

The boss walked back to his circle, where the small trader was standing, shivering.

"In other places," the bookseller continued, "taxes are used for social services and visible development projects. But here, this uncivilized lot do what they like with our money."

I looked from the puddles to the potbellied boss and wondered if he would pass as uncivilized. If civilization was defined by what one wore, he was the most civilized of everyone on Souzey Street.

"No, na too much money. Too much for tax," the small man was saying in protest to the tax vultures waiting to consume him in taxable bits.

"How much are they collecting?" I asked the bookseller.

"It depends," he said. "The boss tells you what to pay. And that's all."

The small man continued to stand his ground. "No, the money too much," he was saying, shaking his hands as if to punch both air and earth. The boss paid no attention to his little protest. The assistant, and another who looked like the assistant's assistant, pounced on the small man's goods: a bag of rice, a half bag of beans, and six tubers of yam arranged into a pyramid. The assistant's assistant hefted the half bag of beans. His superior officer went for the rice. The small man raised both hands to heaven, brought them down clasped together as in prayer, exasperated and helpless.

"Are you ready to cooperate?" asked the assistant.

The boss was a few feet away, texting. The small man's face tightened in frustration. Now the tears I had anticipated gathered. He did not let them drop. He pulled out a small wrap of naira notes bound by rubber band, and peeled off a few. The boss stopped texting, inched closer, went for the notes and counted away. His assistants waited for the signal. He waved and nodded. The small man's goods were carefully returned to their positions. From the boss' folder emerged a sticker and a receipt, which he gave the trader ceremoniously. The team walked away, the boss strolling behind.

The bookseller walked to his neighbour who had just been relieved of a substantial sum. There were other sympathizers, most of whom had also endured this arbitrary imposition of taxes. He patted the small man's shoulder.

"See that book over there?" It was Margaret, pointing at a yellowish-gold book on the top of a pile. I left the bookseller's bench and squatted next to her. "My dad has a copy," she said. I picked the book. *The Surreptitious Speech:*

Présence Africaine and the Politics of Otherness, edited by V.Y Mudimbe. "I think it was published the same year or a year after Dixon's translation of Senghor's collected works came out," she added.

"Sharp memory," I said.

"Well, my dad never stops talking about his books. You should see his room. He moved back with more books than any other belongings. Ten years later he still orders his books from The Strand on 12th and Broadway, and pays more money to have them shipped to this obscure town."

"The Strand on 12th and Broadway. That's in New York, right?"

"Yes, he spent half his New York days there."

"Well, we may have to show him how to hunt for books around here. See, there's a Salinger on that side of the mat, next to Mailer and Malamud."

"Good," she said unenthusiastically, reading the back cover of a book.

I looked at the preface to the edited volume, written by Senghor in '88 in Dakar. In my head I drew an imaginary line from West Africa to North America, and romantically pictured the flowing and flowering of ideas from here to there, and back. I imagined myself in that free flowing stream of ideas. "Dear Professor," the letter began. I returned to the bookseller's bench. He joined me. I inquired about the small man next door.

"He has not paid his children's school fees," he said.

"How many children?" I asked, half-concerned since a part of me was still picturing the transatlantic crossing of ideas.

"Eight," he replied. "Wait a minute, isn't that the bastard that just left here?"

I looked up and saw the tax collector's assistant walking briskly towards us. His trouser, way too wide for his small waist, folded out in different belt-angles. His first stop was at the kola nut seller's. The conversation did not last long. He moved on to two other stands before coming to the small man's stand. "Did you see a black phone charger?" he asked the small man.

"Charger?" said the small man, in a tone that was, surprisingly, as bold as the question that was posed. "Charger?" he repeated and stood up.

"The boss is looking for his charger. He might have left it somewhere here."

"Here?" the small shop owner said, moving towards the assistant.

The assistant took a step back. The original confidence with which he landed waned with each turn of the conversation.

"You think I have your charger?" inquired the small shop owner, beating his chest for emphasis.

The assistant was caught off guard by the small man's burst of boldness. He looked around, perhaps to see if he was questioning the wrong person. The assistant had overrated his own worth. He forgot that he was a mere pawn in a lopsided system, that he was nothing without his boss and the entourage.

The small man balled his fist, as if ready to hit. "You take my money, now you accuse me of stealing?"

A small crowd gathered.

"Slap the bastard," a voice from the crowd suggested.

"That idiot must be mad," said another voice.

"I only asked if you saw a black charger," the assistant said and took several steps back. "Okay, forget it."

"Forget it?"

"Never mind."

"Never mind? You take my money and now you call me thief?"

The assistant was smart enough to sniff what would befall him if he waited another second. He stepped away from the small man's stand, amid insults and jeers.

"Thief. All of them. Thief. Big and small thief. All of you," the small man chanted at the receding figure.

"Bastards," another voice added.

"Only God will save this country," the bookseller said and announced that he was travelling next week, in case I didn't see him around.

"Where to?" I asked.

"Onitsha, then, Lagos."

"From here to Onitsha and then Lagos? That's a little zigzagged. South, east, south, then west."

I thought of the planned trip with Osagie that never happened and wished I could catch a sight of him strolling down the street. I looked up and scanned the area.

"I know," the bookseller was saying, "my family lives in Onitsha. I have a daughter there. She is three and lives with my mother."

"Nice. What about her mother?"

"She's no longer with me," he said.

"Oh…"

"She's with her ancestors."

"Sorry, my friend."

"I'll see my daughter, leave some money and then go to Lagos."

"Good plan, family first."

"Yes, my daughter before business. I'll bring you more

books from Lagos," he said, more as a reward for my empathy than a mere marketing stunt.

"Brilliant."

"*My* importer says his warehouse is filled with books from the UK and the US."

"Is that so? How do they get these books?"

"Ah! Long journey." He pulled a serious face, perhaps to show how long the journey was.

"How long is this journey? It appears you have embarked on one yourself. Yes?"

"No, not at all. Actually, the importer has friends and partners over there." He pointed north.

"He must be a good businessman, an international one for that matter," I said, more interested in this transatlantic journeys of books.

"Well, this is Nigeria," he said.

"What do you mean?"

The meaning of his expression was clear. But I did not want to generalize. Margaret joined us on the bench, shuffling me towards the bookseller.

"You are my friend, so I will tell you about this journey. I'll start with the businessman. He's the principal and founder of a school near the wharf in Apapa. The books come to him as donations through a charity he started alongside the school."

"His charity?"

"This is Nigeria, my brother. Anything is possible. So, his partner in the US collects the books from all over: Boston, New York, all over, from libraries, churches, everywhere. They are told to donate to this literacy program in Africa. All that good stuff."

"Under the impression that the books will go to his

school?" I asked, impatient.

"Yes, including universities. See those books," he pointed to a hardcover," they are for universities. When the books land, his friends at the customs clear the containers. Some are stocked in his school's library. The rest are for business."

"Are you serious?"

"Yes. That is why I'm going to Lagos, and so are many distributors from Aba, Abuja, Benin, Calabar, Enugu, all over." He paused and took a long breath. "My little girl and her grandmother…" He did not finish the sentence.

"But it's a big scam," cried Margaret

I looked at the Mudimbe on my lap, a totem of my romantic, transatlantic free-flow of ideas. As I looked at it, I wondered if the Atlantic, that neutral space, ever cared to check the intentions of the cargoes it bore safely across its tides. For centuries it bore vessels that transported cargoes of all sorts, humans and produce, from one edge of the globe to another, innocently lending its hands to the transactions that tilted and messed up the history of our race.

Margaret paid for the books. I shook hands with the bookseller, patted his shoulder, and left.

8

Morning. I am too tired to write. My shoulders ache for no reason. My head is heavy with the chain of dreams I had the previous night, none of which I remember.

There are two open envelopes on my desk. One is a brown, A4 envelope from a Port Harcourt post office. It did not come with a return address, only the sender's unfamiliar name, Kalu Aminu. The letter itself is a mere two-page note, typed and stapled to loose pages with scribbles, some of which are completely illegible, visibly old, like papers left to rot in the archives of a forgotten library.

I read it last night, the two paged note, and I figured out, after reading the first sentence, that the mysterious Kalu Aminu was no other than Pa Suku.

"Dear Son," it begins, "I know the scream of silence, and your silence since moving away tells me you're 'in good hands.'"

I knew it was him. My heart had leapt in anticipation of what was to come, the message that lay below those initial lines, so I quickly scanned to the last line— a wrong move, and I regretted doing so. I should have left it there, on that first paragraph, where he ponders "the scream of silence." I should have stayed there. But how was I to know what was coming? His opening lines were baits, and I fell for them. At the end of the letter I felt like a cow fattened before facing its fate at the abattoir. The sense of loss that followed had no remedy, as there was no return address to which I could respond; and even if there was an address, there would be no one there to receive my response.

"I left the blocks a month ago," the letter continued, "and have since settled into a flat in Diobu, in a neighbourhood that's not far from where I was born. I faintly recall telling you about this place, but not sure if I did justice to that description. The streets where I played are visible from here, from my back window, and it's refreshing to be reminded of a time when I ran around these corners flying kites, watching boys pick fights, and girls playing Oga after school. It was here that I dreamt of becoming a pilot—remember that story?—and I was here when the war broke out. The building that collapsed during that war used to stand around the corner from this flat. The spot where its ruins were left untouched for almost two decades is now taken over by a building that's half church and half elementary school. That seems to be the trend now: churches that are schools and schools that are churches, pews serving as school furniture, and Sunday school boards as class room chalk boards

"There used to be some exquisite colonial houses around here. They have all been torn down and replaced by mounds of ugliness that I would jubilantly flatten if given the chance. The saddest part is the colours these houses bear, mostly yellow in harsh variants, the edges blue or red or green. Some are jarringly white in horrible contrast to the overall tone of this area. A short course on aesthetics could save this country a lot of heartache.

"But I'm glad the street names have stayed the same, and have not been changed to bear names that peddle religion or direct us to its potency: Miracle Street, Lord Redeemer Street, Eternal Healer Street. It's not the religion in the name that annoys me, but the thoughtlessness therein. I'll take Methuselah Street over Miracle Street, since the former returns us to a point in biblical narrative, which gives us an opportunity to learn something new, or reminds us of what we already know.

"In any case, I'm extremely happy that the old names have not changed; there is joy in spotting an old street sign that has stayed the same. I walk around and search for those old signs. I consider this an indirect way to return and reacquaint my mind to this place. I have returned to roost like a creature driven by instinct.

"Walking this neighbourhood, you might say, is the same as flipping through an album that holds one's past experiences, one's memories of childhood. The other day, for instance, I was on Bonny Street and saw that the tailor's shop, where I recall being measured for my first suit, was still there. The building is the same. Repainted. 'Cambridge Tailors', reads the sign, like it read seventy-something years ago.

"I walked in, and the man I knew—who ran his measuring tape around my shoulders—was unmistakably present in the face of the current owner. 'How may I help you, sir?' he asked when I stepped in. I must have struck him as a rather bizarre old man, as I lingered at the door, looking around like I was taking stock of his shop. 'Any problem, sir?'

"'Not at all,' I replied. 'I used to come here as a child, and I'm only glad it's still standing.' He must have been forty or so, the young chap, born many years after my first visit to the shop he now owns. I left the shop and followed the bend to Creek Street, where the old sign was still standing.

"I pay attention to each sign I *meet*, pondering them as one would ponder a piece of art on display. Some signs are hunched over like men twice my age, weighed down by sediments of dirt, or by random bags of garbage. Some have tilted to the side, pointing the public to the wrong direction. They are all just charming the way they are. And I get a kick from observing their contribution to the character of this area. Time, as I now believe, imposes charm and character on a place. And I'm convinced that street signs are memories in their own rights. Not only do they announce where you are or where you are going, but they also remind you of a past you share with everyone who's walked that path. We enter—and become—memory each time we read a street sign, just as we enter an author's imagination through his or her work.

"Speaking of authors and books, I recently ran into an old friend at the state library, which is not far from here, and left with my heart sunk and shredded in bits. I won't say much about the state of the library, as I'm sure the situation is no different where you are. I would be surprised if you're able to walk into your faculty library and checkout a recent translation of Walser or Dostoevsky. Wouldn't *that* be a miracle, you step into your library and at the entrance are displays of new releases from top publishers around the world? I hope it happens in your lifetime. It's not an impossible transformation, since we once saw that in this country.

"So I ran into Tamuno Briggs at the library. I don't recall telling you about this childhood friend. I certainly did not share his story. We called him Tammy in those days, and the boys teased him for this female-sounding name. I often stood up for him but gave up after a song was spun to go with his name. I don't remember the whole song, but know there was a 'Jammy' and a 'Bammy' in-between, carefully inserted for rhythmic effect. He hated it. I hated it too, but we were both powerless.

"His father worked at the state library, and I remember going there with Tammy to watch his old man hefting books from shelf to shelf, his button-down short-sleeve drenched in sweat. He always wore the same short-sleeve shirt and grey trousers, and his glasses were always left to sag down his nose. Whenever Tammy got in trouble at school or at home, which happened almost every week, his dad would have him work at the library, running small errands between offices, re-shelving books...

"He hated it. He hated the library. 'It smells like shit,' he would announce on our way there, 'and those shelves are like small devils. I want to stand at one end and tip them over.' He did try to tip those devils. I stopped him. Not because I cared what the consequences were. I was only protecting a place I loved more than anything else.

"Stepping into the library, I would draw a lung-full of air, exhale satisfactorily, and make my way to the shelf with picture books. There was a sign that announced the section designated for children books. The sign is still there, wrinkled and faded. I would go for *D'Aulaires' Book of Greek Myths*. I don't remember telling you about this book. I have forgotten most of what I shared with you. My memory is fading. *D'Aulaires Book of Greek Myths* was my favourite book as a child, followed by *Brown Bear, Brown Bear, What Do You See?* I don't remember why I liked them so much. But as the years went by, I'd recall them while reading other books. Did I mention Ola Rotimi's *The Gods Are Not To Blame*? I'm not sure but I know you must have read it now. The first time I read that play, I saw the connection to Oedipus, and then recalled the first time I met Oedipus in *D'Aulaires*. *Brown Bear, Brown Bear...* was my introduction to the beauty of colours and experimental fiction. It's strange how these things work. Anyway, where was I?"

Where was I? I could imagine him asking that question at the blocks, to which I would respond with silence, knowing he would reel back to where the subject had forked. He had written it here deliberately. I believe it was deliberately done to create a fake sense of proximity, and I can see him smiling as he wrote down that question, an unfinished cigarette burning next to a small stack of book on his desk. I momentarily stopped reading the letter, walked to the window and studied the darkness outside. Margaret was asleep. The night was silent. I returned to the letter.

"Street signs and memory. There is freedom in sameness, in returning to find that change—that whore that imposes itself on our existence—has not completely erased everything that constitutes our past, everything that we know from our childhood..."

I picked the envelope and flipped it. Sender: Kalu Aminu. Why did he choose to write pseudonymously? The letter was sent three months ago and arrived here two weeks after, waiting for me at the English department on campus.

I have started strolling into campus once a week to see if I will run into Osagie. I have had no success in that regard, and I am not yet ready to walk into Adam Hall and knock on his door.

Despairing after yesterday's walk, I headed for the English department where I impulsively started reading posts on the notice board outside. There was a list of newly admitted students, about a hundred of them. There was a university-wide list of rusticated students, evenly divided among those caught in exam malpractice and those involved in violent gangs. And then there was the list of those who had mail to pick up. This list is updated every day, with new names added to names with waiting mail. I was on the list. I knocked on the administrative secretary's door. She asked me in. I said I had mail. She gestured to a corner, where the box of letters, unsorted, heaved and begged for rescue. I left with my letters.

On the way out, it occurred to me that those in adjoining offices, professors and support staff in the English department, did not as much as whisper when they saw me. It was as if I had not disappeared from the fairly small department. They had not noticed that I had dropped out, and that made me sad.

I did not read the letters when I got home. I saved the reading for nightfall and started with Kalu Aminu's letter.

"Anyway, where was I?"

That question. Written to refresh memories of when he asked it in person. I read it again and moved on.

"Yes," he continued, "at the local library. I saw my friend Tammy walking towards me with a stack of books, wearing a white, button-down short sleeved shirt, drenched in sweat. Age had conferred weight on him, and there was a noticeable twitch on the left side of his face. He did not remember me. Time had blurred what we looked like before moving on to explore the world. I wanted to introduce myself, but was burdened by too much emotion. I let him finish his task. He pulled out a handkerchief, just like his father, wiped his brow and walked to the office his old man had occupied. He was breathing heavily, exhausted, taking in the same smell he hated but now inhaled from nine to five. The desk was the same. The walls have been repainted. There was a portrait of the current state governor, a portrait of the chief librarian who also happened to by my ol' pal Tammy, and a landscape painting that was quite impressive.

"'Good afternoon, you need assistance?'

"He still did not recognize me. I could feel the tremor on my lips. He was looking into my eyes, a forced smile on his face. How did he end up here? He hated this place. He hated the smell, the shelves, the staff and users.

"I said I wanted a library card, that I had just moved to the city centre from O., and needed a place to study for an adult literacy programme organized by the state government. 'It's not too late to learn, you know.' He was impressed by this story, an old man returning to school to learn how to read and write. 'Take a seat. I'll be back in a second.' He sneezed and left. I studied his office. There were no family photos. Tammy is not married, I thought, perhaps for the same reason I'm still single and not searching for a companion. Did he consider marriage? Too many questions waiting for answers. He returned with a form. I filled it out and handed it over. 'You'll need a passport-size photograph,' he said. 'I'll give you a temporary card for now.' He encouraged me to take my studies seriously. And there was no condescension in his voice. The voice itself had undergone transformation, and seemed to rise from a pit dug by age and years of silence.

"I thanked him and left to explore the shelves. I went in search of *D'Aulaires Book of Greek Myths*. It was still there! No joke. The same copy. I picked it up, my hands trembling as memories surged. I flipped the pages and could see my childhood on each page. I held it close to my face and sniffed. A small laugh escaped my lips. I sat there, reading it, a stream of tears descending down my cheeks.

"Peering into the past on those pages, into my own past, it struck me that *D'Aulaires Book* was also a reminder of my friendship with Tammy, for it was here, in this space, that we bonded, despite his dislike of the library. Back then, he would momentarily escape his father's sight and run over to playfully snatch *D'Aulaires Book* from my hands, and toss it on the floor. It was a game. It was his way of reminding me of how he hated the library. Recalling those silly incidents, the tears welled up again. When I looked up from the page, I saw Tammy's frame ahead, between shelves. Was he watching me? I could have walked up to announce my identity. I did not. He walked back to his office. I followed him, building up the will to announce myself. I changed my mind when I spotted him pouring pills into his left palm, a glass of unclear liquid on his desk. The twitch on his face had intensified, perhaps the reason for the pills. It thus occurred to me that there might be a medical explanation for his non-recollection. I wondered why he was still in service, and not retired to a house somewhere. I left the library, fondling the temporary card in my picket, drained by all I had seen and experienced.

"I'm sure you're wondering why I left the blocks. I'll tell you why. Before that, I'll start by saying that my new place is nothing like where we first met. I don't think you can imagine me in a two-bedroom flat with running water, cable television, a small yard with a rocking chair that does not wobble arbitrarily… and there's a garden boy that trims the flowers outside, he looks fifteen or thereabouts, and there's a vendor that brings me the papers. Can you imagine me living this lavishly? I like the air: it smells of freedom, and freedom is the only thing I've known all my life, since I've not cared to take roots anywhere. Here, my day begins with Rossini. Did I ever tell about my Rossini phase? I don't think so. Anyway, I bought a CD of his "Sins of Old Age," and play it every morning before I set out for my long walks. It would ring in my head all day, as I slowly cross the streets, walking until my knees ache, at which I would return and replay Rossini before settling to the window, from where—eating lunch—I would watch humans milling about in the sun.

"I know you can't imagine me at this new place, with the luxuries I've described. Neither do I, and I'm only here for a short time. And if you're reading this letter…" He continued, I read to the end and wished I had not. Why did he write to share this tragedy? I did not expect it from the tone of the opening paragraphs, and the whole letter had merely read like the jolly memoirs of an old man.

He does not want me to worry, he said at the end of the letter, and went ahead to draw a parallel he must have considered funny.

"You know, sometimes I imagine myself making a grand scene like Nietzsche in his days of madness. Let's see, convinced you are Jacob Burckhardt, I write you a letter in which I call myself Dionysius, and claim that I created the universe and everything in it. On reading my letter, you'll come find me—won't you?—only to find out that I'd been making a fool of myself by hugging and kissing a horse flogged by its owner, by showing up at funerals and claiming to be the dead. But I'll spare you all that, my boy. I'll simply pass without fanfare."

My eyes were dry. I shut them and could see his face the

way it was the last time I saw him, the day before I left for university. I had gone over to his place to say goodbye. He did not talk much, and I suspected there was something wrong. I knew he was gradually recoiling from himself and the world, even from me, and had begun to repeat old stories, to share new ones that made no sense. Now this letter. The instruction was not to worry, that he had thought it through and had everything sorted. Sorted how? He had no family. Did he? Now it is too late to find out.

The second letter is from Osagie. There is a sender's address on the envelope, an address in Benin City, which makes it clear that he is not in town. Why did he leave town when exams are going on? Should I write him a letter? What do I want to say to him? Nothing comes to mind, except a sense of emptiness and displacement. He had copied out Henri Cole's "Sacrament," and clipped it to the letter. He had also written me a short story. I read the poem, and it finally struck me that he may have known my whereabouts, my life with Margaret, which he may have interpreted as a rejection of what we shared, a disapproval of his sexuality. My God. And he chose to set the story in Port Harcourt, the only city that adjoins O., making it clear that the story is more or less what would befall me. Reading the story, I see him creating two characters out of what he thinks of me; the betrayed and the betrayer, the victim and the villain. I reread "Sacrament":

On the way to Mass, by chance,
I spotted you on the boulevard at a café
with your wife and her mother.
You were wearing the lovely gold cross
my father gave me when I was a boy.

There was no doubt that he had seen Margaret and me. I tried to draft a response to his letter, but somehow could not get myself to do so. I will try again this morning. Though I am fairly certain that something inside—a fear, a doubt, perhaps shame—would incapacitate me.

EPILOGUE

Monologue for Ex-Neighbours
By Osagie

… the world outside is still there—ugly and
merciless; and those factors always create anger
and sorrow beyond one's own feelings of personal
happiness. —John Rechy

Self-confined to my room, immobilized by grief, I listened. Down the blue-walled hallway, ignorant of my presence, they shared words that were like shards of glass forced down my throat. I listened silently.

"What is he going to do now?" Tam asked.

I pictured him standing at his door, his eyes scanning the corridor as he analysed what he believed I was and what would become of me. Earlier on he had attempted a narration of homosexual intercourse, stumbling through incoherent assumptions and eventually concluding with a brazen remark: "It is nothing but absurd and contradicts every law under the sun." Someone sighed. Pat. Tam's girlfriend. I knew it was her. She was rather quiet the whole time.

"I think this law is not harsh enough," added a frail voice. Daniel. The primary school teacher. A room away from Tam's.

I pictured him: shirtless, a smirk on his narrow face, his eyes enlarged as though in fatal shock. He'd lived in that room for a year and had been reasonably friendly. There were times I stopped at his door to say hello. "How are you today?" I would ask. Rising from his red rug, where he often sat grading papers, he would respond with a smile as wide as his doorframe. We were good neighbours. But as I replay the words he freely shared last night, confident that I wasn't home, I wish I'd read more into his exaggerated smile.

A can popped. Someone drank with a loud slurp. The entrance to the hallway creaked open, followed by the jiggle of keys. It was Steve, just back from work. He joined the rest.

"What's the excitement about?"

"Our possessed friend is in trouble," Dan said.

Another can popped. Someone coughed. They fell silent for a minute or two.

"Is it the new law?" asked Steve. He must have tossed his Chianti satchel into his room and planted himself at his door, unknotting his tie and unbuttoning his shirt from bottom up.

"Is he home?" he inquired.

I sensed exhaustion in his voice. He must have had a terrible day at work, at the local branch of a national bank, where he ran the SME unit. Smart guy no doubt. If only his head had room for the making of meaning outside numbers. I wished he'd be different from the rest, maybe say a word that'd make me spring out and hug him. I knew that wouldn't be the case. I hoped, nonetheless. Assured that I wasn't home, he spoke his mind.

"Well, what do I care? Bloody worms with base instincts."

Pat hissed and started a sentence—something about

God's ability to heal, to deliver, to make one normal—but fell silent, as though hushed by an invisible force.

"They are a disgusting lot, anyway," Steve added.

Tam pretended to retch and asked for a lighter. Dan laughed and clapped as though cheering for all three. I pulled away from the door, stepping on a small pool of tears that had gathered at my feet, my pond of blood, my misery.

Dan's clap rang and jarred like crashing cymbals. My head spun. I steadied myself against the wall next to my bookcase. Their voices and Dan's clap, as if not grotesque enough, became the stomp of parading soldiers down the hallway. And the soldiers were at my door. I slid under the bed. They kicked down the door and poured inside, hovering like apparitions, their guns at the ready. One went for the chest I rescued from the streets six months ago, which I'd transformed into a stand for my gramophone. He picked up the gramophone, smashed it against the wall. "Who buys gramophones these days?" he asked the assaulted wall. The gramophone's horn sat still, a severed earlobe waiting to collect raindrops. The blow had crippled the crank. The turntable was in pieces. Then he squatted next to his helpless and dismembered victim and probed the horns with his index finger, fingering with determined vigour, heaving as though burdened by an unknown weight.

Having had enough I came out to confront them, shivering as I rushed to stop them from knocking over my bookcase. They saw me and stopped at once and began to laugh. Their voices collected into a group-clap that seemed to rise from invisible pores on the walls, trickling into a familiar voice. "I know him well," said the familiar voice.

It was Steve. He was still at his door and I was in my room, crouched on the floor next to the bookcase. I was beginning to see faces that weren't there and to imagine the worst. I was beginning to lose my mind. "I've known him since we were boys," Steve was saying.

He was right. We grew up in the same town I'm leaving now and will soon discard from my memory. I'm on the bus to Lagos. Where in Lagos I don't know. I've never been to Lagos. But I'll get there. I'll get there like everyone in this bus: the twenty-something-looking girl in the front seat, dozing off; the old man in a felt hat clutching a folded newspaper, silent; three chatty boys discussing girls and politics, their views as divergent as the colours of their trousers; the woman next to me... As they say, Lagos is a city the size of a mad man's idea, vast as the mysteries of death, complex as the arbitrary boundaries of Africa, an indescribable mix that breeds anonymity, where, as John Koethe said, "disorder leads to unexpected patterns..." I shall find out for myself.

I'm sitting by the window and can see shadows racing past as the bus hurtles through the fogless morning, consuming the kilometres between Port Harcourt and Lagos. At noon the speeding shadows will become homes and stores, trucks and trees, city souls stumbling to nowhere, colliding, drowning in their own sweat, in the hovering stench of clogged gutters. I contemplate what I am leaving behind: a space with double-faced neighbours, their cackles as sharp as the edges of a butcher's knife.

There were days Dan asked if I wanted to read a paper by

his favourite student, and days he asked if I could play him something on my gramophone. I often indulged him, and would play him a danceable piece from the '40s. Glenn Miller was his favourite. He would whistle and dance down the corridor. We were *good* neighbours, but his neighbourliness was a front for the repulsion he shared last night.

"I've known him since we were boys," Steve said.

I listened, wanting him to say more. I wanted him to tell them we played men-at-war on Ebele Street, back when the plot that became our apartment building had six garbage heaps on different spots, with rats and vultures feasting freely, before the street was paved. He wasn't exactly nice to me then, but he was a child, and we were both kept from the world by our innocence. He's an adult now, and that innocence has been replaced with the ambivalence we all learn to cultivate. His was evident when he returned from Shamsbury with two degrees and a mammoth ego. I'd stayed back in Nigeria and had gone to the College of Art and Science, thirty kilometres from Ebele Street. I dropped out a year later to manage a bookshop, a move that was an excuse to sate my appetite for books and work on my own writing. I remember the look of disgust and indifference on his face when he randomly walked into the bookstore and saw me at the counter. On seeing him, an irrational urge to hug and welcome him back to Ebele Street flared within me. But I restrained myself and was glad I avoided embarrassment. Without a single word he turned and left, abandoning whatever brought him there. He also had that look on his face when he saw that I lived in the building he was moving into. I kept my distance. I kept the hug to myself. He grew more indifferent. I avoided him but so badly wanted to catch up with him; if for nothing else, to ask if he ever got my letters, ten or more letters I sent to the address he left that cold Harmattan morning.

In one letter I informed him of recent changes on Ebele Street: the buying up of the empty plots we called our Kingdom; the appearance of the new middle class, with their fairly used cars, gadgets from China, and pampered children. "Oh Steve," I wrote, "their kids are not like we were. They don't play in the sand and do not dance in the rain. You should see them walking to school in their spotless shirts, picking their steps like fragile ceramics on toes. I wish I had applied for that scholarship at Shamsbury. That would have kept me from enduring these changes. I suppose gentrification is a universal thing, no?" In another letter I told him about my novel in progress and the chapter that'd been accepted for publication outside Nigeria, in faraway Texas. "I read somewhere that John Rechy is from there, from a town called El Paso," I wrote. I also shared where the idea for my novel came from: "It's drawn from that time in junior secondary when we saw the science teacher peeing into a Pepsi bottle, remember?"

He never replied. I chose to believe he didn't get them and that they never left the country. I chose to believe they were stuck in the basement of the Postal Service on Ebele Street where hopes and agonies are left to rot, where I once spied a mailman surreptitiously unboxing and re-boxing a package after extracting what he wanted. I never got around to confirming otherwise from Steve. I also never had a chance to—and actually could not bring myself to—remind him of his twelfth birthday and the blue flashlight

I bought him with my savings. He'd always wanted to sneak out at night and climb the mango tree in front of the Mosque on Ebele Street, to reach the bird nests "and see if there are birdlings." The mosque and the tree are no more, an unfortunate fact I also conveyed in one of my letters. "I can still see the vile face of the bulldozer thrusting and forking its tongue into the innocent mosque," I wrote, "knocking it over until it lay lifeless." I further wanted to remind him of how his father—now dead after suffering a severe heart attack—despised me for no tangible reason and how he was my defender, shielding me from the onslaught of his father's gaze. His mother was silent but observed me with detached curiosity. Sometimes she squinted, burrowing into me, searching, questioning.

What his parents saw and whatever it spurred in them, revulsion or disdain, I didn't care to note. Instead I paid attention to the maturation of my impulses and how it differed from the boys around me. For instance, I noticed that Nora, who seized every chance to hold my hands, didn't stir or shift my moods. I liked her the way one liked a friend's sister or a cousin. Nothing more. I recall when she asked to kiss me and how I instantly longed to kiss Steve instead. It was a longing that I begged to stay away from me. It persisted, blooming and pulling me away from Nora, from everything that society expected of me as a boy that would be a man.

Nora went ahead and kissed me. We were twelve or so. After the kiss she stood back waiting for something in return, for what boys were supposed to do at our age. I didn't know what to do in that moment and wasn't sure how to respond. There was no harmony between us, neither was there the palpitation between the legs. I simply stood there, impervious, unblinking and pondering her: a body with moving limbs, a face with brilliant eyes, a neck with fine lines, a chest with growing breasts, a being that drew from the same stash of air, who must be loved, one breathing being in love with another, as simple and free as that. Aghast as a tree struck by thunder and sure that she had kissed the wrong boy, she ran off. I followed her, as confused as she was. I saw her behind her parent's house, crawled into a ball next to the chicken coop. I sat next to her, stroking her back, confused. A shudder ran through her. She managed to say something through her sob. I strained to hear but failed. I sighed. She lifted her head and looked at me.

"What did you say?" she asked.

"Nothing," I said.

When I'm ready, I thought silently, I'd plant a kiss on Steve. I imagined it. It gradually began to feel good. I let it grow. I smiled. The acidic stench of chicken excrement wafted between us, assaulting our nostrils and threatening to shorten whatever time we had to sort our emotions. I disregarded the smell, and paid more attention to the idea of kissing Steve, an idea I would later give free rein to bloom into a full-fledged attraction. Whenever it came up, I would let it stay, turning it from side to side until it was comfortable enough to find expressions in my dreams and wild imaginations. In a sense, that idea—and how I chose to express it—became one of the ways I came to terms with who I am.

Steve is now a man and has grown to hate the person that I am, disgusted by what he knows about me and legally free to channel that hate and disgust.

I'd shut my door for four days. They assumed I was away, but I was in my room listening to their *neighbourly* chats each night, wishing I were a mouse digging into the poisoned floor. Last night I packed what I could fit into two duffels and left for the bus station, where I shared the concrete floor with eight passengers waiting for the bus to Lagos. We are now a hundred kilometres out of Port Harcourt. The sun is rising. Before us the murky and ominous River Nun sprawls, winding like a flattened snake. We are approaching Kaiama Bridge which divides the Nun. I strain to magnify the boats sprinkled on the river like ants rolling a grain of brown sugar. Is this the Nun that ferried slaves from Aboh to the Gulf of Guinea and then to the New World? How many died here? How many enjoyed the journey to nowhere, singing and applauding as they were carried away? Knowing that their freedom was gone, did they pause to bathe in the mild river breeze? Did they smile at the lush greenery on both sides of the river? Should I contemplate sunrise and flowers in a space that denies my humanity? Does anyone care that I've been excluded from the living, and that I'm as good as dead? If I was imprisoned, or perhaps stoned to death for being me, would there be mourning in the land? Of Giordano Bruno, Czeslaw Milosz wrote:

> On this same square
> they burned Giordano Bruno.
> Henchmen kindled the pyre
> close-pressed by the mob.
> Before the flames had died
> the taverns were full again,
> baskets of olives and lemons

again on the vendors' shoulders.

Before packing and leaving for the bus station, I contemplated suicide but was turned off by the logistics of self-hanging. Not only will the chair, kicked away by my nervous legs, crash and attract the neighbours, the cutting off of air from my throat may unleash muffled but loud-enough noises that would draw their attention. I didn't want to give them the opportunity to be heroes, to knock down my door and rescue me. What I wanted was for the stench of my bloated remains to wake them up at night, displacing their share of fresh air; for maggots, sliding under the door and out into the corridor, to crawl into their rooms, into their pots, into their tea cups...

The other option was to starve myself to death. While this sounded like the most executable option, without possible causes for *neighbourly* attention, the absurd idea of waiting for death, like a criminal, was repulsive. I discarded that option and took a short nap. I dreamed that I was on a train to an unknown destination. On my wrist was a purple band. I was immobilized by a chain on both legs and watched by two soldiers. The train plunged into a tunnel, and darkness enveloped us. When it emerged into the light, the soldiers were nothing but a heap of bones, and the surrounding landscape had changed from ash to green. I woke up, packed, and left.

The woman next to me is breastfeeding a child. The child is squeezing the mother's breast, forcing strands of vein to emerge around the nipples. The bus hits a pothole as we get on the bridge. The woman's shoulder brushes against mine.

"Sorry, sir," she says.

"No problem," I reply with a smile. "What is your child's name?"

"Lucky," she answers and stamps a kiss on the child's forehead.

"Lucky," I repeat after her and pinch the child's cheek. Here's a child who doesn't know to what category it belongs. If it turns out to be mine, and if Nigeria is still what it is, it may have to crawl into a crevice or face the gallows. I flinched at this thought, and the grotesque picture it generated and displayed before me.

The bridge is now behind us. Lagos and whatever it holds is five hundred kilometres away. Lucky has bitten its mother's right nipple and seems to smile at this little triumph. I look away, drained, resisting the tug to sleep, afraid of what might appear in my dream.

About The Author

Born in southern Nigeria, in 1984, Timothy Ogene is the sixth of seven children raised in a two-room tenement block. He attended St. Edward's and Oxford Universities, and is currently completing a Master's in Creative Writing at the University of East Anglia. He is the author of a collection of poems and his writings have appeared in *The Missing Slate*, *Harvard Review*, *Hong Kong Review of Books*, *Numero Cinq*, *Tincture Journal*, *One Throne Magazine*, *Poetry Quarterly*, *Tahoma Literary Review*, *The New Engagement*, and other places.

Acknowledgements

Many thanks to those whose words and lives have been a blessing: to SES, JPH, and L. Curtis, for opening their doors and hearts; to Clare, for her insights and feedback; to Henri Cole, for the permission to use the ninth line of "A Half-Life" as the title of this book; to Sir Antony Gormley, for the permission to use his work on the cover of this book; to Robert Peett, for giving me a chance. Many thanks to the editors of *One Throne Magazine* and *The Missing Slate*, where excerpts appeared in slightly different forms.